After the
Darkness

BETTY
CODY

POOLBEG

Published 2023 by Poolbeg Press Ltd.

123 Grange Hill, Baldoyle,

Dublin 13, Ireland

Email: poolbeg@poolbeg.com

ISBN 978-1-78199 513-6

www.poolbeg.com

ABOUT THE AUTHOR

Betty Cody was born in Cork City but moved to Dublin after her marriage. While her children attended school, she did a PhD in Psychology at University College Dublin.

Apart from her family, sport has been her main passion in life: table tennis, followed by squash, golf and now pitch and putt. She has written a golf psychology column for the *Irish Independent* and features, plus celebrity interviews, for *Irish Lady Golfer* magazine. Her self-published book, *The Road to Perfect Golf*, sold out its print run.

Playing bridge is a new passion in life for her and last year she had the unusual experience of winning an event that allowed herself and her partner to compete in the Irish International Camrose Cup trials.

She has now returned to her first sporting love – table tennis. In July 2024, she hopes to compete in the World Masters Table Tennis Champions – for her age category – in Rome.

During Covid lockdown, she wrote her first novel, *The Brightest Star*.

Her motto has always been: *Don't ever give up on your dreams, even if on occasions 'Life' gets in the way!*

ACKNOWLEDGEMENTS

I want to thank most sincerely the dedicated team at Poolbeg for their amazing support yet again, by commissioning my second novel. Their wonderful editor Gaye Shortland is a historian with such a great breadth of knowledge that it is humbling. My thanks also to the lovely Paula Campbell, who unfailingly answers my emails, even when they are not remotely to do with the book! She is my go-to for everything regarding the industry. My thanks also to the rest of the staff in Poolbeg. I'm astonished at the fact that they have such great patience when dealing with me! I really do appreciate their support.

I want to thank my kind and helpful writer friend in Florence, Lisa Clifford. Her enthusiasm for all aspiring writers is wonderful to experience.

Finally, I want to thank my family and friends who encouraged me to write a sequel to my first novel, *The Brightest Star*. I hope they enjoy meeting the characters again.

DEDICATION

I wish to dedicate this book to my beloved family. To my husband Michael, our children Gillian and Alan, their spouses Ken and Laura, and our grandchildren Chloe and Joe Cody and Lia, Jack and Louis Kirwan.

I wish also to dedicate the book to my friend Monsignor Caoimhín Ó'Néill, late President of Carlow College, who sadly passed away before this book was published.

Finally, to Doctor Ethna Swan who has been both a mentor and friend for many years.

Thank you all for your support and encouragement.

Chapter One

August 1844

When morning throws its shards of light
The steeple it stands tall,
And when the church doors open wide
The light brings peace to all.

* * *

As the congregation sat in their seats in the parish church in Midleton, County Cork, the rector walked to the pulpit, opened his notes and read.

"*We are gathered here today to remember the life of Robert Turner. It should not be seen as a sad day, but one that celebrates the life of a good man. He was born in Midleton and lived here throughout his long life. A man of faith, a great family man and a supporter of many good causes. Yet he never looked for the limelight. He quietly ran a successful farming business, but his main interest in life was always his family. As a young married man, when sorrow knocked on his door he accepted the death of his beloved Kathleen and thereafter spent his time working and concerning himself only with being the centre of his children's world while, at the same time, quietly helping those less fortunate than himself. He was also a lucky man, because he had the wonderful Meg who made it her life's mission to bring up his daughters, Eliza and Lily, as Kathleen would have wished. To the delight of his daughters and everyone who knew him in the county, he married Meg when the girls became self-sufficient. His world was truly complete when Meg bore him another beautiful daughter, Alice, who was to be in his later years his pride and joy. Today, Robert will finally be reunited with his beloved first wife Kathleen, knowing that she too would have been proud of the wonderful care he bestowed on his family throughout his life. May he rest in peace."*

His youngest daughter Alice sat with her head bent as tears streamed from her eyes. She was being comforted by her husband Richard. Nearby her eldest sister, Eliza, sat next to Meg, her hand firmly grasping that of Robert's widow. Eliza knew that Meg was always grateful to have had a child of her own and she hoped that she would gain comfort from the long life she had shared with Robert. Lily, the middle sister, who had lived in Hertfordshire for all her adult life, sat with her husband Neville. They would return to England after the funeral. Margarita Beconsford, Eliza and Jack Ryan's only child, sat close to her husband, the Honourable Victor Beconsford. She spent the time remembering all the good days and evenings she had spent with her Grandpa Robert. She said a prayer of thanks that she was able to ease some of his final days by singing to him, as he lay in a weakened state during the last few months of his life.

Although the funeral of Robert Turner was sad, once everybody returned to the large farmhouse, where Meg would now live alone for the first time in her life, most of the people that joined them for food and drink wanted to recall the good memories they had of Robert. Listening to their stories started the healing for Meg, because on that day she heard good things about her husband's quiet charitable donations, of which she had known nothing.

Molly Ryan, the mother of Eliza's husband Jack Ryan, who lived close by in Rose Cottage, had spent the last few days beavering away making meat pies, curing ham and baking hot bread, helped by Mrs. Sexton from the bakery. They had even prepared apple-and-cinnamon pies with cream to round it all off.

By the end of the day, when the visitors had finally left the farmhouse, Alice and her husband Richard Staunton sat down by the fire to talk to Meg.

Alice held her mother's hand and said nothing for a while. Then she took a deep breath.

"I need to talk to you, Mama," she began, hesitating before she continued. "Richard and I have some very good news for you. But first I want to let you know that we told Papa this news before he died and he asked us to keep from telling you until after he had passed away."

"Why would he want that, Alice?" Meg asked, looking bewildered. She had little energy for anything after the long-drawn-out sadness of living for months with the knowledge that her husband was fading before her eyes.

"Because he asked us to make a few suggestions to you about your future. He insisted on that. Then, whatever you decided to do with your life after you heard the news was grand by him."

"I've lived here all my life, Alice. So, what decisions would I have to make?"

Richard put a protective arm around Alice and announced: "Alice is expecting your first grandchild, Meg. It's due before Christmas."

As if propelled by a bolt of lightning, Meg jumped from the chair and threw her arms around her only daughter.

"Since the day you were born, I've wondered if I'd ever live long enough to see my own grandchild!" As she cried, she could barely get the words past her lips. "This is wonderful news and I'm so glad Robert knew! You were right to keep the news from me because, if I had known this before he passed, I would be twice as upset at the thought of him not living long enough to see the face of his grandchild. That would have broken my heart even more. Now, after all we've been through today, hearing this news has given me some hope for the future."

"Mother, he had a final request and asked us to put it to you. As you know, Richard now has to oversee the family farm in West Cork, as Jerome his father is suffering from rheumatics and his only brother Barry is in America and says that he will only return to Ireland if he's ever really needed. For now, Richard will still be singing in concerts but we will be living in West Cork, supporting his parents Grace and Jerome, as they need help around the farm."

"So, what's that got to do with me?" wondered Meg, as she always knew the day would come when she would see less of her daughter. Yet, she had hoped it would not be so soon.

"This farm is now yours. That was agreed by Papa, Eliza, Lily and myself. We all have our own lives now. Papa suggested that you could either sell up and move to West Cork with us or perhaps rent out the farm for a few years. He thought you would love the chance to be with us before and after the baby is born. As you know, Richard's mother would love to have the company of someone nearer her own age and, if I wanted to travel with Richard, I couldn't think of anyone better than you to take care of our new baby."

Meg sat back in her chair. "So much has happened in my head today that I'll need to think about it all and talk it over with Eliza and Jack. They have two good heads on their shoulders."

"Of course, you must, Mother. I just didn't want you not knowing about the baby before we head to the farm and without explaining Papa's solution to the problem."

Meg was always going to have a sleepless night but, as she tossed and turned in the bed, she realised in her heart that she was going to be lost when Alice left Midleton. She knew also that she didn't have to ask for anyone's advice on the matter.

As dawn broke and the first rays of light peeped through the curtains, she finally fell into a peaceful sleep. She wanted to spend her life with the daughter and grandchild she never expected to have. As she wrapped the warm blanket around her, she could almost feel the touch of her only love, Robert Turner, and could hear his voice in her head urging her to live the best life she could and not spend her future mourning a love who would never return to this earth.

Before leaving Midleton, Meg made the decision to rent out the farm and her home. The Beconsford estate offered her a good rent. They would use the lovely farmhouse for the under-manager of the estate and they generously allowed Sam Byrne, who had served the family for most of his life, to remain living in the farmhouse. He would continue to help the under-manager with the horses and carriage. Everyone was happy, especially Eliza, as her old home would stay within the family, for now.

Moving to the townland of Eoinstown, situated between Ballydehob and Bantry, was going to be a big change for both Alice and Meg, although Alice knew that she would live anywhere to be with her beloved husband.

In late September, when Meg finally left Midleton in the Beconsford estate's carriage, she felt some trepidation. During the journey there were fewer trees and forests than she was used to in Midleton and many of the houses they passed appeared to be built of mud bricks and looked barely fit for habitation. The people who walked the roads also looked poorer than those around Midleton. Yet she knew already from Alice and Richard that there was a close bond in the community. When times got too rough for any family, help was provided for those in need. Even for those who wanted to emigrate to America, a hat went around and people who had a spare penny helped the young men or women who were trying to make a better life for themselves and the families they would leave behind. The money they would send back to their families could be lifesaving. She liked the thinking behind that.

She arrived in Eoinstown and saw the two-storey farmhouse for the first time. The exterior was of grey brick that looked sturdy, its stone walls strong enough to withstand the winds and harsh winter weather coming in from the Atlantic. The garden gate led up to a brightly painted blue front door. A chimney sat on the slate roof at either end of the building, with puffs of smoke rising from each. Flower-beds blossomed with well-tended sweet-smelling roses on each side of the door.

As Cillian the coachman knocked on the door, Meg knew that her decision to come to West Cork was the right one.

The door was opened by a smiling Alice, with Richard, followed by his parents Grace and Jerome close behind. Heat emanated from the kitchen, giving her a warm feeling from the moment she entered the hallway. Meg knew immediately that this house was filled with love.

Later that evening, having dined as a family, Alice was very pleased at how easily her mother fitted in with her new family and she knew how happy she was with the way her life had turned out. She was, however, aware of the fact that she was one of the lucky few.

When Alice first arrived in Eoinstown, it was confirmed by Richard that since she had been in West Cork the previous year, poverty had increased for the rural population. The small mud homes, with paltry pieces of land attached, appeared to have more children running around in clothes that looked like rags they would use for cleaning in Midleton. What shocked her even more was that jobs in the region were now few and far between. Grace told her that public works seemed to fill some void but men complained that there was little purpose in many of the works they carried out.

As she lay in bed with Richard, she asked him to explain where this poverty had come from in the past year.

"It's because the land isn't good enough for the intense use the people have to put it to, in order to grow enough to eat, plus enough to sell at the markets to pay the rent. Some of the land needs to be rested. We're close to the mountains here and it's a harsher landscape than you're used to in Midleton, love. My father is always rotating crops and we have enough water in the wells to keep our farm working well. I feel very sorry for the poor around here and, I agree with you, it's got much worse in the past year. But I want you to concentrate on our baby for now and perhaps later you can begin to help them. How you can do that, I don't know, but for the moment we'll just continue giving a few shillings to the families where the sons and daughters are taking the boats to America. It tides them over until the envelopes start to arrive from across the Atlantic. Some folks are already receiving money from America and it's keeping them fed and clothed."

Alice pondered on his explanations and promised herself that with her mother and Grace now in the household she would make sure that she made a difference in the area, like her sister Eliza had done in the past in Midleton. She had taught at the school there and later her daughter Margarita had transformed it by teaching singing. The benefit the kids got from learning to sing and play musical instruments was remarkable. The school choir had gone from strength to strength under the instruction of Master Johnson, the local music teacher, and the input of Margarita. It taught Alice that people who care do make a difference.

In the middle of December, Alice went into labour. The local midwife and Doctor Kiely from Ballydehob were both there to help bring the baby into the world. For many hours before the birth, Richard and Jerome were on tenterhooks. Richard thought it would be easier if only he could be busy like the women in the family who helped the doctor and midwife. Yet, even though she was helping, all the while Meg was praying in her heart. She wanted nothing to go wrong for her only child and grandchild.

At two o'clock in the morning on a bright winter's day, Meg thought that her life yet again had meaning, as she watched the arrival of Gregory Robert Staunton. She prayed that she would have a long life to spend years in this happy state, helping yet again to bring up a child.

Chapter Two

Margarita had grown content with her new life at Beconsford House. Their twins, Violet and Louis, had been born in February 1844. Louis had a head of black hair like his mother and a tranquil disposition that reminded Margarita of her own beloved father Jack. Violet had blonde curls just like her sister Rosita, and was more vocally demanding than her brother. The happy parents had enjoyed picking out their names. Margarita said that Victor's late wife Fleur would love another flower in the family, thus Violet was named. Richard said the boy would follow Fleur's French ancestors and they would call him after King Louis!

By late autumn, the twins were sleeping each night and settled into a routine. It was around then that Margarita became restless. She had been busy during the last months of her grandfather Robert's life, spending a lot of time talking and especially singing to him each afternoon. His loss she felt deeply. There was a restlessness in her now that she needed to address. I want to sing again, she thought. She realised that the wife of the future Lord Beconsford could not work in concert halls singing for payment, unless they were worthy charity events. Yet she couldn't see herself sitting with an embroidery needle or visiting local estates and having afternoon tea with the ladies. She had not been reared for such pretentious pursuits. She knew she had to deal with the problem.

The following morning, when the children were taking a nap, she sat down with her husband for their morning chat, while they enjoyed tea and hot buttered scones. If the sun was shining, they regularly took a walk in the Secret Garden. On that morning there was still a warm glow from the sun. They entered the garden and Margarita always could immediately smell which flowers were blooming and herbs smelling sweetly, whatever the season. They sat beside the fountain that her father Jack had designed for Victor's father, Lord Isaac, as a gift for his new wife Deborah. This garden was opened after her wedding to Isaac almost thirty years before. On warm days, from late spring to the end of autumn, the sun spots in the garden were a glorious haven of peace for all who sat there. Old John, who died during the Big Wind of 1839, had taught her father the relaxing value of rippling water plus the heady smell of herbs. Breathing in the camomile, thyme, sage and rosemary never failed to calm the body and quieten the minds of those who loved that quiet space.

Today, Margarita hoped that their presence in the garden would make Victor understand that her needs were not like those of the normal gentry.

When they were seated, Margarita took a deep breath. "I want to talk to you about my music, Victor," she began, somewhat anxiously, as she took his hand, squeezing it gently.

"What's wrong with your music?" he asked, smiling indulgently as he turned to her, raising his eyebrows in anticipation.

"Well, nothing is wrong, it's just that I'm looking for a future role in which I can still be involved with singers in a small way. Oh, I'm explaining myself badly. I know that it would not be appropriate for me to be singing professionally anymore but I've had an idea that I want to share with you. I'm hoping that you see it as I do, Victor, because I want to feel that what makes me happy isn't going to upset your position in local society."

Victor laughed heartily at that idea. "My dear Margarita, I have such a reputation because of my past problems with indulging in too much alcohol that I don't think there can be much worse to set the county gossips talking."

Margarita smiled. "You know how settled the twins now are with their routine since bringing in Hilda Bowe's eldest daughter Florrie to help

Nurse Jean. Florrie is a very hard worker with a lovely kind nature and we owe such a debt to her mother who nursed Rosita through her childhood after the sadness of losing your beloved Fleur."

She fell silent and they both took a moment to remember Victor's first wife who loved the Secret Garden where they had created a special corner filled with red roses in her memory. Victor put his arm around his wife, holding her close.

"My dear, remember that you were even more important in helping to raise Rosita to be the beautiful independent young girl she is turning out to be. I'll be forever grateful for the sacrifices you made to stay with my daughter after her birth. Therefore, Margarita, it would want to be something very shocking for me to refuse you anything."

Margarita looked into his smiling eyes and felt very excited about her project.

"That's good," she said enthusiastically. "You know how you are always asking me to hire a lady's maid? Well, I have a better idea. I think Nurse Jean is now beginning to feel somewhat surplus in the nursery and, as you know, I've had a great relationship with her since Rosita was born. I think I could persuade her to help me with various things. I know from Master Johnson that he is looking for an extra voice-tuition teacher for some of his best young female pupils and he believes that I can help him. Would you mind if young music students were to come to the music room in my father's house, where I could help them improve their singing? I would, of course, do it free of any charge, for just some hours each week. I feel that I need a purpose away from the children and I think that this might work out. What do you think?"

She waited anxiously as Victor looked at her.

"Well, Margarita, I wasn't expecting that, but it all sounds grand to me. However, I don't think Nurse Jean would like being called a lady's maid. Florrie will do very well with the twins because she's used to helping her own family, with her father so ill all these years. How about calling Nurse

Jean your companion? If her presence at your side will give you more time to enjoy your life then, I'm very happy."

Margarita was delighted at the thought of Jean becoming her companion.

For the next while they both sat in contented silence, each with their own thoughts until Margarita hugged him while thinking that she must be the happiest woman in the whole of Ireland.

Jean was very happy with the idea of her new role and she admitted to feeling a bit superfluous as the twins were getting bigger by the day.

"I think Florrie Bowe will be honoured with the promotion but I believe that she needs a young nursery maid to help her while she finds her feet. We could always give a position to young Lizzie Bowe, Florrie's younger sister. I know she's young but she's a strapping young girl and is used to looking after her own younger sister Esme. Esme will still be home to keep an eye on the father during the day while Hilda, their mother, works in the house."

Margarita agreed that it just might work.

And work it did. Margarita began to spent a couple of afternoons each week teaching young singers at her parents' home, much to Eliza's delight. Margarita began to feel needed again, mingling with some of the community of Midleton and meeting people with whom she had grown up. It wasn't long before she was getting high praise from Master Johnson due to her ability to teach the girls how to breathe better and she also explained to them how to present themselves on stage, during their journey towards becoming working singers in the future.

"The ladies you are teaching are finding it much easier to hold a high note. I have to admit that some of their parents were originally sceptical about learning from you, but you have proved them wrong. I could find myself replaced very easily by you, Margarita!" He laughed, seeing her face reddening with delight.

"I would never want to do your work, Master. You are a one-off, according to the best singers in Cork and that includes my brother-in-law Richard," she joked back, as she always felt relaxed in Master Johnson's company.

Christmas seemed to creep up on them very quickly and was spent quietly in the Big House. Deborah, as always, organised the beautiful tree in the hallway of the house and everyone enjoyed the lighting of the candles and the present-giving ceremony. Deborah's father had witnessed this custom in Germany and she had introduced it to the Big House. Young Louis and Violet, who crawled around the sparkling decorations, were captivated by the shining candles surrounding the tree when they were lit. Everyone in the household and the estate enjoyed the seasonal break from their work.

In West Cork, by the time Christmas Day arrived, Gregory was proving to be a contented child and Alice was delighted to see that her mother had a new spring in her step. Also important to Alice was the fact that her mother and Grace Staunton became good friends, as well as in-laws. Christmas was a happy time in the farmhouse, where each recalled a memory of Robert. His passing was still raw for Meg and Alice.

As Alice watched her family all sit down together for a feast of food prepared by Meg and Grace, a different kind of fear took hold of her which she found difficult to shake off. A cloud of uncertainty sat about her, mingling with her sense of happiness.

Before Christmas she had seen the levels of local poverty continue to grow as those seeking a bit of help to leave the country increased. This saddened her very much. As she looked around, the thought of any member of her own close family going away, with little chance of seeing them again in her lifetime, horrified her. She knew how much Grace and Jerome missed their son Barry. Amid all her happiness, for a moment she felt a shiver of real fear that she could not name.

Chapter Three

As 1845 began, there was an extra chill in the air. Alice spent a lot of time pushing the perambulator around the townland, getting to know a wide circle of people of all social classes. Thankfully, she was already able to help many of the people in ways that didn't make these proud families feel they were receiving charity. Some of the children would run errands and make small deliveries and they would return home with food that would allow the families go to bed with food inside them during the cold days of winter. Meg was receiving regular rent from the farm in Midleton and it was mainly her generosity that contributed to giving the payments helping those who needed it most. Alice often lifted her eyes to the sky in thanks for her luck in being able to help. She often remembered Jack's Granny Sheila and she knew that herself and her mother remembered the way Sheila quietly helped those in need.

Alice continued having concerns about the people who had been touched by poverty. Some of those looking for aid from the State through works schemes weren't always paid enough to cover the cost of feeding and clothing their large number of children. Some of those men were going without their own food so that their children could eat. Alice knew this wasn't the answer, because during that winter the health of even strong men weakened and poverty was growing, especially as the number of children living in each household continued to increase.

Richard continued to work as a singer in Big Houses around the county and their household ran smoothly with the addition of Meg to help with the chickens and the kitchen. She seemed to have the energy and enthusiasm of someone half her age. Richard worried about his own parents as his father was now constantly in pain with swollen joints in his hands and legs. Although he had to help on the farm, Richard was glad that they had made the decision to live in West Cork.

Alice knew of one great difficulty that was causing problems in the community. It started when the local landlord, Sir Graham Stewart, died in 1841. He had just one child, a daughter, the rather shy Sylvia, who was just nineteen at the time of her father's death. As a child she had a head of auburn curls that was the envy of many young girls. Yet now she wore that hair in a severe bun. She wasn't a true beauty but Richard knew that she was a lovely young lady with a kind heart. They had met on many occasions in the past since he had begun singing in public. She had attended many of his recitals with her father, who had been a good squire to his tenants. It was a surprise to the locals when just over a year after her father's death, her forceful and overbearing aunt, who was appointed her guardian until she came of age, arrived from London and announced that she had found a husband for Sylvia. The man she browbeat Sylvia into marrying, although she was still mourning her father, was nearly fifty years of age. Sir Graham Stewart had been a decent landlord and a gentleman but, since the arrival of Toby Ramsay, the community had watched in dismay as their new landlord turned out to be an unpleasant man and an incredible snob. They all felt sorry for Sylvia, because she looked cowed and almost fearful from soon after they wed in early 1843. What worried them even more about her unlikeable husband was the way he was beginning to treat his workers and tenants.

When Alice told her mother the name of the new squire, Meg was amazed.

"I heard from Grace about Sylvia and Toby but didn't know his second name. I knew him when your sisters were young, Alice. He was a friend of Isaac Beconsford and I know he took a fancy to your sister Eliza. Robert didn't like him and he was very relieved when Ramsay disappeared and didn't return to the area again. They all agreed in Midleton that he had notions above his station. Fancy, he's now the local squire! That will come as a surprise to them back in Midleton, so it will."

"I think we should keep our counsel, Mother, for the moment. We don't want to spread innuendo about the man until we see for ourselves."

Alice had only heard rumours so she decided to keep an open mind until she knew the family better. Richard had known Sylvia since they were small so Alice knew that they would very shortly become acquainted.

Later that week Alice informed the family that she had been invited to take tea with Sylvia. Sylvia had insisted that Alice bring Baby Gregory with her, which pleased Alice.

When they met in the drawing room of the house, Alice took an instant liking to the lady of the manor. Sylvia greeted her warmly as she looked longingly at the young child in the perambulator. Alice knew that Sylvia had not yet become pregnant.

As they had sat chatting amicably, the door burst open and Toby Ramsey entered and without drawing breath appeared to be criticising his wife in a rude manner.

"Have you not shown our guest around the house yet, Sylvia?" he demanded, before introducing himself to Alice by taking her hand and raising it almost to his lips.

Alice felt an instant dislike of this man. Toby didn't even look at his wife as he seemed intent only on impressing the visitor with his fine home.

"I have only just arrived and we have both been absorbed in keeping my young son quiet."

"I'm sorry my wife entertained you in this room as it needs so much work to make it attractive to visitors," Toby announced, barely concealing a smirk. "Unfortunately, my wife wants to keep it like this as a memory of her late father."

"Please don't apologise, sir. The room is very welcoming, as is your lovely wife."

"Unfortunately, her father had such bad taste in furnishings, didn't he, dear?" he continued with an arrogant air.

Sylvia's face began to redden as she looked embarrassed. Alice just thought, what a silly, pretentious man, who is devoid of good manners. So, she intervened. "Your wife has been the perfect hostess, sir, and has allowed this young fellow to roll around and enjoy the freedom of your lovely cosy rug. You have a beautiful home." She turned to Sylvia, giving her a sympathetic smile. "I think it's time for me to get this young boy into his perambulator for a sleep."

This brought a scowl to Toby's face and Alice had to hold back a satisfied smile as she saw the annoyance on his face.

When Toby took his leave, Alice and Sylvia enjoyed tea and refreshments, enhanced by the absence of her boorish husband.

Toby re-entered the room as Alice was leaving.

"Do come over to the farm whenever you get a free afternoon, Sylvia," Alice said. "The family would love to see you again and I promise that my husband will sing a couple of songs for you! I know how much you love going to his recitals."

Toby scowled at that but insisted on seeing her out. She knew that she didn't imagine it as he helped her with her cloak. He stood far too close to her.

"I'll see your husband tonight in Lord Kenmare's house," Toby said, as he shook her hand and patted it far too intimately for Alice's liking.

"I won't be attending, but I hope you and Sylvia enjoy it," she responded, giving him a less than genuine smile. They are right about him, she thought. What an odious man he is!

As she made her way home, pushing Gregory's perambulator, she decided that she'd say nothing about her discomfort with him as she didn't want gossip getting back to Midleton. He didn't know that Alice was

Eliza's half-sister. She thanked her lucky stars that she was married to Richard and not someone like Toby Ramsay.

When she came through the front door of the farmhouse, Grace was sitting in the kitchen and came towards her. She was all smiles as she lifted her beloved grandson out of his pram.

"I missed you, darling boy, and your daddy is waiting to say goodbye before he goes to his concert in Ballylickey House."

"Are you talking about me, Mother?" said Robert as he entered the kitchen, laughing as he embraced his wife before going over to kiss his young son, who was now snug in Granny Grace's arms. "I'll be home late tonight and we can chat then about your first day mingling with the upper classes, Alice. I'm sure you'll spend this evening writing to Eliza and your parents, telling them about your day."

"I will, my love, but it will only be news about our little Gregory," she said, laughing back at him.

Chapter Four

Later that evening when Richard returned, she told him of the obnoxious squire but said that she would keep it to herself for now.

"I have enough on my mind at the moment and don't want to waste my brain on such a man. I need to start thinking of something that could really make a difference to the poverty levels around here. I'm especially worried about the burden on the women, having to care for so many children, as I now feel that my energy levels have fully returned after the birth of Gregory."

"Why don't you have a serious talk with my mother and Meg? Put your heads together and, with all your experience of getting things done when myself and Margarita went to sing in France and Italy, you should come up with something."

"That's a good idea, love. It certainly beats moaning about the local squire!" she said with a laugh.

The following morning after breakfast, Alice asked Grace and Meg if they could come up with ideas of ways to help the community deal with the rising poverty around them. Having put Gregory down for a sleep, Grace suggested her close neighbour Mary Sheehan, who earned a few extra shillings helping out in the farmhouse regularly with the heavy washing.

"She knows everyone in the townland," Grace said, agreeing to call on her later in the morning while Alice was out walking with Gregory.

As she walked into the farmhouse the following morning, Mary Sheehan was like a breath of fresh air. She was small and rotund with silver hair but, as she bustled around, she looked like a ball of energy and she had a smile that would make her agreeable to anyone she met.

When Grace introduced her, Alice smiled and shook her hand.

Widowed at a young age, Mary devoted her life to working hard to give her son and daughter a good start in life. Her son Liam was happily married to a farmer's daughter and lived in Macroom. Fiona, her daughter, was married to a good labouring husband, Fergus Maguire. They lived close by with their two young children.

As Meg was still busy making tea and cutting slices of fruit cake for the guest, Alice invited Mary to sit down.

"I want to pick your brains, Mary," Alice said, as they all finally sat down around the large kitchen table.

"I hope there's nothing wrong, Mrs. Staunton," Mary enquired.

"Will you please call me Alice?" she said, smiling. "No, Mary, there's nothing wrong. It's just that I want to get more involved in the community, now that Gregory is a bit bigger. Shortly, I'm hoping to get a reliable young girl to spend a few hours each day with him."

"Well, I might be able to help you with that as my Fiona's daughter Maeve is nearly fourteen and she's still at school. They could do with a few pence extra each day coming into the house. Her husband's labouring job gets quiet outside the planting and the harvesting seasons. I always loved spending a few hours with my grandchildren when they were younger, but they are now growing up fast. I like to pass Fiona a shilling now and then, although she doesn't like taking it, that I do know. She's always so proud of her children. A little job would help young Maeve. She's very good with her schooling and Fiona is right proud of her."

Alice thought that they sounded a nice family. She smiled as she thanked Mary.

"I'd like to meet her soon, which brings me to getting involved with the community. I know there are rumblings about the increase in poverty in parts of the country and I thought it might be helpful to check out how we could help some of the poor in this locality."

"You're certainly right there, Alice." Mary nodded. "You don't need to have to look too far from here to see how poor some of our landless labourers in this townland are. Many of them who worked for the Stewart estate before Sir Graham died are now being worked to the bone by that despicable Toby Ramsay for half the money. They all need help and I know many of their wives and some of them don't have enough food to keep their children from half starving."

"That Toby Ramsay has a lot to answer for. I've only met him on one occasion and I was not impressed. Have you any suggestions?" Alice was realising there was a lot more poverty around than even she expected.

"Maybe there is something we could do for the wives," Mary said. "Many of their children are going around in rags and without shoes. I've been told that you are a professional at making clothes, Alice. Do you think it would be possible to get some materials and needles and threads to show some of the mothers how to make things? It wouldn't be seen as charity by the proud ones if you were just showing them how to make clothes."

"Mary, you are a genius! Why did I not think of something like that? What do you think about that, Grace? You're the local."

"I think it would be a great start. And let me take you out to the back of the farm, where I think there is somewhere you might be able to use to do your teaching."

The three women looked at Grace, intrigued. They all stood up and walked towards the back door of the farm. They made their way through the busy farmyard where the views of rolling hills stretched to the horizon. Alice always felt at peace listening to the sounds of cattle competing with the hens who were pecking at their food close to the farmhouse.

The sun was shining and Grace got the ladies to sit on a bench in the garden, close to a wall which shielded them from the winds.

"Look at the stable down there. Well, it's been empty for a few years since we got rid of one of the large carts when Barry went to America. Now it's an empty building. If you let me talk to Jerome, I'll ask him if he's happy for us to use it. I know it has even got an old fireplace in it from the days when farm boys lived there in the past."

"Well, ladies, that's great progress for this morning!" Alice beamed. "Let's get together again early next week and if any more good ideas come to mind, we can discuss them then. Now let's go in and have another cup of tea before the real work of the day has to be tackled!"

When Mary returned to the farm the following week, Alice met her with a beaming smile.

"I have good news for you," she said as she walked Mary in the direction of the large old stable that had been out of use for a few years.

They went in and Alice turned to Mary with a grin on her face. "Jerome has agreed. He thinks it's a great idea. He has even offered to pay for a clean-out and to pay for some distemper to help spruce this place up."

"That's wonderful." Mary looked around her and then nodded her head. "It will need a good cleaning, but I can do that with the help of a few women from the village. However, we have another problem. I was checking around to see if people would be interested in the sewing and when I went over to the townland of Ballyormond, I was shocked at the way the living conditions of many of the people have deteriorated. It has got so much poorer since I was over there last summer. Some of the people are living in what you could only describe as mud huts and even the farmers with a half to an acre of land are nearly as badly off because they have to pay rent for the land. I spoke to the wives but the problem is that most of them have small children. The mothers' eyes lit up when I told them about the sewing lessons because they all dreamed of dressing their children, especially for the cold weather, but they will have nobody to mind the children if they come over here."

Alice thought for a few moments. "Do any of them have girls around twelve years of age?" she asked.

Mary nodded. "Yes, some do."

"Maybe we could put aside a section of the stable and they could bring the children with them. We could give a few pence a day to the older girls if they kept the younger children occupied."

Mary nodded again. "That sounds like a great idea. Your time organising the opera singers is certainly standing to you, Alice! You have a solution for everything!"

"Right, let's get back to the kitchen now and start making our plans with Meg and Grace. We could even do it as a trial over the spring months and then see if they want to continue after that."

The days that followed were a hive of activity around the farmhouse and stables. Mary got a group of women to help her wash, clean and even make the windows of the stable sparkle. Fiona's husband Fergus came down and helped clear out the rubbish and put some white distemper on the walls. He also brought some old tables and chairs he'd got at a house sale, which Meg paid for. The women and their children would come from nine each morning until around midday. Meg suggested that she could supply tea and a bit of food to the ladies and milk and biscuits to the children when they finished the sewing at the end of each morning.

Jerome had finally accepted that because of increasing pain in his joints he needed to be seated for most of the time. The family were then really touched when he asked if he could be brought over in his brand-new Bath chair to the stables.

"I could stay seated and teach some of the children how to read," he suggested.

Alice was delighted with the idea. That evening she wrote to Eliza in Midleton, to tell her all about the scheme. Eliza replied by return and told Alice that they would send a carriage in a few days' time, with books for teaching and a selection of good old clothes that could be cut and shaped to fit their new owners. She also confirmed that Isaac's trust fund would supply all the sewing needles and threads. They would include also enough pencils and paper for the children to write on.

Fiona's husband Fergus went into Cork, armed with cash from Meg, and bought a variety of children's second-hand shoes for a great price. Alice was overcome by the generosity of everyone.

The carriage arrived from Midleton on the following Saturday. After Cillian had enjoyed their overnight hospitality and given them all the news from the Beconsford estate, he returned to Midleton bearing letters and presents from Alice and Richard.

In the meantime, Mary had spread the word around the townland and when the teacher heard about it he agreed that it would help Maeve's chances of later becoming a schoolteacher if she gave tuition to the young children. He also allowed a couple of reliable girls time off to help with the very young children. Alice was delighted with the positive response to the scheme from the local community.

On the following morning before nine o'clock, Alice again felt almost overwhelmed at the sight of more than fifteen women walking into the farm clasping the hands of small boys and girls and some of them with infants in arms. They all looked uncertain and uncomfortable but Mary immediately put them at their ease.

"I'm glad to see you, Lolly Murphy," Mary said to one of the first women. "It's useful that you know everyone, especially those from other townlands!" She laughed as she greeted everyone with Lolly by her side.

"You can tell us all about yourselves when we get inside the warmth of the sewing house," said Alice.

Lolly looked to Alice to be in her thirties. She was tall and strapping with a beam on her broad freckled face.

"Mrs. Staunton," said Lolly, "because Mary asked me, I have already picked out two great young girls to help care for the young children. Come over here, Eily and Catherine! Also, young Madge here is good at minding young children. Sure, she can turn her hand to anything!"

Alice laughed as she grasped Lolly's hand to thank her, feeling breathless already and thinking that this just might work. She saw that the others now began to feel more at ease, as they all looked around the building in amazement. The children were already running over to the place where toys and rugs were on the floor for them to sit there and play. Immediately they were closely followed by Eily and Catherine who were already warning them to behave.

Alice sat the ladies on benches at the table as Meg and Mary arrived with large pots of tea which they began to pour into mugs lined up on the table. Mary went back for biscuits which she gave out to everyone. She smiled as the children's hands all rose at the one time, as she arrived in their corner with a plate of biscuits.

"You'll all get a nice glass of milk before you leave at lunchtime and if you're all really good you'll get a little treat each day with your drink." She smiled, knowing the littler ones didn't understand what she was saying. "Now, children . . . let me introduce you to your teacher, Mr. Staunton."

The older children looked in awe at the man who was being wheeled towards them by his wife Grace. He smiled as they walked up to him and thanked him for giving his time to help them, just as they had been instructed by their mothers to say.

"Thank you, girls and boys. Now I want to introduce you to my assistant Maeve Maguire but I will need another assistant to help give out sheets of paper and pencils to the older children and to assist the little ones in drawing some pictures. Who would like to give out books and jotters for me?"

Mary's ten-year-old grandson Micky Maguire walked forward, not to be outdone by his older sister Maeve.

"Me, sir, and I know some words and my sums," he told Jerome.

"Well then, lad, maybe you'll be our helper and, if you enjoy it, you can be called my assistant." Jerome noticed that Micky seemed to grow taller in front of him at the compliment.

"Now, if the older ones can sit on the rugs at the back, then the younger children can come forward and sit in front of me and the first lessons can begin."

At the end of the morning Grace came in carrying chunks of bread and butter, followed by two farmhands carrying a cauldron full of hot vegetable soup. The room was still a hive of activity with Jerome conducting the children in singing a song. When it ended everyone clapped.

Alice had spent her morning showing the ladies how to cut out clothes from paper patterns that Margarita had sent, while a couple of the women preferred to use the wool provided to knit jumpers for their children. There were piles of clothes donated from local Big Houses as well as the generous donations from Lord Beconsford. All the women eyed them enthusiastically, knowing they would work on them over the coming weeks. She then gave out the second-hand shoes to the delighted children.

Alice looked around with satisfaction as all her anxieties about the project were fast disappearing.

The training continued until the end of April and, according to everyone in the townland, the project was a great success. On the day before they finished, all the children were presented with sturdy boots that, again, had been purchased second-hand in Cork by the ever-helpful Fergus Maguire, thanks to a further donation from Isaac's trust. The children were now in possession of two pairs of shoes each which, Alice knew, would later be passed on to younger children and cousins. Her own goal, of ensuring all the women made at least one garment for themselves and at least one for every child on the course and some for their friends, was met. They were also given clothes purchased second-hand in Cork for their elderly family members and their menfolk.

When the final day arrived, it was a glorious late spring day. From early morning, the farmhouse kitchen was a hive of activity with cold meats being cut, bread being buttered and fairy cakes arranged on plates for the children to eat with their cups of milk. When the families arrived on the Friday morning, the sun was shining as they all made their way to the sewing house dressed in their new clothes and shoes. There would be no work done as everyone was expected to just enjoy themselves on the last day.

When everyone was seated the food was brought in by Alice, Grace and Meg. They were followed by Richard who was holding a plate on which sat a large cake. Everyone, including the children, cheered with excitement but, before the promised party began, Alice spoke.

"I want to thank all of you for making the journey here these past few months, sometimes in bad weather. As you know, we've had inquiries from lots of women further away in other townlands and we hope that they will learn from our example. We hope also to continue to support you and other people from the townland after the summer and when the harvest has come in. Hopefully we can resume then. In the meantime, I know that your skills have improved. Next winter, we will be making sure that we have all the equipment to continue to improve further and we will create additional spaces to accommodate more women and children. I know that some of you ladies are already passing on your new skills to neighbours and friends. Hopefully, some of you may make some money with your new sewing skills because the work you have done is exceptional. Finally, I want to thank you all for coming and I hope it encourages you to continue to use your skills in the future."

Alice stopped speaking and stood smiling as everyone clapped and cheered.

Then Alice and Mary walked over to the children. They each carried a large sack.

"We have a little gift for all of you children, but first of all I want a big cheer for Mr. Jerome and the young helpers."

Everyone cheered again and, as Mary began to give out the presents, Lolly shouted from the top table.

"Let's all raise our cups of tea in a toast to Alice, Mary, Meg, Mr. Jerome and Mrs. Grace!"

As the cheers rang out again, young Gregory was brought through the door by his proud father. This morning young Maeve Maguire was at his side as she was by now a regular babyminder for Gregory in the afternoons when she finished her day at school.

Alice couldn't stop smiling, but she knew that it was likely that in the future support would be needed more than ever with the rising poverty levels, a problem for which she had no easy answers. She looked up to the sky and offered a silent prayer that they would be able to continue to meet the needs of those good people.

As the grateful participants left the farm, Alice knew what she wanted to do. It was to read a letter that had arrived earlier from her sister. As she happily sat in the farmhouse kitchen, she basked in the warm feeling that the sewing classes had given her. She was going to enjoy sitting by the cosy fire with nothing of consequence to do or even think about. When she opened the letter that had arrived earlier in the day and began to read it, she immediately called out to her mother with excitement in her voice.

"Mother! Richard and I have an invitation to celebrate the marriage of Jack Ryan's niece Cara in Cork at the end of next month! And that includes you!"

She read Eliza's letter and discovered that all her family from East Cork would be joining the festivities. When she read it to her mother, Meg just smiled and said that maybe it was about time Alice made a nice outfit for the two of them to fit the occasion.

"I agree with you, Mother!" Alice said excitedly. "We'll go next week to get some material in Bantry."

When Grace was told the news, she immediately said that she would be delighted to keep Gregory if they wanted to stay on in Cork for a full weekend.

"I'll bring young Maeve Maguire in each day to help out," she said. "So that should keep your mind at rest. You deserve a break after all the effort you have put into the community recently."

Alice ran and hugged her, delighted with the idea. Later that evening, when Gregory was asleep, Alice sat in the warm kitchen with a cup of tea and wrote a letter to Eliza.

My dearest Eliza,

I hope everyone is well. As you know, I have not had time to write over the past while due to the project here in Eoinstown. It was an incredible success, especially with the input of funds from East Cork. Thank everyone for me, please!

My husband keeps asking me to find out if your beloved daughter Margarita is ever going to sing again with him. He says that she must surely be able to leave her three children in the safe hands of their father and grandparents, especially with the number of servants available in Beconsford House!

I'm very excited about the wedding invitation you passed on and we hope to spend the whole weekend in Cork, thanks to Grace who has agreed to mind Gregory! That is so exciting for me. I've got a real yearning to meet my family again before I restart my sewing classes in the barn in October.

As you know, I have settled in really well in West Cork. I've now got a good friend in Sylvia from the Stewart estate. The house is a splendid size and its gardens are laid out with many species of flowers that are blooming early. However, most of the land is now rented out to tenant farmers since the new squire arrived. When I first took tea with Lady Sylvia in their house, I knew that I had found a true friend. She's a lovely, rather shy person, who loves playing with Gregory. In fact, she seems a little sad and maybe I discovered why when her new husband appeared, all bluster and bumptiousness with, dare I say it, slightly wandering hands when he helped me with my cloak before I left! By then I already knew that he wasn't liked by his tenants and he certainly did not make a good impression on me. I'm very happy that Richard's family own their own land as I would not like to be beholden to him! His name is Toby Ramsay and he's around fifty years old, I believe – much older than Sylvia. I think he married her only to get hold of the estate! Meg said that she remembered him around Midleton with Isaac many years ago, before I was born, and that our papa didn't like him. You might remember him? Richard is singing regularly in places such as Kenmare House and I feel that Toby Ramsay only allows me into his house because Richard is rather famous in this area. But, enough about that odious man!

On another uncomfortable topic, we have heard from the farming community here that some of the potato crops are not thriving, but Richard says that his Opera friends in Europe have experienced some similar problems and he thinks it will be fine. I worry because the small farmers and labourers in the surrounding townlands in these parts are dependent on the potato crop to feed their families. I hope that I'm being too pessimistic and that Richard is right.

To finish on a happier note, Gregory is now taking spoons of soft bread and milk and he loves rolling around on the rug in the kitchen! I can't wait for him to take his first steps, but that's still a long way off. He's looking more like his father each day – handsome of course with his black head of hair!

Send our regards to everyone and make sure that all of you stay two nights in Cork, when we are there for the wedding.

Looking forward to meeting with you all, sooner rather than later,

Love,

Alice

Chapter Five

Jack Ryan was sitting at the breakfast table in Midleton, enjoying his breakfast in the relaxed company of his beloved wife. Eliza sat opposite him with her usual cup of tea on the table. She was enjoying the peace of early morning before the chores of the day began. She smiled as she opened the envelope on her plate.

"I can't wait to hear Alice's news and I hope she's thinking of making the journey to Cara's wedding now that Gregory is getting a bit bigger."

Jack smiled, knowing how much Eliza loved having all her family around her.

"What news has she except the wonders of her son?" Jack said, laughing. Then he saw a look of consternation on Eliza's face. "Is there a problem?"

"Read if for yourself," she answered, as she thrust the letter towards him. She watched his face as he read.

"*That viper, Toby Ramsay!*" he exploded. "How did he manage to inveigle his way into marrying a squire's daughter? Are you going to tell Alice about your ordeal at his hands all those years ago?"

Tears came to Eliza's eyes and Jack moved closer. When he held her hands, he found they were trembling.

"I'll have to think about it. I thought that I'd never hear his name again."

As the minutes passed, they were both lost in thought. Finally, Jack touched his wife's chin and gently lifted her face and looked her in the eye.

"I think she needs to know, love. She needs to make sure that she can keep herself safe when she's around him. He attacked you and goodness knows what would have happened if you hadn't fought back. I think it would frighten him to discover that she is your half-sister, as he was gone from East Cork before she was even born. He'll want to keep in with all the gentry in West Cork and most would be horrified by his past. It was awful that he attacked you but to follow it up by paying the O'Leary brothers to set fire to Rose Cottage, with me inside, was abominable. Brendan O'Leary would always confirm that if it was needed. So, stop worrying. Write to Alice and give her a hint about Toby and wait until you next meet her to tell her the full story."

Eliza looked into at her husband's eyes with a watery smile.

"I can always rely on you, Jack Ryan. I keep being surprised at just how much I love you! I have to put that man out of my mind. At least Alice has one bit of good news. She's joining us in Cork for Cara's wedding and I can't wait until we all meet up again. Come on, Jack, let's put Toby Ramsay out of our heads and instead walk in the woods so that I can clear my head before we have to deal with what the rest of the day will bring."

Margarita Beconsford sat in her cosy upstairs lounge in the Big House and smiled as she watched her three young children playing with Florrie Bowe and the young nursemaid Lizzy, in the newly created children's play area just outside the Secret Garden. Her father, Jack, who had originally created the Secret Garden, had now designed a safe play area for their eldest daughter Rosita and the twins. Violet and Louis were now getting sturdier and they loved playing in the fresh air. Florrie had drawn chalk lines and Rosita was playing hopscotch. Margarita shook her head as she spotted that Violet was grabbing most of the attention from her gentler brother.

She decided to take them in their perambulator to her parents' home in the estate.

Within two minutes of arriving at her childhood home, close to the forest, Rosita was already talking non-stop, until her grandmother Eliza asked her to slow down.

"Mama says that Papa will still not let me go to the forest and swing on some of the trees. I've seen Letty Patterson having great fun with her brother on their farm and it's not fair that I can't do that."

Eliza smiled indulgently at her granddaughter.

"I'll talk to your papa again later," Margarita said, "but you know how much he wants you all safe and not getting hurt. Let me see what I can do – I'll talk to him again. For now, Rosita, just go into the parlour and read your book while I talk to your granny. Then, if you behave yourselves, you'll all get a biscuit before we go home!"

"Thank you, Mama," Rosita said angelically, looking first at her mother and then with a cheeky grin at her Granny Eliza.

Margarita smiled at Rosita who was in many ways far too grown up for her age, but her sunny temperament made everyone in the household love her. She had an opinion on everything and everyone. The child really does need a few more freedoms, she thought.

When Rosita left the room, Margarita sat back to reflect on her dilemma. Eliza knew the problems they had in the big house with Victor's intense need for everyone to be safe.

"I think you do need to deal with that, Margarita," Eliza advised her. "Children must take some risks if they are to learn any life lessons, even if their parents' hearts are almost stopping when they take their first step towards independence."

Margarita nodded in agreement. Although she adored her life and loved her husband Victor dearly, his insistence that the children were at all times allowed only to indulge in safe play was becoming a problem. The twins were still too young to be left out of sight but Rosita certainly needed more freedom.

As Margarita lay in bed that evening, she reflected on how she would approach her husband regarding Rosita's lack of freedom. She decided to broach the subject when she and Victor took their mid-morning break together. On the following morning, when her husband joined her for coffee, he was followed by the kind-hearted maid Jenny, who was promoted to the job of cook's helper. She carried a tray with tea and coffee, plus hot scones that had come straight from the oven.

Victor kissed his wife as tea was served. Margarita loved this time with Victor as they both watched through the window while the children played and their shrieks could be heard. However, today she was working out how to broach the problem of getting a little more freedom for Rosita, and indeed the twins when they were no longer so young.

Margarita took hold of her husband's hand and squeezed it. "I need to talk to you about the children," she began.

"They're alright, aren't they?" Victor immediately asked with anxiety in his voice.

"Of course they are," she said, laughing. "Can't you see how healthy they all look? But I've had Rosita pestering me for months now, as you well know, wanting to go climbing a few low trees and swing with ropes. Her friend Letty keeps asking her to join in when we go for a walk past their farmhouse. Yesterday, I promised her that I'd talk to you again. I know that your anxiety stems from the death of your beloved first wife Fleur, while she was giving birth to Rosita, but you simply cannot allow all your children to be wrapped in cotton wool until they are adults. Have you forgotten how many risks you took as a young boy? I know you don't remember me crying when you tried to climb to the top of a large tree so that you could see the church steeple in the distance. I had to beg you to come down. Yet you survived. You must at least give Rosita a little bit of freedom, or she'll begin to resent you. She's such a caring girl but she is also independent and strong-willed and I would hate if the time came when she resented you."

Victor looked at Margarita and she could see that he had tears in his eyes. He always hated conflict and stress, she thought, remembering how he had disappeared to Europe after the death of his wife and took to drinking excessively to block out the memory of her death.

"Victor, things are different now. We have so many people to support us and all we both want is what's best for the family. I am as conscious as you are of keeping our children safe but as they grow older, we have to adjust as their needs change." Margarita paused.

"Yes, yes, I've listened to you and know you're right. My mother and father have been nagging me as well. Let me go over and check the trees on the Pattersons' land and perhaps we'll go around there as a family next Sunday?"

Margarita threw her eyes to heaven as she smiled, shaking her head.

"You're making it sound like a military manoeuvre – but it sounds like a good idea. Afterwards we can go to my parents' home in the estate. That should make everyone happy! Now why don't we go down and bring the twins up to the nursery and have a bit of fun with them before their nap?"

Victor smiled and kissed his wife. "How was I lucky enough to have you agree to marry me?"

Margarita linked his arm and they made their way outside to their family.

Margarita was wishing that life would be calm and relaxed, for the time being at least.

I hope that no problems lie on the horizon, she thought, as they each held out their arms to the twins who let go of Florrie's and Lizzy's hands.

They took the twins up to the nursery and played with them for a little while before Florrie brought them a small snack to have before their nap.

Victor left then and Margarita kissed the children and handed them over to the capable hands of Florrie and Lizzy.

Since starting to work in the nursery some months earlier, Lizzy Bowe gave even more time to looking after the twins than she was paid for, because she loved her job so much. Margarita secretly thought that the newly promoted Florrie, who was growing up fast, already hero-worshipped Victor, but she would be afraid to tease him about it as he would be disturbed. Margarita knew that Victor despised squires who abused the young members of staff. Sadly, she knew many of these obnoxious men who held places in society but had no morals.

Alice smiled as she received a letter from Eliza – she recognised her writing on the envelope. She walked back to the kitchen, happy that Gregory was in the capable hands of her mother as she made herself a cup of tea before sitting by the fireside. She opened the letter, thinking that it was a very quick reply from Eliza.

My dear Alice,

I am so pleased that you will be attending the wedding in Cork and look forward so much to meeting you there! We will, of course, also spend two nights in the city.

Unfortunately, I have to tell you of the shock I felt when you mentioned having come in contact with Toby Ramsay. Suffice to say that he is a very nasty man. Ladies need to avoid him and I cannot help but feel sorry for his wife. Please discuss this only with Richard and not with your lovely mother Meg and when we meet I will give you more information.

I am so happy that Gregory is thriving, as are our three grandchildren up in the Big House. Aren't we both lucky to have such wonderful families around us?

Your loving, much older sister!

Eliza

I knew I was right about him, she thought. I'm going to keep my distance from him, but I'll just have to continue to be a good friend to Sylvia. How awful that such a man ended up in a position of power!

She would have to be careful around him in the future.

Later, Richard walked into the kitchen exactly on time for his midday meal.

"I think you can smell the food wherever you are." Alice smiled as Richard seated himself at the table.

"Where is everyone?" he asked, looking around.

"Your mother is with your father in the parlour and they're both entertaining Gregory by teaching him music with a new rattle and the lid of a pot. Meg is down visiting Mary. I gave them their lunch earlier because I need to talk to you."

She put a large bowl of vegetable soup on the table for him and buttered a couple of slices of bread.

She fetched some soup for herself and joined him. Then she handed him the letter she had received from Eliza.

"Read that. It's from Eliza."

"What is this about Toby Ramsay?" Richard asked, when he finished reading the letter.

"I don't really know as I wasn't even born, but I've decided that I will keep out of his way and still stay friendly with Sylvia. She certainly needs a friend now. I'm waiting until I talk to Eliza in Cork to hear the details. I'm just grateful that I'm not married to such a horrible man and I just hope that he doesn't find out that I'm Eliza's sister.

Chapter Six

On the advent of summer 1845, the weather in County Cork had a chill in the air that was unusual. Shrewd farmers felt an extra concern, knowing that famines had appeared around Europe and worried that ominous signs of crop failure were appearing in Ireland. With the population exploding throughout the Irish countryside, the last thing they felt the people could cope with was a similar situation arising in Ireland. Yet things still seemed alright. Concerns of rising poverty seemed to be a topic on many people's lips and this was never helped when many absentee landlords of the big estates worried only about the export of their best crops and the ready availability of cheap labour. Most Irishmen, even those with a half-acre, were always ready to take on extra work to feed their growing families and to pay the rents on their holding. Now the word poverty was on the lips of many peasant farmers and unskilled labourers.

Jack Ryan was in his home in Midleton enjoying the warmth of an early morning sun. It was sending rays of bright light into the kitchen. He was about to enjoy a peaceful breakfast with Eliza when the words that were unspoken became for him a reality. *Potato blight*. He sat reading a letter from his good friend Gerry Harris who had trained him many years ago in the Dublin gardens. The contents of the letter made the hair stand on his neck and cold goose bumps chased the feel of the sun from his arms. Gerry explained in his letter what might now become a reality in Ireland. It seemed that the Belgian government imported seed potatoes from America and a crop in West Flanders was subsequently found to be diseased. Soon after, a similar problem appeared in Kent in southern England. It appeared that the blight might now have reached the farms of Ireland.

He immediately shared the news and his worry with Eliza. As he stood and pulled his wife of more than twenty-five years into a tight embrace, she could feel his heart racing as she wondered if he was overreacting to the contents of the letter.

"Are you seriously worried, love?" she enquired, looking at him and seeing fear in his eyes that she rarely had seen since the months after he survived a shipwreck in Tramore back in 1816. "Maybe the harvest will be lost in some parts of the country, but we have so much rich land it shouldn't be a disaster, surely?" she asked, hoping to calm him down.

"Of course I'm seriously worried, love. I have a bad feeling about it. I think it could quickly lead to a full-scale famine in Ireland because more than half of our population relies solely on potatoes to keep them alive!"

"Then explain it to me more carefully and do not go running up to the Big House and have them all in a panic – because they're all worried enough as it is with the rumours going around."

"Gerry Harris, although now retired, has insider knowledge. If it gets bad Gerry doesn't appear to have an answer to the problem. It's believed that it might be a fungus. There is no easy remedy or quick fix to this, he says. It's very unlike him to say that we all just have to hope and pray! We might be about to experience a famine in Ireland, Eliza, and I say those words with a very heavy heart."

They held each other close for a few minutes more before Eliza suggested that they sit down with a cup of strong tea.

"At least let us go to the wedding in Cork next week and then we can deal with it," she begged him.

Alice was consumed with excitement at the prospect of spending a weekend in Cork at Cara's wedding. The wedding breakfast would be in the Imperial Hotel in Cork, following the church service in St. Ann's church in Shandon. All the East and West Cork relatives would gather there. Food still appeared to be plentiful in Cork, especially for those with extra money to spend.

It was with some trepidation that Alice was leaving the baby even for a night.

"Come on, love." Richard smiled as he helped his wife onto the carriage. "We want to try to arrive in Cork before dark."

"Imagine two nights for us both without worrying about Gregory waking up!" she said.

Meg was already in the carriage with her small bag on her lap and their finery was in a trunk on top of the carriage. She too was excited at the prospect of again meeting all the family from Midleton.

Margarita and her mother Eliza were standing inside the hotel door, waiting for the carriage from West Cork to arrive. As it drew up in front of the hotel, they ran outside and passers-by smiled as they saw the excitement in the faces of the families as they greeted each other with kisses.

"Come inside and join everyone!" Margarita said as she led the way to a small salon close to the entrance. The excitement grew as Jack, his mother Molly and Margarita's husband Victor were spotted enjoying drinks and refreshments. They stood up to greet the travellers.

"Imagine us all here together without any demanding children and for two days and nights!" Margarita said, putting an arm around her husband as she sat beside him.

Within minutes, it was like old times as they shared reminiscences of their years in Midleton. Richard was laughingly being educated on the number of young men that had hoped to marry his Alice before he won her heart some years earlier. A warm feeling enveloped the group as they were fed and cosseted by the hotel staff until it was time to get some sleep which was needed by all.

The wedding of Cara to Conor O'Hanlon was watched by many northside Cork residents as they had heard that Lord Beconsford's family were in attendance. The crowd watched in awe as the well-dressed groups arrived in their carriages. Margarita had offered a grateful Cara the opportunity to wear an ivory wedding gown made with imported satin and a veil adorned with a wreath of flowers which had been worn by Margarita when singing in Italy.

Later, when the newly married couple hosted the celebrations in the Imperial Hotel, Cara hugged Margarita and Eliza and told them how grateful she was to have had such a fairy-tale day for her wedding.

"Things are getting tougher in the city," she explained, "and although Conor has a good job delivering the turf and coal, money is getting tight. We're lucky to be able to live with my parents Hannah and Jarad in First Avenue. They were always so grateful to Great-granny Sheila for giving them the house when she sold the market garden and moved with you all to Midleton. So, I've little to be worried about and a lot to be grateful for today."

Margarita assured her that it was the least Jack could do for them. "After all, it was Granny Sheila who first set him up so he will always make sure his family in Cork is alright."

In the evening, local musicians had the party dancing with lively music and such a day could not have ended properly without songs being sung by Margarita and Richard. Tears were in many eyes as the duo finished with a love song during which they drew the new young married couple into the middle of the dance floor to sing with them.

By the time they left Cork at the end of the weekend, Alice knew that she had truly needed this break. Herself and Richard had been shocked when Eliza told them how Toby Ramsay had attacked her and tried to burn Jack's home, all those years ago but the trip to Cork had given her time and breathing space away from the rising poverty in West Cork. It gave her a new resolve to help the people in her neighbourhood, as Jack and Eliza's family did for their Cork relatives.

When they finally reached home, Alice was grateful to Grace when she saw how contented her young son was. He seemed as happy as when she had left. Secretly, she knew that she had enjoyed the break from him and had to admit to herself that, like Margarita, she would always need a little more in her life than rearing a family.

It was late August when Alice received a letter from Eliza. Its contents upset her so much that she did not share them with Meg and Grace but waited until she was alone with Richard before showing it to him. His face turned white with shock as he digested the contents.

My dear Alice,

I want to say first of all how much I loved our time in Cork, but Jack has insisted I write about a concern that he's had and is only now sharing with Isaac. I don't want you to get too worried, but a few days ago Jack got confirmation from Gerry Harris in Dublin that potato blight has spread throughout Ireland. It is worse in some areas than others. Jack hopes that like many of countries in Europe it will be over in a season but, even if that is so, the poor people who rely almost totally on the potato will need help if they are to have enough food to survive. Please discuss this only with Richard for now, as we believe that the idea of a long-drawn-out famine is being played down in certain governments circles.

I'm sorry to be the bearer of such disturbing news, but I know that you are a problem-solver and that you would prefer to know rather than avoid the inevitable. I just hope and pray that it is short-lived.

Your loving sister,

Eliza

When Alice and Richard retired to their bedroom later, they quietly discussed the bad news.

"I knew there had been problems in some areas of the country. I've recently seen where crops have failed during my journeys to sing. But remember me saying that there have been famines in many countries and they are over quickly?"

"Well, Richard, I am a realist and I don't wait until things are broken before I start to try to fix them. I want to ensure that our townland here in Eoinstown is prepared for problems and I want to help where necessary, but I need some guidance as to what I can do. I have spent much of my time since I arrived here concerning myself only with the family and our beautiful son, apart from the sewing project in the spring. I was looking forward to restarting the sewing classes, but I think that it will now have to be shelved because there is a bigger crisis already beginning to happen around us."

Richard felt a cold sweat coming over him. As the silence settled around him, he put his arm around Alice.

"Alice, love, we are fine with our lovely farm with its diverse products and I believe we could weather a famine for a year or so. The biggest problem in this locality is that Toby Ramsay's presence is likely to cause issues for those dependent on his estate to survive. He now charges high rents to all the farmers in the district and, like you, I wouldn't want to rely on someone like him to support the community in a crisis. I am certainly impressed with the passion you are showing, but I hope this problem doesn't turn into a catastrophe. I need to discuss it with some of the men in Bantry and Ballydehob. Maybe then we can see what help is required and where it is needed most. I know how capable you are, Alice. Didn't you steer myself and Margarita around European opera houses without any calamities befalling us? And that was one of the reasons I fell deeply in love with you." He put his hand on her cheek and caressed her, then gently held her worried face. "I will support you in anything you do to make the lives of people here better, and so will my mother and father. You know that Margarita's Great-granny Sheila would be proud of you because she came from this area before she moved to Cork city many years ago."

"I know what I will do first," Alice replied happily, thankful that her smiling, easy-going husband was on her side.

"I'll talk to Mary when she next comes in to help with the heavy cleaning. She's a wise woman and knows a lot of the locals and is well liked by most. If anyone is seriously down on their luck, she'll find out about it. We are so lucky, Richard, with your income and a successful farm. We can afford to offer help, at least in the short term."

As summer came to a close and the crunch of autumn leaves began to mingle with the heady smell of lilac blossom still smelling sweetly, Alice discovered that many of Mary's enquiries around the local townlands told of a steep rise in poverty everywhere in the region. Finally, she was forced to share her knowledge with Meg and Grace and Jerome. Alice felt that she had to be honest with them. The blight was here and the loss of the potato crop was happening in farms throughout the country.

For a long time after her trip to Cork, Alice was still glowing but this news frightened her. I think it's more than sewing classes that the women will have on their minds this winter, she thought. Maybe some of the prouder people are hiding their difficulties already, she reflected as she sat back on the chair and tried to formulate some kind of a plan in her head.

The following morning, she sat down with Meg, Grace and Mary.

"I have some difficult news, ladies. From my investigations, I have been told that the potato blight is now confirmed officially in Ireland. It looks like a blight has hit the potato crop and famine is around the corner, for those relying solely on the potato for sustenance. Gerry Harris in Dublin says we can only hope and pray that it is over in a year, but he has his doubts. I need us to talk and come up with real ideas as to how we can help the people locally without it seeming too much like charity. Jack Ryan has already warned us not to restart the sewing classes. He says it could cause a spread of disease if people come from a distance in a weakened state of health. That saddens me but we have to make sure that we keep all these families safe plus ourselves and, if he thinks it's too risky, I have to take his advice."

The ladies were all ears and deeply shocked by the starkness of Alice's words. They agreed that they needed time to think, as they all suddenly began to all worry about their own families and even their lives. It looked as if a catastrophe might be coming down the road over the next few months.

Jack Ryan had by now taken enough time mulling over Gerry's letter before finally deciding that it was necessary to share the information with Isaac, because many of the large country-house owners still didn't recognise the seriousness of the situation. Isaac, of course, knew that the potato crops were failing but Jack wasn't looking forward to the conversation, to having to tell him that the country was already facing a widespread famine.

Isaac was in the office when he arrived and they greeted each other as the friends they had become over more than twenty-five years of working together.

"You look anxious, Jack. Sit down and join me for coffee before we start our day's work."

Jack sipped the coffee slowly before turning to Isaac.

"Gerry Harris has finally confirmed our worst fears. The blight has been officially confirmed and he believes we need to prepare for what he thinks could be a long-drawn-out problem for this country."

"I heard from the powers that be that there has been an issue with this year's crop in parts of the country but that it should be over in a short time," Isaac assured Jack.

Jack began to feel his temper rise – not at Isaac but at the so-called civil servants who ran the country from London.

"They don't know what they are talking about!" he answered angrily. "I've been in this business now for nearly thirty years and I know enough about the plants and vegetables that are grown in this country to tell you that we may have a massive crisis beginning to unfold in this country. The number of families who rely for their entire food on the potato is massive. The population explosion in the past ten years means that there are far more mouths to feed in every household. Now I might be wrong but –"

Isaac put his hand up and stopped him. "I hope that you're wrong but I know you well enough, Jack, to take heed. You have me seriously worried because I have heard the rumblings from around the county. As you know, most of the rich and powerful don't worry about things unless their finances are put under pressure and that hasn't happened yet."

"Not yet," said Jack.

"Nonetheless, I don't want us to say anything to Victor for the time being. I'll talk to his mother first about how we'll tell him," Isaac concluded with a sigh, knowing how anxious his son got when he had to face any difficulties in his life.

The late summer evening sun was glowing in the sky as Margarita left the Secret Garden to go in for dinner. She had left the twins in the capable hands of Florrie and Lizzy earlier and Rosita was enjoying her tea in the kitchen today, where she regularly got treats from Cook, before retiring to her room to enjoy reading her book before bedtime. It was adults only who sat down for dinner most evenings because estate matters could then be freely discussed and mulled over, if required.

Victor and Isaac were already seated when Margarita entered. She was quickly followed by Deborah.

"I'm always late," Deborah said with a chuckle, as she sat down next to Isaac. "I love this time of the day, when all the children are quiet and I don't fall over a toy whenever I turn a corner!"

Their meal was always lively, usually including stories of the children's antics and the gossip from the farms around the estate, as well as business. Time usually flew as they enjoyed the usually delicious meats with a rich supply of vegetables, and potatoes creamed to perfection. Tonight it was followed by a succulent apple pie topped with creamy custard. Afterwards the family always took coffee at the dinner table, where they enjoyed Cook's thin chocolate squares as an extra treat before they enjoyed a chat and sometimes even a song from Margarita.

Yet tonight, Margarita noticed that Isaac looked subdued throughout the meal.

"You're not your usual chatty self tonight, Father-in-law," she said.

"It's because I have something that I need to talk to Victor and yourself about and Deborah agreed that it would be better to discuss it with all of us present."

"Now you have me alarmed, Father," Victor said.

"Jack believes we may be in for difficult times in Ireland, but hopefully we in Midleton will be alright. As you know, there has been talk of the potatoes failing in parts of the country. Well, the potato blight is officially confirmed in Ireland. I don't have to spell out to you the effect this will have on the many landless labourers and farmers with small acreage. It could result in the emergence of a major famine and we want to be prepared here if the worst happens."

Margarita felt a jolt of fear in her stomach that worsened when she saw Victor's leg begin to tremble, which happened when he got fearful. She was trying to work out whether she felt more worried about the poor or her husband, who got upset even about things in which she saw no danger.

"Victor, love," she said, "we are all very resourceful in this house and we should be fine, so perhaps we should be concentrating on the poor who will be most affected if they go hungry. You have always supported good causes, as did your father and mother. Let us focus for the time being on being positive but preparing for any emergencies that may arise."

"Maybe we should move the children to England?" Victor said.

"Whatever for?" Deborah protested.

"Son, we can deal with this," Isaac said. "Why don't you ladies get together with Eliza tomorrow in her house and Jack can join us up here. I think that we should call a meeting with our farm tenants and see how we can work on some plan. They need to know what's happening locally. However, I hope that our efforts will be in vain and that this blight will pass quickly. Yet we have to prepare for whatever life throws at us. We can only do our best given the circumstances we find ourselves in, whatever that will be."

As they all looked towards Isaac's drawn face, they thought of the uncertain future coming down the road.

As autumn closed and winter brought its cold winds and rain to the western seaboard, the people of Eoinstown and surrounding townlands had been hit by a disastrous harvest of potatoes. The fields were a stark reminder that famine had wrapped a cruel hand around the country. Many fields were now filled with potato stalks of a sickly colour and smell. The dark fungus made the potatoes inedible. It had only slowly dawned on the people that the crop they relied on to feed themselves through the cold winter months would not be there for them this year.

Those who could among the young people began to scrape together enough money to emigrate. They could be seen every morning walking the road towards Cork, with their bags of belongings and tears in their eyes. Those left behind didn't know if they should be happy or sad for them. Yet it seemed to be their only hope. To go to America was the option open to those young men and women.

At home in her farmhouse, Alice was close to exhaustion as she tended to her son and tried to keep on top of everything that threatened to overwhelm her. The cursed famine affected many areas and the news from Skibbereen and other townlands in West Cork was more than worrying for her. Plus, the news from the northwest of Ireland was even more dire.

When Richard opened the bedroom door, he immediately noticed the distress exhibited by his young wife as she lay in the bed. He took two strides and enveloped her in his arms. He said nothing for a while as he allowed her to shed the tears he knew were bottled up inside her.

"What is worrying you most, love?" he asked, knowing full well that there was very little he could do to relieve her anxiety.

She laid her head close to his and for just a moment a feeling of calm came over her. If I could only stay like this forever, safe in his arms, with my son close by, I wouldn't have any worries, she thought. But real life had to go on and she just didn't seem to have the energy to embrace it as she had in the past.

He dried the tears from her eyes with a handkerchief and planted a gentle kiss on her brow.

"I always thought I was the luckiest girl in the world when I married you. I even embraced our new life here in West Cork and thought everything would stay the same. I love that beautiful brown-eyed little cherub in the cot, now sleeping so soundly. But what kind of a world have we brought him into? And I don't seem to have the energy to look after him because there is another reason why I am worried, Richard. I think I might be with child again but I'm sick thinking of the madness of bringing new life into this country when it's gripped by fear."

Richard looked at her in shock, before taking her again in his arms and holding her tight.

"Richard, I feel old, tired and not in control of my life anymore!" Alice said in anguish.

"Alice, my love, this pregnancy is the most joyous news I've heard in the last few months. Just listen to me for a moment. The doctor will agree with me that you have worked yourself to the bone, making sure that all the people you had in the classes now also have some food each day. Hopefully, the crop of 1846 will show that this was a one-off year. The people all appreciate your efforts but you must now return to taking care of yourself and our second child. You can direct operations from the house, my love, but no gallivanting around the townland for the moment. Another child does not have to be the end of the world. It can be a new beginning! Everyone in the house is coping very well and we have food enough to feed ourselves and to help as many neighbours as possible. This too will pass and I'm not leaving to go singing again until you are back to yourself, my love!"

As he held her close, he was grateful to find that she had already fallen asleep in his arms and, as he lay there praying that Gregory would continue to sleep, he tried to work out how to ensure his wife returned to good health and how they could cope with a new arrival.

Chapter Seven

In the town of Midleton when the bitterly cold winter had passed, Brendan O'Leary made his way in trepidation to the gate lodge of the Beconsford estate. He had many years ago helped his bullying brother Dermot set fire to Jack Ryan's house but when he eventually removed himself from his clutches, Jack Ryan had not only forgiven him but had helped him set up with a horse and cart to shift goods in East Cork. Now he was doing so well and had not only saved his mother and his family from poverty, but had acquired a carriage and four horses and carried both goods and people. He was making good money from the gentry and rich farmers in the region even though the potato blight had begun to decimate areas of the country. He saw it all in his travels. Now he wanted to do something for the poor and he knew that Jack Ryan and the Beconsfords were helping people, especially in West Cork. As Brendan had expected, the gatekeeper was reluctant to let him enter the estate. With that in mind, he had written a note and asked him if he would be good enough to hand it to Mr. Ryan. The gatekeeper told him to return the following day at noon and he'd let him know if Mr. Ryan had written a reply to his letter. As he walked home, he said a silent prayer that Jack would believe him when he told him that he was now an honest man.

The following morning Brendan arrived at the estate and was informed that Jack would see him. With reluctance, the gatekeeper escorted Brendan to the estate manager's house.

"I wonder what Brendan wants?" Jack asked Eliza. "I know that he's making a great success of his business and his mother is out of poverty due to his now diligent work."

"I'm proud that you gave him a chance to get a life away from Dermot. I'll leave a pot of tea on the table and let you have a chat with him while I go up to visit Margarita," said Eliza, bending to kiss her husband on the cheek.

"What's that for?" he asked.

"For being the kind man that you are," Eliza responded as she went to put her cloak on.

<hr />

Brendan saw Mrs. Ryan walking up towards the Big House as he knocked on the estate manager's door. Almost immediately it was opened by Jack.

"Come in, lad. How are you?" Jack said.

"I'm good, Mr. Ryan."

Jack pulled out a chair at the kitchen table. "Here – take the weight off your feet and tell me what's causing that frown on your forehead."

Jack sat opposite him across the table and poured him a cup of tea. He pushed the milk jug and sugar bowl towards Brendan.

"Now, what can I do for you?" he then asked.

"I am a bit worried meeting you, Mr. Ryan."

"Well, don't worry, just tell me what's on your mind."

Brendan took a sip of tea before breathing deeply and saying, "I'm still sorry for the pain my brother and me caused you all those years ago, so now I want to try to pay you back for your kindness in setting me up in the carting business."

"Not at all! You've more than paid me back the money for the horse I got for you and even though I haven't seen much of you for the past few years, I've kept my eyes open and know that you look after your mother well. I'm glad you are successful, lad. Everyone in life needs a second chance. That's my view anyway."

"Thanks, Mr. Ryan. I have also been hearing that you and Lord Beconsford are trying to help a lot of people during this wretched blight on the country. Now I want to do my bit to help. I've saved money and I'm still regularly moving people and goods in my carriage. Even the rich people in the region are using my services by travelling with me and getting me to do a lot of their deliveries around County Cork. I think I could help you but I believe that Lord Beconsford might not like to take my help."

"What do you have in mind, Brendan? Tell me, and let me decide if it's worth bringing to Lord Isaac and Victor."

"Well, I have been delivering deep into West Cork and one day I met your carriage when it was bringing help to the people near Ballydehob. I have been giving people free lifts plus a bit of help around the county, mainly when I'm returning from my deliveries. I've picked up some exhausted travellers on their way to Cork to start their journeys that will get them on ships going to America. I usually give them a bit of food and sometimes a few shillings if they're short for the ticket. Not much, mind, but I make that decision when I'm dropping them off at the harbour. Mr. Ryan, I could deliver some of the produce that you send regularly to your wife's sister Mrs. Staunton for free and maybe there are a few people in her townland who need a bit of help getting to the city instead of having to walk. I also get jobs in East Cork to bring people to Waterford harbour and again I try to fill the carriage if I meet people in need of a lift. I explain in advance to those who are paying their own fare that I might be picking more people up on the way and they are usually happy to see others saved from walking the roads. I could do that for you, Mr. Ryan. I only want enough money to cover the horse's keep during my trips and I'll make that with the goods I carry. My family and I are all going to be alright for food, at least for this year."

Jack sat back as Brendan stopped talking and quietly thought about what he had heard. Brendan drank his tea, casting a few anxious looks at Jack.

Finally, Jack spoke. "I like your ideas, Brendan. Would you let it with me for a couple of days and I'll send a note to your cottage when I've had a word with a few people."

"Yes, sir. Thank you, sir."

Brendan stood up and Jack followed suit, stretching his hand out to shake Brendan's before walking him towards the front door.

"I'm so grateful to you, Mr. Ryan, for hearing me out. I am a changed person, thanks to you, and I hope over the next while I can meet your expectations and help some people from around the county."

"Don't worry, lad. One person can do only so much but anything is better than nothing when we are all faced with hundreds of people with no hope of a future each day. We can only do our best."

Later Jack spoke to Eliza who always had practical ways of making things work, usually with the help of her women friends and neighbours. He remembered how his Granny Sheila had made a difference to many of the locals in Midleton and, like her, his Eliza was always looking for ways to support good ideas.

Eliza was delighted that some fresh ideas were emerging to help the people. "I'll talk to Deborah and Margarita if you are having any difficulties with Isaac. I think it's a great idea and the families with old relatives who are now contemplating going to the workhouses might be able to keep them out if they emigrate and send back money."

Jack sat with Victor and Isaac in the estate office in Beconsford House. Jack knew he'd have opposition when he told him what Brendan O'Leary had proposed.

Victor looked bemused as his father banged the table with annoyance.

"How do you get a guarantee from an O'Leary that he can be trusted, when that family caused so much disharmony in the estate before they tried to kill you?"

Jack decided to stay calm as he answered. "I've kept a good eye on Brendan since he started the carting business and you have my assurance that he's a changed man. I think he needs a chance and, before you ask, I will give you a guarantee that he will not run off with the supplies going to West Cork. He would have too much to lose."

"What if he pretends that the load was stolen from him?" Isaac continued angrily. "I never did agree with you that we shouldn't hand that pair over to the law."

Victor, who always wanted a peaceful life, looked at his father before speaking up.

"I think, Father, that it is Jack you need to trust in this and I'm all for any help that can be given to Alice's townland." He looked from one to the other.

"Fine, Jack but, if any of the first consignment goes astray, the Beconsford trust will have to cut down on its spending and more people will suffer. On your head be it, Jack, but make sure that someone you know travels on that journey with him and I'll agree to his proposal."

Breathing a sigh of relief, Jack took his leave and returned home. He immediately sent a note to Brendan asking him to call to the estate house that evening.

A week later Brendan had a load of produce that filled all of the back section of his large carriage with more strapped to the roof. He had a couple of male passengers, who were regulars going to the city of Cork on business. They were sitting in comfort inside the covered centre and Brendan was joined by Jody, Cillian the coachman's son, who sat next to him. Young Jody at eighteen years of age now tended the horses for the estate carriages and could help out on the journey if problems arose. Brendan knew him from seeing him around the town and he was happy to have him along, knowing that His Lordship had sent him to keep an eye on how things went over the following days.

The carriage arrived in Eoinstown at noon the following day.

Alice and Richard had been looking out for it, having received a message from Jack the previous day.

Alice was beaming as she greeted Jody and Brendan.

"Come in for some food before you have to unload that lot," she said, her face lighting up at the sight of the large load.

"I'll guide them to the back of the house," said Richard. "We don't want the load disappearing before we work out where it will be most needed."

He took them to a barn at the back of the property and, after they had tended to the horses, led them back to the house where they were served soup and bread in the kitchen.

Alice and Richard were joined by Meg and Grace and they all sat around the long kitchen table. Meg wanted to know all the news from Midleton.

No fancy food in West Cork, Brendan thought as he ate. Having been in West Cork homes a few times since the famine had started, he knew that more and more well-off families were training themselves to live on reduced rations while the locals' needs were great.

"I'm delighted that you're going to help today with the distribution," Alice said with a smile as she looked at the two visitors who were enjoying their meal. "There's a back room upstairs for you both to stay tonight."

"Thank you, Mrs. Staunton, but there is something else I need to discuss with you," Brendan said, hesitating as he saw the eager faces around the table. "I have an idea. I put it to Mr. Ryan and he said that the families in Eoinstown needed a lot of help and support. As you can see, I will return to Midleton with an empty carriage. I have only a few deliveries going back from here to Cork but I owe a debt of thanks to Mr. Ryan and I want to help some of the locals who are looking for a free carriage ride into the city."

"You're helping just by bringing the food, Brendan," Richard assured him.

"Well, in the last while I've been transporting some emigrants from East Cork to get on the ships going to England and across the Atlantic to Canada and America. I feel that many of those who get a ship from Cork Harbour aren't all that sure that they'll get across the Atlantic alive and I agree with them. I'm told by the sailors in Cork that many of the ships have brought timber from Canada and they take passengers when they are returning. But most of those ships aren't fit for the purpose of transporting people. I try to get the men with a trade, plus the women who are sought after as housekeepers to try to get to Liverpool and take a liner to New York. The poorest and unskilled end up in Newfoundland, if they manage to survive the crossing. They're calling many of these ships 'coffin ships'. Yet they're all wanting to emigrate so I give some of them a few shillings to help them on their way – those who don't have sufficient money for a ticket."

Everyone around the table was amazed that an O'Leary could be saying and doing this, because they all knew about his brother and his past.

"So, what can you do for these parts?" Richard asked.

"As I said, I have an empty carriage and I can give those in your local area a free ride to the city or even beyond. I try to persuade the people who are emigrating to try get to Liverpool for the liner and I can give them a bit of extra money and food to help them on their way. Almost everyone I've driven so far have nothing on their minds except to get to America. I also found that too many who've had to tramp the road to get to Cork are so exhausted that they are unlikely to arrive at their destination in a healthy state. Some look so weak that they are more likely to die on the way or just give up because they have no energy. Hope leaves people who don't get help. I found that years ago when I was ruled by my brother Dermot. I feel for these people, both men and women. Some are rogues, of course, but then that's life. Not everyone you help is good. So, if you could check around the townland, I can take eight people back with me and if there aren't enough in this area, I will pick people up on the road back."

Meg was the first to answer as they were all reflecting on what Brendan had said.

"I'll go down and talk to Mary straight away and we'll put our heads together and see what happens. I'll be back before tea and we'll go over it all again. I don't want everyone to know because there could be a queue around the farm and we don't want that."

"I'll go with you," said Alice.

"Don't you dare come with me!" said Meg. "You have your unborn baby and your own health to worry about. Just leave this to me and I'll deal with Brendan and Jody."

Alice smiled, shaking her head, knowing that her mother was excited, even in these strange times, at the thought of a second grandchild.

"How much in cash do you have to give out for this trip, Brendan, because we have some funds from Lord Isaac's trust still available."

When Brendan mentioned his contribution Meg leaned over and patted his hand as she shook her head in amazement.

"I'll give you an extra few shillings, Brendan. After all, you're helping the people of East Cork also, where I lived for most of my life."

"Can I tell you something?" Jody said, looking at the kind faces around the table. "I know two East Cork families that Brendan helped a few months ago and they wouldn't have got on the boat without his help. The families are grateful even though they haven't heard word since. They live in hope and I think unless you have hope for the future, you have nothing in Ireland now."

"Brendan, your mother must be very proud of you," Meg said as tears came into her eyes and she felt a lump in her throat. She rose quickly from her seat. "I'm going to get my cloak and leave at once."

By seven o'clock the following morning. four men and two women were at the front door of the farmhouse. They had bags carrying their meagre possessions but Alice noticed that they all had proud and determined looks on their faces.

The family stood at the door and waved to the intrepid travellers.

"Please, God, look after these people and keep them safe," Meg said, clasping her hands in prayer, as she looked up into the sky.

There were tears in the eyes of the travellers as the carriage made its way out of Eoinstown towards Cork. They had all left their families with very little notice and were all quiet, knowing that they were never likely to see their homeland again. It was a sobering thought.

The following evening, Jody was called to the office in Beconsford house to let Isaac, Victor and Jack know how Brendan had got on.

"The people loved the food, sir, and all the other people that he took back in the carriage were all crying and thanking him for everything. The two men he picked up near Cork were given food by the others that Mrs. Alice had given them all before leaving the farm. These two were crying the whole way to the harbour and then Mr. O'Leary made sure they had enough money to get on a ship out of Ireland. He's a good man, Your Lordship. I know that I'm young, but I'm well fed here and seeing the poor people in parts of West Cork had me thinking that I need to help more people. I just hope they all reach America safely because that's where they all seem to want to end up."

The gentlemen at the table thanked Jody and let him return to his home to rest.

As they looked at each other Jack smiled and said, "Well, there's no answer to that, is there? You've got your answer, Isaac, and hopefully we can do this again, while continuing to pray that the next crop will herald the end of this devastating blight. I was told last week that there are thousands of passengers boarding ships around the country each week and that it may get worse. Imagine all these people leaving the country who will never return! Plus, you know what they're calling some of those ships? Coffin ships! Many of the people never even reach America. Yet what's the alternative?"

He realised that the worst was probably not yet over.

Chapter Eight

It was late September in 1846 when shock waves reverberated around the country as it appeared that the entire potato crop in the country had blight. The good harvest that everyone had prayed for had not happened and hope disappeared from the eyes of the poor and needy. People were being kept alive with the arrival of Indian meal from North America and inadequate help from the Imperial Treasury.

Back in Eoinstown young Maeve Maguire had kept her head down, focusing on her studies. She had spent the last year learning to improve all her writing and reading skills with help from Jerome, whenever she was in the house minding young Gregory. Jerome knew that her heart was set on becoming a teacher and the school had indicated that if she continued to learn she could help out officially in another few months.

Now she was in the kitchen, having spent the day helping Alice look after Gregory. As she   put Gregory into his perambulator for a rest, her young brother Micky arrived at the kitchen door, shouting for Maeve to come home as their dad was poorly.

Alice hurriedly put some provisions in a basket for Maeve and gave her a big hug before the young girl ran after Micky. She watched as they tore off in the direction of their cottage. Alice said a prayer that Fergus would be alright.

When they arrived at their home, Maeve discovered that the door was locked. She shouted out to her mother. Fiona told her to come to the back door. When she hurried around the house, she found her mother outside, with the door closed behind her.

"You can't come in," Fiona explained to her daughter, as tears spilled from her eyes. "Your dad isn't good, love."

"What's wrong with him, Mam?" Maeve cried as panic rose within her. "He was grand yesterday!"

"He hadn't been feeling too good for a day or two but last night he started to burn up with a bad fever. Nothing I do is bringing it down."

"Did you get the doctor?"

"Of course I did, love. I went down earlier in the day and he gave me a medicine for him. He said to keep him cool and that's what I'm doing now. The doctor said that neither yourself nor your brother were to come into the house until he's better."

"He will get better, Mam, won't he?" Maeve asked. "Here, take this – it's food Mrs. Alice sent for us."

Fiona shook her head sadly. "He can't eat at the moment, love – just take it down to Granny Mary and eat it with Micky. Stay with her and don't let either of you come home tonight, I'm warning you now. Do you understand?" Her anxiety was showing in her eyes.

"I'll go down and have my tea with her but I'm coming back after that and I'll stay out in the front if you won't let me in," Maeve said, with exasperation in her voice.

It was with a heavy heart and tears in her eyes that she made her way down to her granny's cottage with Micky.

"Dad has the fever," she announced when she arrived.

"*Shush*, love, I know – but don't let your brother hear as he doesn't know it's the fever."

Maeve threw herself into her granny's embrace and let the tears that were building up flow freely down her face.

"My mam won't let me in to see him."

"Hush, child, take my fresh hanky and dry those tears and we'll say a little prayer for your dad. He's a good strong man and your mam will do her best to pull him through," said Mary with little conviction in her voice.

Mary and Maeve looked on at the joy on Micky's face as he enjoyed the buttered bread and the ham that was in the basket. Maeve's stomach was in a knot and she couldn't face the food. She whispered to her granny that she was going up to sit in front of the house until after sunset. Mary just nodded and made her put a shawl on before walking back up the hill.

When she got to her home, her mother had put a chair out in the front for her to sit on. Before she sat down, she went to the window of the bedroom where she could see her mother bending over the bed and gently wiping her beloved dad's brow with a wet cloth. She tapped at the window and her mother gave her a smile, but her dad never even moved in the bed. She brought the chair closer to the window and sat down and said a prayer in her heart, begging whoever could hear her to save her dad. She had brought a book to read as she had found it was usually the only thing that took her away from worries but having read only a few pages she put the book away. The book didn't work its magic on her tonight, so she settled down, regularly peering through the window, hoping that her father would move and smile at her. Yet nothing happened and, as darkness began to fall, she got up to leave. Then she heard an anguished cry. She could see her mother in the light of a candle, standing over her father and shaking her head.

She heard her mother's wail, as she walked from the bed to face her daughter at the window. She was crying, and couldn't talk for a few moments.

"He's died, love, he's just died. He was strong. This awful famine is to blame. He had a fever and the dysentery. Go and fetch your granny and send her up to me and tell her try to get the priest to come up. Let you stay with Micky until your granny gets back later." As she saw her daughter hesitating, she begged her, "Please go down and get me help! I need your granny, love."

As Maeve raced down the hill, all she could do was howl into the sky, asking how could this happen to her dad who had only ever done good deeds for everyone he knew. It just wasn't fair.

***

While Alice was helping with breakfast the following morning, Mary came into the house with the terrible news. Her son-in-law Fergus Maguire, Maeve's father, had been doing a job helping up in the workhouse and he contracted a fever there that he died from late last evening.

"Fiona was distraught when he got so ill and she sent Micky and Maeve down to me," Mary said, breathless, with anguish in her voice. "She didn't want the children to contract the fever but she insisted on tending him herself. Last night Maeve ran out of the house after tea and came back hours later in tears. The priest is saying a Mass for him tomorrow morning."

Alice put her arms around her to offer comfort. Then she drew back and said, "I'm going to give you some money because the family will have things to pay for over the next few days and I'll help out where else I can. You know that you only have to ask."

Sadly, Alice also knew that Maeve's ambition to be a teacher was now over as she'd have to work, because Fiona's priority would now be worrying about how she would provide for herself and her children in the future. It was but one of many deaths in the townland since the beginning of the famine, but it was a death that brought Alice the most pain as it seemed to bring the famine right up to their own doorstep. What an awful mess the whole thing is, she thought. Nobody should suffer such hardship and death in a country so rich with green fields.

The funeral of Fergus Maguire saw people from all over the townland come to pay their respects. He was well liked in the community where he was always offering help to others. When the time came for him to be laid to rest, the men with most strength shouldered the coffin to the graveyard on the hill above the church. There was a stillness in the crowd when he was lowered into the ground and after Father O'Neill finished the prayers, he asked for quiet as young Maeve wanted to read a poem that she had written after the terrible death of her father.

Alice noticed how Maeve seemed to make a big effort to keep her voice strong as she read the poem that came straight from her heart.

"As his illness took its final toll, his life slowly drifted away
It was in the year 1846 that dreaded killer came to stay.
I watched him through the window pane, I was not allowed inside
I saw his eyes close at nightfall as my mam sat with him and cried.
Now alone we stand and think of Dad, our unseeing eyes are dry but sad,
As the seconds tick without a sound, I hear the silence all around."

You could hear a pin drop as the mourners, with eyes closed to hold back the tears, absorbed the young girl's words, before the wails of pain came from the graveside. As the body of Fergus Maguire was lowered into the grave, the tears of a whole parish were shed in sympathy with the family who were now enduring the sadness on the passing of a good husband and father.

Later, as Alice helped feed the mourners with soup and bread in the garden of Fiona's small home, she promised herself that she would do what she could to help the family in the future.

As Alice sat in her home, she pondered on how she could help the Maguires, but was conflicted in her thoughts. Although she despised Toby Ramsay, she knew that Sylvia needed a good young girl to work as a kitchen maid in the manor. Sylvia had already asked Alice if she could recommend someone. Alice had raised her eyebrows when asked but the blushing Sylvia promised Alice that any new girl entering their home from now on would be well cared for by her. Alice thought that if Maeve earned enough money to go to America, it might be a way out for the family. Like everyone in the area the only thing they all truly feared was the workhouse. Alice promised herself that it would never happen to her friends while she had a breath in her body.

⚜

Just a few weeks after the death of Fergus Maguire, Alice went into labour and without any fanfare, Emily Margaret Staunton was born. She was the image of her grandmother Meg who couldn't keep the smile off her face for weeks and, while Alice was recovering from the birth, the two grannies took over all the minding of the young children and the household.

⚜

Up at the manor, Toby Ramsay continued to rule the roost. As his temper got worse, his wife got more fearful of him and fully withdrew emotionally from his weekly demands in the bedroom. She had never seen what people described in books she read as loving relationships but knew enough to realise that her husband was the opposite. An uncaring brute whom she should never have been forced to marry. She had now taken to locking her bedroom door each night, as she finally decided that she'd had enough and hoped that his regular trips to Cork city would keep him away from her as much as possible. She missed the calls from her friend Alice who was resting after her beautiful daughter Emily was born. What she missed most was not having children. As a child she always promised herself that she'd have many children, as she knew the loneliness of being an only child. She had given in to her husband's excessive demands in the earlier stages of her unhappy marriage but, having failed to conceive a child, she became reconciled to her loveless and barren state. The one thing she was most grateful for was that her grandmother's trust fund was held so tightly by her lawyer in Cork that Toby could never get hold of that money. The thought of that money made her hope and dream that sometime in the future she could carve out a life away from him.

She was also looking forward to telling Alice, when she next called to the farmhouse, that she had interviewed Maeve and was pleased to offer her a position in her household. She knew that money, food and a roof over people's heads were all in short supply in West Cork and she would make sure that young Maeve would go home with some provisions each week on her day off – although she had to remind herself to be careful that this didn't antagonise other servants. She recalled how sad Alice had been when Fergus died and maybe she could now do some good herself for that family. She knew how bright young Maeve was and hoped that she could support her if she ever wanted to better herself.

Two weeks later Fiona walked her daughter up to the squire's house, talking to her very seriously before they reached the servants' door.

"Now remember everything I've told you. Mind your manners and be respectful to everyone. Most of all, keep a distance from the rough lads in the yard and stay out of the way of the squire. He has a bad temper and is not a nice man. Is that clear?"

"Yes, Mother, I'm not a child anymore and you know that I'm not stupid. I can look after myself!"

Oh, the arrogance of youth, Fiona thought, as she shook her head, knowing that she was losing control of her lovely girl and she would just have to trust her.

"Alright, Maeve, but I want you to come straight home on the Sundays you are off and I'm only three miles down the road if you ever run into any trouble."

As Maeve knocked at the servants' back door, Fiona hugged her and prayed that she would be safe from the famine for now.

Fiona said a final goodbye to her daughter just as a timid young girl opened the door and stood back to allow her to enter.

Maeve found herself in a small room inside the door, with shoes and boots stacked up against the wall. She was relieved when her mother went home because she was looking forward to the excitement of living with other maids and not with her young brother.

"My name is Bridget and I'm to take you to talk to Lady Sylvia in her parlour."

As they walked through the kitchen, she heard one maid asking how Maeve had got the position when she herself should have been promoted from scullery maid. Maeve just stood taller and nodded her head as she walked past, with a hint of a smile on her face. Put that in your pipe and smoke it, Peggy Reid, she thought, smiling to herself, remembering how nasty Peggy had been to the younger children in the little village school before she was asked by the schoolmaster to leave because of bad conduct. As she went by the cook, Úna Hayes, who knew Maeve's family, Úna put a hand on her shoulder and gave it a squeeze.

"I hope you enjoy working here, lass. I knew your dad and he was a great man. You should be proud of him."

Maeve's eyes were moist as she thanked the cook. Looking around, she noticed that some of the girls looked very unhappy with the good reception she was getting.

When she left the kitchen, she was greeted in a side room by Noreen the laundry-room assistant who told her to stay there while she got a new uniform in her size. Only then would she be introduced to Lady Sylvia.

"Thank you, miss," Maeve replied, while respectfully inclining her head as her mother had taught her.

When Noreen went out, young Bridget whispered that some of the kitchen girls weren't too nice. Maeve told her with not a huge amount of confidence that she was well capable of looking after herself.

"While you're waiting for Noreen to get your uniform, I can quickly show you where you'll be sleeping," Bridget said.

They swiftly climbed a narrow stairway and entered a large room where Bridget explained to Maeve that she would be sleeping with five other young maids.

"I'll be next to you so we can look out for each other."

Ever the optimist, Maeve smiled brightly when she saw that there was a large window at the end of the room from where you could see the top of the mountains far away in the distance.

After they returned to the laundry room, Noreen arrived with a set of clothes for her.

"You know, Lady Sylvia is a good employer as was her father," Noreen whispered, "and you will be warm in that room as long as the estate can afford to keep it heated in these times. The master is a mean man."

Maeve nodded as she was handed her new uniform. The dress was of dark material and would be covered with an apron. She was presented with a white cap and shown how to wear it. A pair of warm socks and sturdy shoes were included. Maeve was delighted because she hadn't seen any new clothes for a long time.

Chapter Nine

As December came and went and food got more difficult to source, hope for the future was in short supply in every corner of Ireland. The weary citizens, in particular the poor and the old began to die in their droves. Some even lost their lives at sea, having left with hope of reaching America and a better life. The workhouses were packed to capacity and the death rate was high in them.

The people in West Cork were in despair at the stories coming from Clonakilty where the dead could no longer get a decent burial and were reportedly stacked up to rot in mass graves. Such horrors drove more and more people to seek refuge in foreign lands. Hope of a solution to the problems faced by the poor faded as time passed. The priests and parsons did their best and the help from the Quaker community was exceptional.

Optimism had grown for some that the blight might be gone for the 1847 harvest but the paradox was that few small farmers had the money to plant and most were relying on aid from any source to keep them alive. Financial help continued to come from the Irish Americans. European people had also emptied their pockets and sent money to help alleviate the effects of the famine.

At the same time anger was growing towards the parliament in London as too many strictures were put on any supports they gave. Alice had already seen that in 1846 more and more men and women were leaving the country in despair and the majority of the absentee landlords did not appear to gauge the mood of the Irish at that time. Hostility had grown towards those landlords who still exported produce that should have stayed in the country.

The cold hard ground of another harsh winter moved into a spring that showed little promise of a new dawn for the people of Ireland. They saw the full extent of their tragedy as the effects of the famine went on and on. Lives continued to be lost, mainly through disease passed on from one undernourished person to another.

By then Alice felt she was living through a nightmare. She realised that the famine was causing untold hardship to many who had managed in the past to keep hunger from the door. Their bodies were weakened by starvation, their minds were obsessed with feeding their children and their eyes told the story of their lives. Sadness, uncertainty and despair were clear to see behind the sunken faces and skeletal bodies that walked the road outside the farm. The Staunton family provided a can of milk each morning to the mothers who had new-born babies and Alice prayed that they would find enough energy to face their sometimes long walk home. Many of the men who got employment with the public works hardly had the ability to walk to their jobs, let alone do a day's work when they arrived. Seeing the old forced to go into the workhouse was the most heart-breaking for Alice to watch. Their dignity was gone, their families, some of whom were hardworking farmers all their lives, could no longer feed them and their bent and defeated bodies walked what was for the Irish the ultimate walk of shame to the workhouse. How it had sunk to this for them over a few years they did not know. All they knew was that they believed they were a burden on the young and they wanted their children and grandchildren to live. They knew that they were walking to their deaths.

Alice also met the stronger, hardier sons who saw the answer to the famine was to take the boat to America and send money home to feed the young. She knew of one large farming family with eight children, from the Kanturk area, who had emigrated to the new territory of Hong Kong when their father joined the British navy. Would the Irish end up populating the whole of the world while its own population at home was shrinking? The parish and the townland of Eoinstown continued to help the poorest get enough money for the ticket that would lead them out of the hell-hole that had been their existence during the past few years.

The most personal distress Alice felt, and it left her fuming and angry, was when she saw the cartloads of grain and produce leaving the estate of Toby Ramsay and other large landowners to the west, making their way to Cork harbour to be exported for gain. The people of Youghal had physically shown their opposition to this practice but were thwarted by the authorities. The madness of this exporting hit Alice to the core and their excuse that they had to feed their people with the profits from exporting the grain never sat well with her.

She now had her own problem with a small baby to rear. What she felt was fear and concern for her child, although she knew she had to move beyond her worries and hope that her baby would grow up with the joy of a good harvest soon. Yet she knew that the omens were there stating the obvious. The famine was not leaving Ireland. As she placed a can of milk in the hand of the last of the morning callers, she turned back into the warm kitchen and picked up her young daughter and held her close to her heart.

After what felt like the longest winter in history, the dawn of another new spring with summer around the corner still brought no hope to the hearts of the Irish people.

Would this famine ever disappear, thought Alice, as the resilience shown by the strong and the kindness of people who had health and money, was fast disappearing. As the stronger and younger continued to leave, their mothers shed tears of heartbreak as they looked through the mist at their younger children and wondered if anyone would survive this national calamity.

The mood in Midleton stayed somewhat more positive with the efforts of the Beconsford family. But their help was never enough and the poor spent their time growing anything that would help them survive.

Tragedy entered the O'Leary household when Brendan's mother died, but thankfully it was in her own bed tended by her family and not in the workhouse. These buildings were now dotted around the country since the Poor Law Union was created in 1839 but they were hated by anyone with even an ounce of self-respect.

Margarita Beconsford knew the way people in the district thought, having mixed with many of them when her mother Eliza had been teaching in the village and Margarita had taught the town's children to sing. By late summer the donations and early supports began to drop as the famine persisted. Although the government under Mr. Peel had put in place support of a kind, it seemed to her that Ireland would be wiped out were it not for the help of the charitable donations. With these thoughts in her mind, she turned to walk from the Secret Garden to enter her luxurious home and knew that her battles with her husband were also not going to be easily resolved. He seemed determined that all his family should go to England until the famine was over.

As her father Jack Ryan also walked in the direction of the Big House, he crunched through the autumn leaves covering the estate with their copper and red leaves shimmering in the sunlight. It made him forget for just a moment that its beauty was not the reality of life in Ireland any more. As he entered the house and moved towards the estate office, he could hear the raised voices of Victor and Isaac Beconsford. He shook his head, knowing that there were few answers to their current problems.

He knocked at the door before entering and bid the men a good morning.

"What's good about it?" said Victor belligerently. "Could you please talk to my father, Jack, and tell him that yours and his grandchildren should be sent to England until this confounded famine disappears!"

Jack poured himself a coffee from the pot and sat across from the two men.

"Isn't this a conversation you should be having with your wife?" he asked.

"Well, she is your daughter and she seems to ignore what I say. She says that she wants to help the people in the town and to support Alice in her efforts to feed the locals around Eoinstown. I can't get it through her head that we are not going to save everyone and we must make sure that our own family are safe. She says I'm selfish but I believe that she is the selfish one."

Jack looked at him and felt like telling Victor to fix his own problems related to his escalating drinking and maybe his wife would be more accommodating to his views, but he kept his thoughts to himself.

"Margarita spends her time looking after her children and everyone in this house works to ensure that they are kept safe. She also has a social conscience which myself and Eliza instilled in her and these are the same values that your father and mother taught you, Victor. I am not her keeper and perhaps you need to actually ask her what she wants and then listen to her."

He stood and made his way to the door.

"I have work to attend to in the estate and I'll see you later, when you've cooled down, Victor."

Jack was feeling annoyed at the extra pressure from Victor as he walked down the driveway and through the forest to talk to Nick Jordan, who lived in one of the bigger farms on the estate. Nick was a very intelligent man and he could hear the grass grow when it came to knowing what was happening in farming circles. He knew of the issues concerning all the farmers and their labourers in and around Midleton. Jack and Isaac usually had a weekly meeting with him to keep them updated. Today Jack felt that Isaac had enough on his mind and he'd deal with any problems that arose.

Nick was chatting to a farmhand and he waved at Jack as he reached the farmhouse, then indicated that he should proceed to the house.

"Would you like some tea, Jack?" Catriona Jordon enquired as Jack came through the front door. "Go into the parlour and I'll bring it through."

He sat down at the small but beautifully polished table, as Catriona reappeared with a tray.

"I'm glad you're here, Jack. Nick seems distracted since he returned from the farmers' meeting in Cork yesterday and I couldn't get a word out of him."

Jack was thanking her for the tea just as Nick appeared behind her and put an arm around her shoulders.

"Don't be standing at the door listening," he said, as he steered her out the door. "I'll talk to you later this evening when we're alone."

He quietly closed the door and walked across the room to sit down opposite Jack.

"I won't be telling her everything," he said with a grimness in his face that Jack rarely saw.

"That sounds ominous," Jack replied.

"Indeed it is, Jack, and I'm not going to sugar-coat it for you but it's not to be shared with anyone except Isaac for the time being. We don't want to cause panic. There's enough of that around already, goodness knows. I met up with farmers from all around the county yesterday and the news from each of their townlands is dire. Black fields in the majority of counties throughout the country, yet many of the supports that the people were getting from the parish and government works are disappearing. The monies that were coming from across the world are now not coming, although Irish Americans are still doing their bit. What I found also is that there is a new anger which is directed at the British government and it's feared that it will spill over into the big estates with the Irish nationalists to the forefront. For now, it seems that the anger is directed at the absentee landlords who still live in England and are shouting for their profits, even though everyone here knows the dire reality of the lives of the Irish. Some of the farmers even said that before this is finished there will be millions dead and millions having left the country."

When Nick stopped speaking, Jack silently considered what course of action they could take.

"We cannot allow a worst-case scenario to happen," he said at last. "We have to urgently get the message across to London regarding the extent of our plight. I'll have a word immediately with Isaac as he has quite a lot of influence in taking difficulties to the top of parliament. We have not the time to worry about those absentee landlords but, for what it's worth, I think that actions by Irish nationalists will result only in reprisals and more hardship. I believe that the only thing that should be on everybody's mind is how to feed the people who are starving. Energy is being wasted on the blame game."

When Jack returned to Isaac's office, the two men spent the rest of the afternoon discussing the situation before Isaac made a decision.

"I think I must go to London and bring the powers that be up to date on the thinking of the Irish. Maybe you won't agree with me but I'm going to take Victor with me as his emotive pleading might help in some way. It might emphasise how important the welfare of the Irish is to some of us."

Jack nodded in agreement and the men shook hands, hoping that the trip would not be in vain.

Chapter Ten

Isaac and Victor mounted the carriage steps on a bright early September morning in 1847 as they assured their wives and the children that they would be back from London as soon as possible. Jack Ryan had promised that himself and Eliza would both keep the families safe and the estate working to capacity, while they were abroad. Isaac knew that Victor was drinking again and was happy to have his son by his side for the next few weeks where he could keep an eye on him. As the family kept waving, the carriage with its four horses moved swiftly out of the estate and onto the road to Dublin.

The two men left Midleton with a moderate degree of optimism.

"Victor, this could be a positive meeting in London," Isaac said after some time had passed in silence. "I haven't yet met many of the new government but I hope between us and the members of parliament from Ireland we can get the help that's needed. Mr. Peel tried hard to be helpful with the public works schemes but now we need to get the new prime minister Mr. Russell to understand the needs of the Irish."

"The problems we have now are not just about public schemes. They're about life and death. This affects a whole country! It's not just a question of hunger, as you know. My children could easily pick up the fever or dysentery and my life wouldn't be worth living if anything happened to them."

"Let's just wait and see," Isaac answered in the hope of calming his son. He hoped Victor wouldn't prove a liability rather than an asset on the trip. He had enough to deal with, making this effort to help the people. Thankfully, up to now, he had managed to keep the people on his own estate fed and safe, but he knew that many of the people surrounding it were getting more emaciated as the months dragged on with no sign of a let-up. "We're lucky that my sister lives so close and is friendly with Lord Melbourne in Brocket Hall. It was very important to get an opportunity to actually sit down with as many of top decision-makers as possible. Victor, no matter what goes on at this meeting, I don't want you to be anything but civil to everyone in the room. We can't afford to raise the hackles of those who are in power. Remember, we shall state our case and listen, no matter what transpires. We may need to meet with these people again and it is of little benefit if we antagonise them when we first meet."

After a relatively comfortable trip to Hertfordshire, where they stayed with Isaac's sister Helena, they found that it took only a few days before they had secured a meeting with the prime minister. All their relatives in Hertfordshire wished them well as they set out for the capital.

Isaac scanned the room. Seated with their backs to the wall along the long table were a group of men. What was most shocking was that one of them was Trevelyan whom Isaac knew was no friend of the Irish. This feels like an ambush, he thought, as they were escorted to the table. They took their seats opposite the men.

One of the men addressed them.

"The Prime Minister is on his way but I'd like you to first meet his advisors. I'm Mr Jackson, a parliamentary secretary, and I'm here to take notes for the Prime Minster. I believe you may know Mr. Trevelyan who spends much of his time in Ireland. Seated next to him is Viscount Palmerstown and, finally, let me introduce you to Mr Whitley, a lawyer from the northern part of Ireland."

Isaac and Victor acknowledged the men.

The door opened. Isaac threw a warning look at Victor as Prime Minister Russell entered the room, nodding to everyone before sitting in the middle seat flanked by his colleagues.

"Thank you, Prime Minister, for giving us your time. I'm Lord Isaac Beconsford and this is my son Victor. Do you want me to state why we are here?"

"Of course, I do," he answered gruffly. "My time is precious and I have a meeting with my cabinet shortly."

"Prime Minister," Isaac began, pressing Victor's leg as a warning for him to keep quiet, "the situation we are in is that the negative effects of the potato blight are far from over in Ireland. I now believe it is getting worse rather than better. Ireland is losing hundreds of people every day due to the continuation of famine. With respect, the people of Ireland now believe that there is a huge lack of support from your government."

"Sir," Mr Whitley began but Isaac raised his hand to stop him.

"Please let me finish. Your government under Mr. Peel did send help in the first year of this famine in the form of public works jobs and other supports. In addition, charitable donations were sent from America and Europe. The problem for the landless labourers now is that if they get work, they lack the energy to do so because of starvation. Apart from hunger, the people of Ireland are dying in their thousands from typhus and dysentery. Many donors' contributions have by now dried up and if it wasn't for the Quakers supplying food, many more would be dead. Huge numbers of people have left but you can do that only if you are young, single and strong. Yet now your government is removing some subsidies that from now on have to be paid for by Irish taxpayers and not the Imperial treasury."

"One moment, Lord Beconsford," Mr Russell interrupted with red spots of anger risen in his face. "I have it on the best authority that the famine is waning. I have watched the Irish and they seem to have grown their population way too quickly in the past ten years. That is why Ireland cannot cope with the arrival of a famine. Famines have been happening all over Europe and those countries come out of it very quickly. As one Englishman to another, Lord Beconsford, you might consider that maybe it's God's way of rebalancing the population of the country."

Victor stood up, shocked, and before his father could stop him, he addressed the prime minister angrily.

"With respect to you, Prime Minister, my father and I have a much greater knowledge of Ireland than you have!"

"*Sit down, young man!*" Mr. Russell roared from across the table. "Our government has paid for workhouses and numerous other supports yet the Irish continue to be feckless and workshy. I have my civil servants in Ireland who keep me well abreast of issues there. Mr. Trevelyan is one of those who knows the country intimately whereas you live in one area and you don't look as if you are going hungry!"

"*Trevelyan!*" Victor shouted back, by now totally exasperated. "That man moved grain through Ireland for export that brought the Irish nothing but despair. Does it surprise you that exporting food that is not available for the families in Ireland in the midst of a famine would not be a good solution to the problem? It was the last straw for many men overcome with the horror of watching their wives and young families die in front of them. Do not insult us, Prime Minister, by suggesting that people like Trevelyan are there to help the Irish in their plight!"

"*Sit down immediately, young man, or I'll ask you to leave the room!* I will outline our position before I leave this meeting. You may not care but we have our own fiscal difficulties in this country. We have given as much help as possible to Ireland. Perhaps you should ask the Americans whom you love so much and the charitable organisations to send more aid!"

Shocked at the outburst, Isaac stood up and looked the prime minister in the eye.

"Mr Russell, I thank you for your time but I just have to remind you before we take our leave that this famine is not over. As for charitable donations, the poor in lots of countries have sent as much as they can and they can't afford to give any more help. The Quakers, the Catholic Church and many of our own Church pastors in Ireland are putting their lives at risk to give aid and their time to help the poor. Most of the landless labourers and small farmers renting under an acre of land that had previously lived on the nutritious potato are now starving. With everything gone they have little hope and no energy. When all hope is gone and the only place left for you and your family is the workhouse, they just see such a place provides only a guarantee of an early death. Do you realise that those workhouses that you laud are the breeding ground for numerous infections that lead to death? I hope that you and your government can live with your consciences. You are failing to give adequate help to Ireland in its hour of need. Do you not understand, Mr. Russell, that you have the same duty of care to the Irish people as you do towards your people at this side of the Irish Sea? If this again leads to the Irish rising against your governing of their country, it would not surprise me. Maybe the next time they may successfully rid the country of English occupation, or the 'Saxon yoke', as they call it. Perhaps you should consider that when you speak to your cabinet later, if you indeed ever get around to discussing it at all! Come, Victor, we need to leave and return to Ireland and dash the hopes of those who saw our trip to see you, Prime Minister, as a beacon of hope at a time when many have nothing left to live for!"

They walked swiftly from the room.

Victor, with tears in his eyes, turned to his father, shaking his head in despair.

"I'm proud of you, Father, but this prime minister does not have any respect for the Irish. We're on our own."

Chapter Eleven

When Victor and Isaac arrived back and told their story to the family, Jack was frustrated, but when he saw how much his son-in-law Victor had aged in the space of a few weeks he was worried. He feared for his daughter Margarita and hoped that they could find a resolution to their many problems.

Margarita was well aware of her father and mother's concerns and knew they were right. Victor had become impossible to live with, spending his nights drinking and continuously telling his wife that they'd probably all die if the famine didn't end. Margarita tried to remain positive but, after another week of his distressed behaviour, she got Deborah to keep an eye on Victor while she went to spill her heart out to her mother.

"You need a little break from this, Margarita. You need a clear head to decide how to best deal with him. Why don't you join myself and Deborah at the weekend and spend a night with the Perrott family in Cork? That family are always very welcoming and we will be bringing some provisions to them from the farm as a gift. What do you think?" She was anxious to get her daughter away from the toxicity of the Big House for a few days. Margarita took only a moment to answer. "I'd love that. Maybe if I'd stop worrying about everything for a few days it would do me good. Isaac will keep an eye on Victor and Jean will make sure that the children are looked after."

When the ladies left on their trip early on Friday, they promised to be back late on Saturday with gifts for Rosita and the twins. Isaac held the twins' hands as he saw the ladies off and assured them that they would be well looked after in their absence.

Having eaten his dinner, Isaac kissed Rosita goodnight as she went upstairs to her room and went to see the twins in the nursery before they went to bed. Later, when he knocked at Rosita's bedroom door, he was pleasantly surprised when he entered to find his son sitting by her bedside.

"I'm going to read a story to her before she goes to sleep, Father. I'll retire then and see you tomorrow."

Isaac was delighted that Victor was doing something responsible for once, while Margarita was away.

"I thought you had got too big for bedtime stories?" Isaac smiled at Rosita.

"I am always delighted to have my papa read to me," she answered, giving her father a peck on the cheek.

Isaac laughed as he left the room, happy that Victor seemed to be taking his parental duties seriously. He retired to his room and had fallen into a peaceful sleep by ten o'clock.

As the dim light of an early dawn peeped through the curtains, Isaac was awakened by a loud knocking on his door. What's happened, he thought, hearing the banging again and running to the door as he quickly threw on a dressing gown.

"It's me, Jean, let me in quick! I think we have a problem. It's Rosita. I don't know where she is. She's not in her room and she's not in the nursery. It's strange but Florrie Bowe isn't in her room either. She isn't with the twins. Young Lizzy says that when she got up Florrie wasn't in her bed."

"I'll go up and see if she's with Victor," Isaac said and made his way swiftly up to Victor's room.

The door was open but there was no sign of Victor. Isaac began to panic as he noticed that clothes were strewn around and wardrobes open. What the hell has my stupid son done now, he thought, exasperation showing on his face as he left the room and ran downstairs, taking the steps two at a time.

"Try and find out where Florrie Bowe has gone and check the rest of the house," he said to Jean. "I'm going out to the gardens. Don't mention anything to the rest of the staff until I return."

As Isaac ran across the gravelled driveway, he stopped as he spotted the door open at the stables. Running inside, he quickly discovered that the large carriage and four of the horses were nowhere to be seen. He raced in the direction of the coachman's cottage and banged on the door.

Cillian opened it.

"Have you seen Victor?" Isaac asked.

"Last evening, sir, he told me he was going away to a friend's house for a few days, that his friend wasn't well, and I prepared the horses and carriage for him."

"What friend?"

"He didn't say, sir."

"Did he mention where this friend lives?"

"No, sir." By now Cillian was looking alarmed.

"What time was this?"

"He asked me to bring the carriage around to the back of the house just before twelve o'clock. I helped him load his trunks into the carriage and then he told me to go home. I've been in bed since then. That's all I know, sir."

"Did you see Rosita and Florrie?"

"No, sir."

"Then get the second carriage ready at once and bring it around to the house."

Isaac raced back to the house.

"Florrie never went to her room last night," Jenny confirmed. "She was very excited because Mr. Victor told her to stay in Rosita's room for the evening as he wanted her to mind Rosita because her mama was away. Florrie was proper chuffed because she was sleeping in luxury for the night."

Isaac began to despair at whatever antics his son was up to and felt out of his depth with his wife and daughter-in-law both away.

"Jean, could you go down and ask Jack to come up? Try to stay calm when you tell him."

Jean nodded and ran off.

Isaac made his way back up to Rosita's room. He looked around and found that some of her clothes also appeared to be missing, plus her books. They were normally placed by her bedside but were nowhere to be seen. He sat down and put his head in his hands in despair and prayed that nothing sinister had befallen his son and granddaughter.

Jack and Jean made their way swiftly to the house. Jean led him up to Rosita's room where Isaac was seated on a chair by the empty bed.

Jack had to sit down with the shock as Isaac began to tell him as much as he knew.

Meanwhile Jean walked anxiously around the room.

"Rosita's winter coat and boots are gone, as are many articles from her wardrobe," she said. "I don't understand. I can't see Rosita leaving this house in the middle of the night without asking lots of questions. She's far too independent to just go off like that." Suddenly she turned around, saying, "What's that smell?"

Sniffing, she walked around the room close to the bed and bent down beside it.

"I can't believe what I'm thinking," she said in a shocked voice.

The men looked at her in alarm.

"He's given her laudanum!" She turned, holding up a small bottle. "Has Victor been prescribed that by the doctor?"

"I don't know. Maybe he has. He's been seeing a lot of the doctor in recent months." Isaac was now shaking as he felt the blood drain from his head.

There was silence before Jack said, "We all need to sit down for a few minutes and try to work out where he might have gone with the two girls."

They nodded their agreement.

"Let us go to the library and work out a plan of action," said Isaac.

Margarita, Eliza and Deborah were sitting eating a leisurely lunch in the dining room of the Perrott home in Cork, still enjoying a relaxing break with their friends, when suddenly a sharp knock on the door was followed by Jack Ryan bursting in, swiftly passing the maid. As he made his way across the room, the ladies began to feel alarmed as they saw his ashen face.

Margarita's first reaction was to think that it was to do with Victor.

"Has something happened to Victor, Father?" she asked.

As her father tried to get his senses together, he hesitatingly answered, "No. Well, I don't think so."

As all the women now began to talk together, Jack interrupted. "Please let me explain. Firstly, the twins are both fine. But when Jean got up early this morning, she found that Rosita was not in her room. She called to Isaac's room. Isaac discovered that Victor had got Cillian to prepare the large carriage and four horses late last night, saying he was going to visit a sick friend – but not saying who or where. It appears he took Rosita and Florrie away during the night while Isaac was asleep."

Margarita was almost relieved because she knew that Victor would never cause harm to Rosita. "Did he not leave a note saying where they were going?" she enquired.

"It had to be somewhere close by if Rosita agreed to go with him. That child always had a mind of her own," Deborah assured Margarita though she was deeply worried, as she knew the mind of her son was not good these days and it had worsened since he returned from the recent meeting in London with the Prime Minister.

"We don't know where he is but we don't think Rosita went knowingly. Jean discovered the remains of a bottle of laudanum near her bed. Nobody heard them leave."

Everyone in the room including Mrs. Perrott was truly shocked. They all looked at Jack with open mouths.

Deborah broke the silence. "Where is Isaac?" she demanded.

"He has gone looking for them. He left in the other carriage, with Cillian driving, early this morning. They decided to go east and make enquiries at any farm or inn they passed to check if anyone had seen Victor drive by. I set out west and stopped regularly on the way but, unfortunately, nobody in Midleton or along the road saw or heard anything during the night. I think we all just need to get back to Midleton straight away and see what we need to do next. We have to make discreet enquires – we can't approach the law as they will not get involved if she's been taken by her father."

The first thing Margarita did when she returned home was to hug the twins. Then she took Jean with her to see what clothes Victor and Rosita had packed. She was happy at least that the child's warm clothing was missing as were Victor's own heavy coat and boots.

It was almost an hour before she got into her own bedroom. How could he do this to me without a single warning, she thought.

"It's nothing short of cruelty!" she angrily said, banging her fist on the dressing table.

As she turned to walk from the room, she noticed that her bedclothes looked ruffled. She pulled back the covers to find an envelope with her name on it. It was Victor's writing.

With shaking hands, she tore it open, unfolded the one sheet inside and read.

My Beloved,

I'm sorry. I'm doing this for Rosita's safety. She's spending too much time with the farm children and I know in my heart she will succumb to a serious illness. I am protecting her and young Florrie is with us. We are going to be fine. It is just like going on a holiday away from the terrible happenings in Ireland. Tell the twins I will see them soon.

I will always love you,

Victor

Margarita read the letter three times before racing down the stairs to show it to the rest of the family. They were all shocked at its contents.

Deborah was grateful that at least her son had the decency to leave a note for his wife. Ah, but why is he putting us through this, she thought, when we have enough problems to contend with here at the moment?

"Hopefully he's going to one of my relatives in Hertfordshire," she said. "Isaac was probably correct to go east if he wasn't seen on the road to Cork. Perhaps someone should check if he's gone towards Dublin?"

"We've asked our farmer friend Nick Jordan to get information from people on that road," Jack said, "but Victor had over ten hours' start before his father set out."

Eliza sighed and suggested that they needed to eat some food and keep their energy up because it would surely be a very long night ahead.

Chapter Twelve

Florrie was excited as she found herself, for the first time, in the large carriage. She was proud when Mr. Victor told her that he wanted her to accompany Rosita on a holiday. He trusted her with the secret that it was going to be a surprise for young Rosita. They were now in the warmth of the carriage and Rosita was sound asleep, lying across a long comfortable seat and Florrie was lying on the opposite one, smiling at her good fortune. She had packed her own and Rosita's bags and given them to Mr. Victor before he carried his daughter, who was fast asleep, silently out of the house.

Florrie was a bit perplexed as Rosita hadn't woken up but was glad to be able to get to sleep herself while Mr Victor drove the carriage through the countryside. Where she was going, she did not know but she was delighted to be part of the surprise, and to be in the company of two of her favourite people, as she drifted off to sleep.

Florrie was frowning as the first light of dawn peeped through the curtains on the carriage window and she saw that Rosita was still asleep. Rosita would never sleep for that long while the carriage was riding over some rough surfaces, she thought. She spoke quietly to her but Rosita didn't stir.

Suddenly the carriage came to a halt and, as Florrie looked out, she saw a vast expanse of sea in front of her. Her stomach began to knot with worry as it dawned on her that they weren't just going on a holiday in Ireland. It looked like they might be crossing what looked like an ocean. Suddenly the carriage door opened and Mr. Victor was there with a big smile on his face.

"Young Patrick here is from the boat that we're going on and he'll take all the luggage on for us. I see my daughter is still asleep so I'll carry her on. You can follow on with Patrick."

"Are we going to America, sir?" asked, Florrie, looking petrified as she had never been on a boat before.

Victor laughed heartily. "No, Florrie, we're just going to England." He gently picked his daughter up and took her from the carriage.

As Victor walked towards the large boat tied up at the pier, Patrick told Florrie to run after them. "I have another job to do too. I'm taking the carriage to the inn yonder before I get back on board. I might see you later," he said to Florrie with cheeky grin.

She smiled back at him and asked him what the name of this place was. He told her it was Dungarvan. She thanked him and hurried towards the boat. She noticed that lots of cargo was being put onto the ship but she couldn't see any other passengers and wondered about that.

An hour later she was in a small cabin where Rosita was lying on a narrow bed. Florrie was shaking her hand and whispering to her to wake up when suddenly Rosita began to twist and turn. She opened her eyes and looking around, asking, "Where am I, Florrie?" in a shocked voice.

"Thank goodness you're awake. I was getting worried about you. We're going on a surprise holiday with your father and the ship we're on has just left the harbour."

The stunned child jumped out of the bed. "Where is my papa and how did I get on a boat without knowing anything about it?" She angrily looked around the small cabin.

"Your father is in the room next door behind this wall and you were asleep while we travelled in the carriage to the harbour."

Before Florrie had finished speaking Rosita was running through the door and banging on the next cabin's door. Victor opened the door to his daughter, who by now looked very upset as she asked him why they were on a ship and where was her mother. Victor put his arm around her as he drew her into the room.

"Your mama is at home with the twins and we are going for a little holiday to England. You can roam around there without ever having to worry about getting sick. You'll have good fun and Florrie is here to keep you company."

Rosita nodded but seemed bewildered as she asked, "Will we be seeing our cousins in England, Papa? How soon before we get to see them? I would love that."

"Well, my love, maybe next week. We're sailing now and we'll be at a lovely place when we finish our journey. I will take you swimming in the sea and later in the week we'll go to see a friend of mine who has a big house before going to your Grandaunt Helena's house in Hertfordshire. It's a lovely day to be travelling on the water. We're going to be on the boat for a few days and then we'll start our adventure in a lovely carriage and we'll see all sorts of places while we drive along the coast. I've packed your books and sketching pads and paints so that you won't be bored on the journey, my love."

"Alright, Papa, but I'm hungry now."

"Of course. Go and get Florrie and the three of us will go up to the captain and he'll get us some food. Don't worry about anything. We'll have a great adventure in England. I'll make sure of that."

Isaac spent most of Saturday getting in and out of his carriage in an endeavour to track Victor's movements and he knew he was going in the right direction due to sightings by many residents along the road towards Waterford. It was late in the day and he was about to head to an inn near

Dungarvan to have a meal when Cillian drew the carriage to an abrupt halt and Isaac could hear him roaring and making a commotion.

Isaac jumped out to see what was happening and then raced forward with delight when he saw his own large carriage and horses stopped at the inn close by, a coachman in front.

He raced to the carriage and pulled open the door. It was empty.

"Is Victor Beaconsfield in the inn?" he shouted up to the driver.

"No, sir, I'm just doing a job. I'm returning this carriage to Midleton in the County of Cork for its owner."

"I'm Lord Isaac Beconsford, the owner of that carriage. Where have you come from?"

"I collected it from the local Harbour Inn. I believe that its owner left on a ship. That's all I know, sir. I just got paid for a job and the innkeeper promised the owner that he'd get it back to Midleton quickly. I've been on a job all day but I assure you the carriage will be back in Midleton tomorrow."

Isaac and Cillian looked at each other before Isaac spoke. "Very well. Before you continue on your journey, will you join us for some food? I will then give you a note to hand into the estate house in Midleton and you can continue on your journey. We will be going on to the harbour after our horses and ourselves have had a rest.

Nobody slept in the Beconsford estate that night. With no word from Isaac, even the staff were on edge, wondering why none of them had realised that Victor had gone. Hilda Bowe had the anxiety of her daughter having also disappeared and when dawn broke on Sunday, most of the residents went to their respective churches to pray for the quick return of Rosita, Victor and Florrie.

As Margarita paced around the front room of her home, she jumped with joy as she saw the large carriage making its way up the driveway. In a matter of seconds, she was racing down the front steps, only to stop when she saw the coachman shaking his head as he walked towards her.

"Have you got my husband and two young girls with you?" Margarita asked hopefully.

"No, madam, but I do have a letter addressed to Lady Deborah and Margarita Beconsford."

By now Deborah and Eliza were by her side. Margarita opened the letter and they all read it together.

"He's obviously taken them to England, as I thought he might," said Deborah, feeling a little relieved. "Hopefully Isaac will be back soon and he'll maybe know where they have gone." She was right.

An exhausted Isaac arrived home very late that evening with bad news.

"Victor and the girls have boarded a merchant ship from Dungarvan harbour. The goods carried were to go to France and Holland. However, the local constable told me that once it leaves Ireland there is nothing to stop the captain letting a passenger disembark anywhere and it could take weeks or months before the boat returns to Ireland again. He believes that Victor would have paid him well for taking them on board."

⚜

Florrie was surprised that Mr. Victor left them in their room alone all the time they were at sea, unless they were having meals. Rosita was happy reading her books and doing her sketching. Sometimes Florrie went for a walk in the air and had met Patrick on a few occasions. He told her that Mr. Victor was downing a lot of alcohol in his room as well as at his meals. Florrie wasn't surprised as she knew about his drinking but worried that he might continue drinking when they were on holidays. It won't be much of a holiday if he does, she thought.

After what seemed like too many days at sea, Victor excitedly brought the girls up on deck to watch as they sailed into a small harbour with an expanse of gleaming fine golden sand that seemed to stretch for miles. The girls were excited as they looked around.

"Are we staying here, Papa?" Rosita enquired hopefully.

"No, love, we are going on a carriage to a lovely quiet area along the coast."

When they left the boat, the girls couldn't believe that carriages for hire were on the beach. When they boarded the grandest carriage available, they left the sandy beach through a long tunnel that went up into the town. Rosita, being inquisitive, read the name of the place and immediately wrote it in her diary. *Ilfracombe*. That's a funny name, she thought, but at least now I know where we are. Rosita loved to detail her day in her diary and had been doing it since she was six. She loved to look at her previous diary the following year to see where she was on that day. She did this every evening in bed and found it great fun.

They all stayed in an inn that night and the girls finally began to believe that this holiday could be exciting.

Soon they passed through another place called Woolacombe and later in the day Rosita noticed a row of very pretty cottages on both sides of the road as they passed through a village with the name Croyde on a road sign.

"This is a pretty place," Rosita said to Florrie.

"We will shortly be at my good friend's cottage. It's close to a lovely quiet sandy beach," Victor told the girls.

As they drove along the road, the girls looked at a view that was truly stunning. The sun was beginning to go down and the clear blue water sparkled as it stretched for miles to the horizon. The long golden beach was deserted below the narrow road on which the carriage travelled.

At last they reached the laneway leading to the small thatched cottage in the distance. The carriage man opened a blue iron gate at a laneway which was barely wide enough for the carriage to reach the front of the cottage.

The girls were delighted to have arrived and ran inside to explore. The coachman helped Victor with the luggage and before he turned his horses, Victor gave him details of when he next wished to have a carriage at the cottage. The coachman agreed to pass the message on to a local carriage owner.

When Victor got into the cottage, Florrie had already opened the large food hamper that the ship's chef had prepared, while Rosita was picking out her bedroom.

Rosita, who had always been inquisitive and loved travelling, was excited at the prospect of enjoying her first holiday for a long time, due to the horrible famine that seemed to have stopped a lot of fun for her in Ireland during the past few years.

Chapter Thirteen

Shock waves continued to reverberate around the estate in Beconsford. Nearly two weeks had passed and there was still no word from Victor. Eliza's sister Lily in Hertfordshire and Isaac's sister Helena had been trying to contact everyone known to Victor from his previous drinking years.

At night in the estate each had difficulty sleeping. Left with these thoughts, they wondered if the girls really were in safe hands but nobody said it out loud. There was speculation that Victor might have gone to Europe and on to Vienna where he had previously been happy in the company of Doctor Bauer. The family knew that the good doctor would never condone Victor's behaviour and, if that happened, he would send word. Margarita's only consolation was that Rosita was the most sensible of children and had a wisdom far beyond her years. She was further comforted by her belief that Victor would never put his daughter in any danger.

Although people in dire need still walked the roads, the Beconsford and Ryan families found it more difficult to empathise with the unhappy situation in the country as they obsessed about the fact that they had heard nothing from or about Victor. They were all consumed with wondering how he and the girls could have disappeared. It was one of the bleakest times ever experienced by Margarita.

Florrie sat looking through the small bedroom window at the damp and desolate landscape outside. By now she had totally lost respect for Mr. Victor, whereas in the past she thought he was the most handsome and kindest man in Midleton. Close by, Rosita was sleeping fitfully. As tears flowed steadily down Florrie's face, she shook her head as she remembered what a fool she had been. The excitement of travelling away from Ireland with a man she admired was now gone. How stupid she had been to agree to go away with him in the middle of the night to give Rosita a holiday! He just needed someone to take care of his daughter.

Everything had been great on the first full day there. He took them for a picnic to the beach and they even made fun drawings in the sand. The following day his carriage collected him from the cottage. Before he left, he warned them that it was a dangerous area with sea pirates arriving at night and that they were not to venture out alone. Late that night he had returned, full of drink and ranting that his friend had left his country estate in a place called Clovelly and had not yet returned from southern Europe where he was still enjoying the warm weather. In the past Florrie had witnessed how vicious some of the village men were when they had the drink in them but she'd believed that Victor was not a bit like them. Usually in Ireland Rosita's papa had been gentle, mellow and sad when he drank, but he seemed different now. On edge, bad-tempered and he looked unhappy.

Thankfully, he had brought home more provisions because after breakfast the following morning the carriage arrived for him and he again warned them not to go anywhere on their own. That pattern continued for almost a week. Now she had to do something or either herself or Rosita would continue to live, hidden away in Croyde, with nobody knowing where they were.

Although Victor returned every evening with bags of food and drink, all he kept promising them was that they would return to Ireland when the famine ended. Rosita was getting more and more assertive as she admonished him. "Papa, how long will it be for the famine to end?" she kept asking, but he just brushed her off.

Florrie turned from the window as Rosita began to stir and cry out for her mama. Florrie joined her in the bed and held her tight in her arms until she quietened down and went to sleep again. Something had to be done soon.

By now, Florrie thought this was a godforsaken place and felt that she couldn't put up with it for much longer. My mother will kill me when we get home, she thought. Yet what to do about it she couldn't work out. Some days when she felt down, she believed that Rosita had more sense than her. They had to do something but what?

When Victor left the following morning, Florrie sat down with Rosita and spoke to her.

"Rosita, I don't think your papa has any plans to take us on a proper holiday or to go home. I know you are a very intelligent young girl and I wonder if there is any way we could get a letter to Ireland without your father knowing?"

"I'm getting worried too, Florrie, but I didn't want to upset you with my thoughts. I miss my mama and the twins so much. Let me think for a while and I'll try to work something out. I always thought my papa would care for me but now I think he must be ill because he's not being nice to us. I have nearly all my books read and I just want to go home."

Then in the middle of the afternoon Rosita came out of her bedroom.

"I have a plan," she said, much to Florrie's delight. "I'm going to write a letter to my mama but we'll post it to your home and your mother can deliver it."

"Why can't it go to the Big House?" Florrie asked, perplexed.

"Because of the plan I have for us to get it into the post. When Father returns each night, it takes the coachman a few minutes to turn the horses in order to go back down the lane. When we hear him arriving up the lane tonight, I want you to go out the back door and around the house and run to the start of the lane and stop the coachman there. Tell him you want a letter sent to your mother to let her know how much you are loving your time on your holidays. I don't want him to think we have a problem. But if the letter was addressed to Beconsford House, he might be suspicious and tell you to give it to my papa."

Florrie nodded, thinking how clever young Rosita was. "What about a stamp though?"

"I found some coins in Papa's room. He won't notice they're gone. It costs a penny, I think. I have the letter written already and I'll read it to you: '*Dear Mrs. Bowe, Could you please   take this letter up to my mama. Florrie is very well and sends her love. She is sorry for leaving but my papa had told her that I was being taken on a surprise holiday. Mama, I want to let you know that I am alright but miss you so, so much. Papa took us to England but I was on a boat before I woke and I thought that you knew that we were going on a holiday. But I think my papa is going to keep us hidden for a long time and I want to go home to you and the twins. I love you so much. This is where we are. We got a boat to a place called Ilfracombe and then a carriage to a place where we live in a cottage high above the seashore outside a village called Croyde. In the village you pass through a lovely row of cottages, and we are about five minutes in the carriage from there to where you can see a blue gate at the end of our lane. Papa's friend who owns the cottage is in southern Europe and Papa is very unhappy about that. He drinks a lot but always makes sure we have plenty of food. Please come and take us home, Your loving daughter, Rosita.*'"

Florrie thought that it was a grand letter and agreed to try to follow Rosita's plan.

When they heard the carriage coming up the lane, Florrie took the letter and ran out. She waited until the master had entered the house before running towards the lane. As the coachman came towards her, she waved her letter in the air and he halted the horses.

"Are you all right, child?" he said, concerned about the girl.

"Oh, I'm fine, sir. I just want to beg a favour. I'm working for the master but didn't want to annoy him by asking him to post a letter to my mother back in Ireland. I have the money here for the stamp and I'd be grateful if you'd do me a favour and put it in the post for me." She hoped he didn't see how nervous she was.

As she smiled up at him, he answered. "Of course I will, child. I won't take your money. I have a daughter of my own in service and we look forward to getting her letters every week. Now go in before you catch a cold."

"Thank you, sir! I'm so grateful to you! Take care going home in the dark," she said as he set off.

As Florrie rushed back to the house, she heard Rosita telling her papa that Florrie had a tummy problem and was in the outside water closet. As she came through the back door. Rosita turned towards her.

"How are you feeling now, Florrie?" she asked, raising her eyebrows.

"I'm feeling alright now, thank you, Miss Rosita. I think I'll go to bed now and see you in the morning. Good night, sir." She smiled at Victor as she made her way to her bed, hoping for a good night's sleep.

In Midleton, the mood in the Big House was very low and all they could do was hope. Eliza and Jack were always by their daughter's side, helping each day with the twins.

When Victor and the girls had first disappeared, Eliza had put her arm around her daughter and said, "Margarita, young Rosita may only be ten years of age but she has the brain of an adult inside that head of hers. The one thing we know for certain is that Victor won't allow Rosita come to harm. Let that thought stay with you and let us all do whatever we can to have a bit of normality, for the sake of the twins, until we know what is going on inside Victor's head. He can't just disappear into thin air."

Those words came back to haunt everyone in the house when two weeks after the disappearance of Rosita all avenues pursued in Ireland, Hertfordshire and London had brought no clues as to their whereabouts. Victor's doctor in Vienna was contacted and all he could do was reassure them all that Victor would not harm a hair on Rosita's head.

On a bright and sunny October morning, the residents in the Big House were still despondent when a sudden commotion in the front hall was followed by the door of the breakfast room bursting open as Hilda Bowe dashed in, breathing extremely heavily, with her chest heaving. Margarita ran to her side but Hilda just lifted her arm and put a letter into Margarita's hand.

As Margarita opened the letter and read it, she began to shake before handing the letter to Isaac, who was by now at her side.

His face lit up as he read the contents. "Thank God!" he exclaimed. "They're safe and well! What should we do now?"

"I'm going to go down and talk to my mother and father," she said. "Something has been spinning around in my mind over the past few weeks. I'll be back in about an hour with my parents and then we can discuss how we can proceed. This is such good news! Rosita is truly an amazing child and I always had confidence that she could deal with any situation. That child will make her mark in the future, of that I am sure."

Margarita returned to the Big House with Jack and Eliza, having discussed her ideas with them. They had reluctantly agreed to what she proposed.

When she put her proposal to her in-laws, she had to give them sound logical reasons in order to persuade them that she was serious about her plans. They too reluctantly agreed.

Three days later, with the weather calm and hopefully settled for a few days, Margarita and Jean, who was by now her best friend as well as companion, left the Beconsford estate in the carriage and headed towards Waterford harbour where they were promised a comfortable trip to their destination.

In Waterford, they boarded a large cargo boat, where passengers with wealth were welcome. They could then decide where they wished to go ashore. The ladies hoped that their sea journey would end safely in Ilfracombe, from where they would travel in a carriage to Croyde, praying that the girls would still be there.

When the ship arrived before dawn at Ilfracombe the weather was changing. Rain was falling and Margarita was glad to get inside the relative warmth of the large carriage. As soon as their luggage was on the seat opposite the ladies, Margarita turned to Jean as she watched the sea which was now beginning to churn up, as bad weather arrived.

"I have had only one prayer on my lips and that is my hope that Victor hasn't moved the girls to some other desolate place."

Jean patted her hand and assured her that someone in the area would know where the carriage would have taken them, if that was what happened.

"Don't think like that, Margarita. We need all our strength and we must keep hoping that we will see the girls before this night is out."

"I still haven't decided what I am going to say to Victor and I'm even less sure if I want him around me at this time. He has put us all through too much heartache and at this moment I'm not in a forgiving mood."

The ladies both settled back with their own thoughts as Jean mutinously believed that she would personally kill him if he had brought any harm to the girl that she had nursed and loved from the day that she had first held her soon after the death of Rosita's beloved mother Fleur.

As the carriage made its way slowly through the muddy roads, they stopped in an inn near the village of Woolacombe for refreshments. Their progress had been slow and the light of day was beginning to disappear as the rested horses made their way into the small village of Croyde. A row of pretty cottages bordered the road as they moved through the village. They followed the road, as directed by Rosita and, in the dim light of dusk, they watched the waves crash onto the vast expanse of golden sand below. The coachman told them the area was known as Saunton Sands and the view was painted by numerous artists during the warmer summer months. They passed a huge farmhouse with its roof of thatch. The surrounds were rich with grass and crops and Margarita wept silent tears as she thought of similar small farming areas in Ireland that were now barren and deserted. She envied the apparent tranquillity of this quaint English countryside. Earlier, Dan, the coachman, had assured Margarita that he had plenty of night lamps for the carriage and could leave the cottage at any hour of the night. He was very happy to be with the ladies as he had been handsomely remunerated for his work.

The carriage arrived at the lane leading to a cottage. To Margarita's relief, she noticed that a lamp was burning inside. The coachman had difficulty as the lane now consisted only of ruts created by previous carriage wheels. As he drew the carriage to a halt, Jean noticed that a curtain had been slightly lifted and she saw the outline of a person inside.

Margarita was already out of the carriage, knocking loudly on the front door. There was no answer and she was quickly joined by Jean who whispered, "There's someone inside the window at the end of the cottage but the light has now been put out. They might be afraid we are highway men."

Margarita immediately ran in the direction of the window of the cottage, banging it and shouting.

"Rosita! Victor! Florrie! It's me, Margarita! Please open the door!"

There was no answer, but Margarita could hear footsteps moving inside the house. Suddenly, a pale face looked through the window. It was Florrie.

"Florrie, please open the door! The rain is drenching us! Get Rosita's papa and tell him to open the door, please!"

The face disappeared from inside the window and after a few moments the door opened, much to Margarita's relief, and she saw the pale face of her young daughter behind Florrie. She rushed to take Rosita in her arms as the girl began to cry noisily.

"Calm down, little one, Jean and I are here to look after you now. Nothing bad is going to happen to you ever again, that I can promise you!"

As she moved with her daughter towards the kitchen, there was a warm glow from the embers keeping the cottage heated. Thank goodness, she thought. At least they're not cold. When she sat down with Rosita on her knee and holding tight to her, she asked Florrie to fetch Victor.

"I'm so sorry, my lady, I should never have agreed to go on holidays – I didn't think we'd go on a ship and I –"

"Go tell Victor we are here, Florrie!" she ordered, exasperated by now, expecting him to emerge from a bedroom.

"He's not here, my lady. He brought us lots of food and fuel two days ago and said he had to take a trip to organise the next part of our holiday. He wouldn't take us with him when we asked. We thought he was coming back when you arrived but the carriage was a strange one and he had warned us to keep the doors locked."

Margarita's jaw dropped as she heard Florrie's words. The relief she had felt was immediately countered by the rage she felt towards Victor for putting two young girls in such a situation.

"Are you telling me that you have been alone here for the past few days?" she asked, trying very hard to stop herself from screaming. Rosita and Florrie both nodded as Margarita looked at Jean who appeared every bit as stunned as her boss and friend.

Jean decided that she needed to take some control over the situation.

"I'm going to tell the coachman to come inside for food when he has attended to the needs of the horses. I think there might be a long night ahead of us. Florrie, will you come with me to the larder and we'll see what food there is to eat."

"Oh, Miss Jean, we have lots of food and I'll be happy to get a meal for everyone."

"I can do that – just show me what provisions you have."

In the larder Florrie spoke, keeping her voice low. "I'm ever so grateful that you came as I was really getting worried about Miss Rosita. She is very upset that her beloved papa has not looked after us like he said he would."

Jean shook her head again, not sure if it was from outrage or disbelief, before she answered the girl. "Don't worry – you're both going to be fine now. Now I'll attend to the food. I want you to go into the bedroom and pack all your things and Rosita's, as we may be leaving here very soon."

Rosita had colour in her cheeks again as they all sat down at the table in the warm kitchen, where Dan regaled the girls with stories of the characters that he had driven in his carriage down through the years. He had seen how upset the young girls looked and felt sorry for them. Being rich doesn't always make you happy, he thought, as he tucked into the lovely spread that Jean had prepared.

When they had finished eating, Margarita asked to speak to him privately. They stepped into the room adjoining the kitchen and Margarita turned to face him.

"I'm going to ask you a question, Dan. I would love to leave this place as soon as possible but do you feel up to a drive in this weather or should we stay over?"

"The rain had nearly dried up when I was feeding the horses and if we get out of the dirt track outside, the roads should be alright. As I said, I have fine lamps on my carriage and there are enough seats for all of you and luggage space, but I have to get some sleep now so that we can all arrive safely at our next port of call. I'll be grand then and maybe soon after midday tomorrow we can get to a good inn for food and rest."

Margarita put a grateful hand on his shoulder. She felt reassured by his answers.

"Thank you, I want the girls out of here quickly and I can't see myself getting a wink of sleep until they are safely away. If everything goes to plan, I want us to get on a London-bound train as soon as possible."

Dan nodded his agreement before going to put his head down for a few hours of much-needed rest.

Margarita spent the next while writing a letter to her husband.

Victor,

I am deeply upset at the trauma you have put myself and your beloved parents through in recent weeks. I have taken Rosita to a safe place and she will not return to Ireland for the foreseeable future.

Please do what I ask. Go to Vienna and get help from Doctor Bauer, who saved you in the past. Until you have done that, I would rather not see you again. At the moment I am far too angry with you and feel I cannot trust you to make good decisions for the family.

Please do everything you need to return in good health before you rejoin our family unit and again become the wonderful father and husband you were in the past.

I do love you, but at the moment I am not in love with the man you have become.

Margarita

She reread it a few times before sealing it and leaving it propped up on the kitchen table.

The following morning, the rain had disappeared and the group left the cottage soon after the sun rose. The girls had slept but Margarita's mind had been racing too fast for sleep. Instead, she spent all her time fretting that Victor would turn up in the middle of the night. She had no idea what she would do. She knew that the law would likely be on his side if he chose a legal route to keep Rosita by his side.

Later that morning, when they arrived in Combe Martin and stopped for refreshments, Margarita sent a letter by mail coach to Isaac and Deborah, who were both in London by now, as agreed before Margarita left Ireland.

The following day, after a night in a comfortable lodging house, they set off for London.

In the late evening, on the day after Margarita had left Croyde, a carriage drew up at the entrance to the cottage and Victor stepped out.

"Could you return tomorrow in the late morning, Charley? Be prepared to be available for two nights as we might be travelling on to somewhere new."

The carriage owner assured Victor that he would return before noon. "We both need a rest tonight after our troubles in Covelly," he said as he turned the horses before driving down the laneway.

Victor nodded in agreement, but frowned as he walked towards the cottage door and noticed that no candles burned inside the dark windows. When he turned the key in the lock, he was very concerned when the cheerful voice of his beloved Rosita did not respond to his greeting. As he walked towards the kitchen, he began to come out in a cold sweat as it dawned on him that the girls might not be in the house. He hastily lit a candle and ran to their bedrooms where he discovered that all their possessions were missing. Panic set in as he swiftly returned to the kitchen. Immediately he discovered a large envelope on the table with his name written on the front.

With shaking hands, he tore it open, needing to sit down as he read the letter from his wife. Relief flooded through his body when he discovered that the girls were safe. As he put his hands up to his head, he shed bitter tears of regret at the way he had treated his daughter. What am I doing with my life, he thought. Margarita is right. As he lifted his head and saw his reflection in the mirror that adorned the wall, he did not like what he saw. Shame seared through his body as he realised that his life had fallen to pieces around him. He should never have left the girls alone. He would have returned earlier except for the accident with the carriage two days previously. He had gone to the Hamlyn family estate in Clovelly where he had hoped his friend might have returned from the Mediterranean. Victor knew that the girls would love to stay in Covelly where a fishing village had been created at the harbour. Victor had hoped that the family would allow him bring the girls to enjoy the wonderful estate set into the hillside high up above the wide expanse of water where the Bristol Channel joined the Celtic Sea. Unfortunately, disaster struck as they drove towards the estate house, when the carriage fell sideways on the dangerous and rain-filled track. They were both lucky to escape injury but the carriage broke two wheels plus a passenger door. To add to Victor's woes, none of the family were in residence in the Clovelly estate but the housekeeper, Mrs. Henderson, was full of kindness and assured them that they were welcome to stay in the house until the carriage was repaired. This had taken longer than Victor had anticipated but he knew that the girls had enough food and fuel until he returned.

What a catastrophe my life is, he thought. As bitter tears flowed down his face, Victor decided to go to bed as there was nothing he could do until the morning. While thoughts of what a terrible person he had become stopped him from getting sleep, he turned, as he always did, to a bottle of brandy that he had in his bedside press. With the help of the alcohol, he finally found the peace that only oblivion gave him.

When Charley arrived the following morning, Victor was dressed and had his belongings packed.

"I'm going to Ilfracombe and I need you to be available for a few days, until I get a ship," Victor explained as Charley lifted the baggage onto the carriage.

"Are you going anywhere in particular, sir?" Charley enquired.

"I haven't decided yet," Victor answered abruptly.

Charley had noticed that the girls were not around, but his wife had already informed him that a carriage had left the area on the previous morning with women on board. He decided to keep his mouth shut because he had become alarmed at the level of drinking by Victor over the past weeks. Even his wife had begun to get worried about the girls. Although the money was good, Charley was almost relieved to see the back of Victor as he sensed that he might be trouble if he stayed in the area much longer. He had experience of driving drunk men home in his carriage but rarely had he met any quite as young and as rich as Victor.

The village clock struck twelve as Victor Beconsford left Croyde. As they drove north, Charley thought that it was likely that Victor's life would end in tears.

When the tired but happy group of females finally arrived at Brown's Hotel in London, Margarita had mixed feelings about the venue because it was there that she had accepted Victor's marriage proposal, after her singing trip to Europe. But she knew that Rosita loved that hotel. At the moment, she had mixed feelings about everything to do with her husband. Was her letter too harsh? She found it difficult to stop worrying about him but knew she now had to concentrate on the children and their safety.

As she entered the hotel, she was brought out of her reverie by the excited girls.

"Are we going to stay here?" Florrie asked Rosita excitedly.

"Yes, we are, Florrie. I have stayed here before and it serves lovely food all day if you are hungry," Rosita told her, feeling suddenly quite grown up.

The hotel manager hurried over and smiled as he greeted the young girl. "We're delighted to welcome you back to our hotel again, Miss Rosita. I have some of those apple slices and hot chocolate drinks available. I remember that you always loved those when you were a little girl."

"Thank you, Mr. Bennison. My friend and I would love some refreshments."

Florrie's eyes widened as Rosita spoke.

"Do you still have the room with all the books?" Rosita asked.

"Of course we do," Mr. Bennison answered, having to hide his smile as he saw how grown-up Rosita was trying to be. "I will send food into the library for you both as soon as you've seen your bedroom."

"Thank you, sir. We'd love that, wouldn't we?" Rosita said, beaming at Florrie.

Maybe they would now have the holiday they'd been looking forward to, Florrie thought in delight.

Upstairs, Florrie couldn't believe her eyes when she saw the lovely bedroom she and Rosita would share. They were delighted to be sleeping in the same room. Margarita felt it would be better as Florrie had told her about the nightmares Rosita had when they were in Croyde.

After they all had freshened up, Margarita gave them permission to go to the library as she wanted to have a private conversation with Jean.

"I don't know how Rosita is going to react to my decision about the immediate future," she said, once the excited girls had almost skipped out of the room and down the stairs.

"Margarita, you have got to be gentle when you tell her, but make sure you emphasise that this is happening and that it is for everyone's good in the long run. She'll be so happy that the twins are joining us that I believe she will be happy about it. I think you should speak to Florrie just before telling Rosita, because you will hopefully be able to reassure Rosita that Florrie will be joining us. These two have built up quite a bond in the last while because they have had to rely so much on each other."

Margarita nodded. "I'll talk to them tonight before bedtime as I don't want to wait until Isaac contacts us. I just hope he's got the letter by now and will be in touch soon."

When they were already in their nightgowns, about to go to bed, Jean knocked and entered.

"Florrie, Rosita's mama wants to see you in her room for a few minutes. While you're gone, I'll sit here and chat to this young lady."

Rosita smiled in delight as she loved Jean who had been her nurse since she was born.

"Come in, Florrie," Margarita said, smiling at the frightened-looking face of the young maid.

"Don't worry, there is nothing wrong. I just want to ask you a question and then you can return and get a good night's sleep."

When Florrie left the room ten minutes later, she truly felt that she was walking on air as she went back to the bedroom.

"Your mama wants you, Rosita. I'll stay up until you come back because I want you to finish reading your book to me. Someday I'll be able to read as fast as you, I hope!"

Rosita ran from the room to enjoy time alone with her mother.

"Come and sit here, my darling girl," Margarita said, holding out her arms to embrace her daughter.

Having bathed earlier, the young girl smelt of scented roses and Margarita had tears in her eyes as she wanted to hold her tight forever. Rosita snuggled up to her mother, before Margarita sat her down on the seat that she had positioned in front of herself. She held tight to the girl's hand as she bent over to talk to her.

"Rosita, you know how much I love you and you know that I would do everything to keep you safe."

Rosita nodded her head and smiled at her mama.

"I didn't know that your papa was taking you on holidays, but what I do know is that he loves you and would never have intentionally caused you or Florrie any harm. I think that your papa is unwell again, like he was for a while after your mama Fleur died. Hopefully he is now going to see a doctor. I know he was very worried about you and the twins getting ill in Ireland. Thankfully you didn't but, in order to keep your papa happy while he is getting better, I've decided that we need to go somewhere where there is very little illness."

"So where are we going, Mama? Is it up to live with your Auntie Lily's family or Grandaunt Helena's? I love it up there."

"No, sweetheart, we are going a long way further than that. And I just asked Florrie would she join us and she was delighted."

"But what about the twins?"

Margarita smiled. "Of course they will be with us and so will Jean."

"Oh, that's alright then. I always wanted to travel to other countries. What country are we going to?"

"America, to New York – you've heard of New York?" Margarita answered.

Rosita beamed. "I have."

As Margarita gave her a big hug, she was more than delighted that Rosita was undaunted and appeared happy to be going so far away.

Margarita had two days filled with concern. She feared that Victor would somehow find them but Jean had yet again assured her that he wouldn't have enough time to work it all out.

As the second day drew to a close Mr. Bennison knocked on her bedroom door.

"Lord Isaac Beconsford's carriage has just arrived at the entrance and it seems to be full of young children and luggage." He smiled, seeing the delight on Margarita's face as she jumped up and grabbed a cloak before swiftly leaving the room and running down the staircase with a big smile on her face.

When she reached the hotel entrance, she was almost knocked down as the twins ran from their Granny Deborah into their mother's arms. Margarita took one in each arm and danced them around the foyer, kissing and hugging them in delight.

Isaac arrived behind them, smiling at the happy scene.

When Margarita put the twins down, her father-in-law kissed her cheek.

"Everything is organised for tomorrow but let us first see Rosita. Deborah has nearly been out of her mind with worry. The letter was such a relief. We'll talk about Victor tonight but let's keep this moment joyful."

Margarita immediately agreed and she held the hands of her children as they made their way to Rosita's bedroom. When they opened the door, the twins seemed as happy to see Florrie as their sister. The delight of the children reunited again was for everyone a joy to behold and the screams of delight in the room as the twins bounced on the beds could be heard on the streets of Mayfair.

Later, when the twins were in bed with both Jean and Florrie minding them, the family sat in the dining room and enjoyed a wonderful meal followed by the delicious desserts which Rosita especially loved. As Margarita looked around, yet again she noticed the stark difference between this laden table and the reality for most of the families in Ireland and she offered up a silent prayer that when she finally returned to Ireland a semblance of normality would have returned. Only then can I tackle the big question of what has happened to my marriage, she thought.

Early the following morning, two large carriages left Brown's Hotel with all the family for the journey to Liverpool, where Margarita, Jean and the girls would board a Cunard Line America-class steamship that Isaac had been informed would take the women to New York via Halifax in just two weeks. The ship was larger and faster than any previous vessels and Margarita hoped that the journey would be safe and that they would find some form of peaceful existence in New York.

Chapter Fourteen

Leaving Liverpool was a sad moment for everyone. Isaac and Deborah both looked heartbroken. They had assured Margarita that they would continue to look for Victor and support him in whatever way he needed. Margarita felt guilty, yet as they sailed away from the shore on a calm and sunny October morning, she was relieved that she was going away with the children and that a troubled Victor had not turned up to block her plans.

As a golden winter sun slipped gently into the calm seas below, Margarita prayed that she would feel at peace in the new world until the lush green fields of Ireland returned to normal.

Exceeding their expectations, all of the females thoroughly enjoyed crossing the Atlantic. They were regularly invited to dine with the captain, while an onboard nursemaid sat with the twins as they slept contentedly in their cabin. Margarita and Rosita slept in a cabin with an adjoining door to the twins while Jean and Florrie were in the cabin adjoining the twins at the other side. The twins and the two young girls played endless games on the deck and in a games room. Only two days of rough seas kept everyone lying down in their rooms, the weather staying relatively calm for most of the trip.

When the ship finally steamed up the Hudson river, they all watched the shoreline with its tall buildings, as Margarita wondered how they would settle in this strange new world. She was deeply grateful for Isaac's foresight as he had already acquired their new home and had even employed a housekeeper.

When they finally disembarked, they all laughed at their wobbly legs as they first stood on firm ground. Two carriages awaited to take their trunks and large bags to their new home. The children watched excitedly through the carriage windows until they finally drove up a quiet tree-lined road with houses on each side. The name of the house was Number 10 Willow Crescent. As the carriage pulled up, Margarita smiled as she saw the large three-storey building with gardens to the front and sides at the end of a cul-de-sac. Flower beds filled with pretty lilac-coloured winter iris greeted them on either side of the short gravel entrance.

My father would love to see this garden, Margarita thought, as she knocked on the oak-panelled front door. She was greeted by the smiling housekeeper and cook, Mrs. O'Brien, who announced that she too had recently arrived from Ireland and she was looking forward to working with the Beconsford family, if they decided she was suitable.

From the moment they stepped inside, Margarita felt the warmth from the many fires burning in several rooms plus the smell of Irish cooking emanating from the kitchen. She was happy for the first time in months and she loved the idea of having an Irish housekeeper by her side.

Christmas was both relaxing and quiet in the house in New York. All the occupants of Number 10 settled in quickly. They all enjoyed the fact that they could eat their fill and more food was available whenever it was needed. The winter weather was much colder than they had expected with snow covering the large gardens surrounding the house. With new warm clothes the twins, especially Louis, revelled in making snowmen and throwing snowballs with his sisters.

Christmas Day was a quiet affair with the family enjoying the celebration meal. Presents were exchanged. Louis played with a new train set that he received, while Violet enjoyed dressing a pretty doll who had blonde curls just like herself. Violet spent hours changing the doll's dresses in the morning and at night. They had been purchased in Tuttle's Emporium.

In January Rosita was enrolled in a private school close to their home and she took it upon herself each evening to help Florrie to improve her reading and writing, as they had by now become good friends. During the day Florrie and Jean took care of the twins as Margarita found that she was sought after as a voice coach for young ladies. This earned her some money to supplement the generosity of her in-laws. It also kept her mind busy from dwelling on the more difficult aspects of her marriage. She received letters every week from Ireland and was saddened by the lack of knowledge of where Victor now lived plus the continuation of hunger and disease in her beloved country.

As the days got warmer, she often sat in the garden to read her correspondence. She was doubly saddened by a letter she received from Alice in early summer.

My dearest sister,

The good news is that both Gregory and Emily are keeping very well, as are Richard and Meg. Jerome's rheumatics are worse but he never complains and Grace and Meg still keep the house running smoothly.

This area of West Cork is still suffering very badly from deaths, poverty and infection. I am finding it harder to watch the crowds streaming towards the large workhouse in Clonakilty where I'm told they still have very little chance of survival. Nothing seems to have changed there. It's a paradox because everyone in Ireland cares about what's happening to their neighbours and friends but are powerless to do anything to help those who enter the workhouses.

The money that has come from the Irish migrants in America allows the Society of Friends to continue doing trojan work but whatever any of the church pastors and priests do it is never enough.

Troubling news also about my friend Sylvia. She is living with a very controlling man in Toby Ramsay and is at her wits' end. She has no near relatives to support her and being such a gentle lady is finding it difficult to know what to do. As you know young Maeve Maguire from the village is working for Sylvia. I'm glad it's working out but I worry about a young pretty girl in a house with Toby Ramsay.

We are all well on the farm and everyone sends their love.

I could fill this letter with more news but it would be all bad and I'll try not to burden you with any more of that!

We are all so happy that you have settled in America, I hope not for too long!

I'll finish as I want to get this to the letter man, who will be collecting them soon.

All my love to you and your darling children,

Your loving aunt

Alice

Having read the letter Margarita immediately went to the study and took out her writing set, wanting to immediately reply to Alice.

My dearest Alice,

We are still all loving our time in New York although I have regular feelings of guilt because I am not with the people in my own country. Victor has still not attended his doctor in Vienna and that saddens me.

It saddens me also that your good friend Sylvia is forced to live with that despicable man. This is why I am replying so quickly. I wondered if she would consider coming over to New York for some months. She is welcome to stay in my home, although there are nearby homes that she could rent if she wanted her privacy. I would be here to support her. It is just an idea and perhaps you might suggest it to her.

At present I am teaching a large number of young ladies who wish to improve their vocal range and have a desire to sing in the concert halls. I already have students on a waiting list to commence their training! I hope that both the ladies and myself get satisfaction from my efforts!

Please give my love to all your family and I hope we can see each other when times improve, both in Ireland and in my marriage.

With love,

Margarita

Chapter Fifteen

Back in West Cork, Toby Ramsay seemed not to have suffered any great hardship throughout the years that had caused death, emigration and hunger to a whole population. Sylvia did her best for their beleaguered workers and farmers but she had another sickening problem inside her own home. She had been watching her husband carefully from the moment that she had discovered that young Maggie Sinnott, their pretty young maid, had left the house abruptly one morning before dawn. After Sylvia made extensive inquiries, she finally got the truth out of the girls who slept beside Maggie in the servants' attic. Young Maggie was with child and the master had ordered her to leave and threatened all the staff with dismissal if they ever mentioned Maggie's name again. Sylvia felt like getting sick when she realised that her husband must have fathered that child. Maggie had already left the area to live with a relative. She knew also that he had now set his sights on young Maeve. She realised that she had to do something about it.

She requested that Maeve should come to her drawing room.

Although Sylvia was furious inside her head, she sat upright on the chair and put a smile on her face when Maeve entered the room.

"Come in, Maeve, and please sit down. I have something I want to ask you."

Maeve looked a bit worried as Sylvia smiled.

"Don't worry, I just want to tell you that I am extremely happy with your commitment to this house. Mrs. Hayes has nothing but praise for you. I've decided that I want a lady's maid, especially to help me with my charity work. I know that you can read and write and that will be important. Would you be happy to accept the job?"

As Maeve bent over with a deep curtsey, Sylvia laughed, thinking that the smile on Maeve's face would light up a room.

"Of course, Your Ladyship. I would love to help you with anything you need. It would be an honour," she said, blushing slightly.

I need someone like this enthusiastic young girl at the moment, Sylvia thought.

"I'm delighted and as I know that your sleeping quarters are not the best, I'm going to ask Mrs. Hayes to prepare a new room for you, closer to mine, on the second floor. It makes more sense to have you nearby."

As Maeve began to curtsey again, Sylvia put her hand up.

"Maeve, as my lady's maid, I don't expect you to curtsey to me! You will shortly know everything about me, good and bad and all I need from you is loyalty."

"You have that already, Your Ladyship, and now I can't wait to go home on Sunday and tell my mam the news," Maeve said enthusiastically.

Sylvia smiled at the excitement in the girl's eyes.

"I'd never get a room to myself at home, but my mam always said that I'd go places!"

Sylvia loved this young girl's zest for life. She would make sure that she got her chance to "go places", as she said.

Within two days, Maeve had moved her meagre belongings to the luxury of the second floor of the house. It didn't go down well with many of the young staff but Mrs. Hayes was delighted for her.

"You're a good worker, girl, and your mind is quick. In no time you'll be able to learn Lady Sylvia's ways and, if you have any questions, just ask me. Your mam will be so pleased for you and the Lord knows that there isn't much good news around these parts at the minute."

"Thanks, Mrs. Hayes. I'm so pleased and I'm getting a pay rise as well. I can't wait to tell my mam on Sunday."

"Come down before you leave on Sunday and I'll set a nice bag of food aside for your family. But don't tell the rest of the maids. I'll give you the bag as you leave and we can say you're running an errand for me."

Maeve felt like giving her a hug but knew the older lady, who had a kind heart, would be embarrassed.

On Sunday morning, Maeve sang as she swung the food bag, making her way down the driveway. She would get to the village church in time for Mass but hoped that Father O'Neill would not spend an hour telling them that God would take care of them. Secretly, Maeve didn't believe him and felt that only hard work and luck had played a part in her getting to be a lady's maid so quickly.

Alice was taking a walk through the village with Emily when she saw Maeve's smiling face in the distance. It raised Alice's spirit to see someone she knew looking happy.

"What do you have to be smiling about, Maeve?" Alice asked.

Maeve was almost breathless as she told Alice about her new job.

"Lady Sylvia is so good to me. She's given me a bedroom near her own. I can't wait to describe it to Mam after Mass." She told Alice about the bag of food given to her by Mrs. Hayes. They both laughed as Alice said that was typical of Úna Hayes.

They waved goodbye but, as Alice reflected on Maeve's good fortune, she frowned. That was a quick move and Sylvia didn't mention it to me last week, she thought. She felt a sudden pain in the pit of her stomach as she wondered if this had anything to do with Toby Ramsay. She would ask Sylvia when she went to the house the following week. Although it's unlikely a wife would say things about her husband, even to a friend.

Maybe she was overthinking it and she should just let Maeve enjoy her new position in the house.

It was a very happy Maeve who returned to the Big House on Sunday evening. She had enjoyed a wonderful day with her family and Fiona had shielded her daughter from the big problems that had now disrupted the lives of most of the inhabitants of Eoinstown. Maeve knew there were huge difficulties but she had the ability of youth to believe that everything would be alright and for that day she refused to engulf herself in the pain and suffering of other people, provided that her own family were alright.

Lady Sylvia was in her drawing room when Maeve returned and when she summoned her there, the girl's enthusiasm and happiness showed on her face as she relayed the news from the village.

As Maeve left the room, Toby Ramsay entered, scowling at her.

"What the hell were you thinking," he demanded of Sylvia, "by giving that skivvy a room on your corridor?"

"For a start, she's not a skivvy. She is a bright young girl and I'm giving her a chance to rise in the world."

As Toby poured himself a drink, without asking his wife if she wanted one, Sylvia looked at him calmly but with a complete feeling of hatred in her heart.

"My father never questioned any of my household decisions and I will not be told how to treat my personal staff," she said, looking directly into his eyes. "I'm retiring for the night now as I'm tired, so I won't join you for a drink."

She stood up and quietly left the room with her head held high and her dignity still intact. How she hated that man, she thought, as she wearily climbed the stairs of the house that she had once loved but now felt was like a prison.

As she had done every night since moving Maeve into her new bedroom, Sylvia prepared for bed, but then sat by the fire and read her book, waiting to hear her husband's heavy steps go up to his quarters on the next floor.

Tonight, she was almost falling asleep when she heard him climb the staircase. He was treading softly and it didn't need a scientist to work out that he was on the prowl. His steps did not appear to be going to his room. She stood up, slipped her slippers on to her feet and listened at the door. He didn't knock at her door but the steps continued along her corridor. Sylvia went and grabbed the heavy poker from the hearth and returned to listen at the door again. What a fool he is, she thought, as she heard him stopping.

Then she heard a handle turning. She had told Maeve to always lock her door when she was going to bed, but she was likely to be still pottering around and not in bed. She may have left the door unlocked. By now, Sylvia was horrified at her husband's behaviour plus his stupidity. He didn't seem to realise that she knew everything that he had been getting up to in the house since they married. Tonight, it would end, she vowed.

Sylvia opened the door quietly, clutching the poker in her right hand. She ran to Maeve's room door, praying it wasn't locked. She turned the handle and it opened.

She lifted the poker as she saw the terrified young girl looking at her in horror with Toby already pressing on top of her on the bed.

"Get out of this room, you brute, or I will hit you on the head with this poker!"

Toby roared like a bull and turned towards his wife. As he did, Maeve picked up a glass vase and threw it at the back of his head with enough force to make him stumble and fall. This gave her enough time to run from the room, with Sylvia following closely behind. Within a moment they were safely locked in Sylvia's room.

Sylvia held the young girl close to her chest. "I'm so sorry, I'm so sorry. I promise you that he will never again do that to you. You can spend the night with me in this room and tomorrow we will talk about how we deal with this."

Maeve still looked shocked and Sylvia pulled the bell to call a kitchen maid to bring them some tea. Sylvia was sad to see how her husband's behaviour had made this smiling girl look so terrified. She just hoped that Maeve's views of other men wouldn't be shaped by her husband's behaviour tonight. Thankfully, she had anticipated correctly that her husband wanted the girl but, luckily, she had stopped it.

After a fitful sleep, Sylvia and Maeve woke early the following morning. As Maeve had slept in her day clothes, she had by then begun to get Sylvia's morning clothes ready.

"Maeve, I want you to eat breakfast here with me. Afterwards, I want you to stay in this room. Lock the door and leave the key in the lock. Put a chair under the doorknob if you are concerned. I will go out but Mrs. Hayes will keep an eye on you."

Maeve nodded and tried unsuccessfully to put a smile on her face.

"I'm sorry, Lady Sylvia, if I've caused trouble for you."

Sylvia was horrified at her words. "Look me in the eyes," she instructed, as she held Maeve by her shoulders. "None of this is your fault. I have to apologise to you because my husband behaved like a monster. Sadly, it isn't the first time, but I will make it clear that it is the last time he'll try to touch any young girls. Unfortunately, I have no control over most of his actions, but I'll do my best to end this now."

Maeve had tears in her eyes as she looked at her mistress and she just nodded her head in thanks.

Having dressed and eaten breakfast, as Mrs. Hayes had fussed over them like a mother hen, Sylvia left and went to the breakfast room where she knew her husband was eating. She marched in, steeling herself to stay strong. She walked over to his chair but stayed standing.

"I'm giving you just one warning today. If you ever again sully the reputation of any of my staff, I will immediately report you to the law. I will do everything to ruin whatever bit of reputation you have in the county."

She stopped as he threw back the chair and stood over her.

"I am the squire of this house and I will do whatever I like and you can't stop me. Nobody would care when they look at the sight of the woman who was lucky to get a husband. Now, get out of this room and remember why I look elsewhere for my women. You are a scrawny barren woman who was lucky to bag a husband at all. So, clear out of my way, I want to enjoy my breakfast."

Although shocked at the nasty words that emanated from the mouth of her husband, Sylvia stood her ground.

"You might be squire of this estate, but I have two things that you will never have. I have a good reputation and am liked by the people in the district. In addition, I am lucky to have a trust fund created by my grandmother that you can never put your hands on. She was a wise woman and knew that all husbands aren't trustworthy."

As the shock registered on her husband's face, Sylvia summoned up all her dignity and marched out of the room, head held high.

When she reached her own drawing room she collapsed into a chair and, with her head in her hands, let the tears flow. Tears for her inability to conceive a child, for her loneliness, and knowing that she had to rely on herself for everything if she was to have a better future.

Sylvia went to the bedroom and informed Maeve that everything would now be fine.

"I'm going out for a few hours to clear my head, so stay here while I'm gone. Mrs. Hayes will keep an eye on you and will bring your lunch up."

Maeve was by now embarrassed by the attention and care Lady Sylvia was giving her and she could only stammer her thanks because she was afraid that she might cry again. Everything was so wonderful yesterday, she thought, but she was now sure that Lady Sylvia would ask her to leave. All she could feel was sadness that her bright future was about to come to an end.

Sylvia donned a warm cloak and hat and made her way down the driveway. She started to walk in the direction of the village. She had spent a lot of the night thinking and now she was making her way to Alice's home to discuss the situation with her.

Meg answered the door and was surprised to see Lady Sylvia.

"Come in out of the cold, love. Is it Alice you're looking for?"

Sylvia nodded and Meg smiled, noticing the strained look on Sylvia's face.

"She's out in the back yard with Gregory. I'll put you in the parlour and I'll take the child for a walk while you chat. Grace is in the kitchen and I'll tell her to send in a pot of tea and some hot scones for you both."

Sylvia thanked her as she sat on a chair placed close to the warm glow of the fire.

Grace was already serving tea to their guest when Alice reached the parlour.

"I'll leave you two girls to talk – if you need anything just shout," she said, smiling at them.

Alice looked at Sylvia as she sat beside her on the couch, realising that there might be a problem.

"Are you alright, Sylvia?" Alice asked gently as tears appeared in her friend's eyes. "Take a moment," she said as she put a hand on her friend's arm to offer some comfort. "Drink your tea and, if you don't want anything more than a sympathetic friend sitting with you, well, that's fine too."

As they were both nursing the hot cups in their hands, Sylvia burst out, "My husband assaulted Maeve in her bedroom last night."

"Did he succeed?" Alice asked, shocked.

"No, I rushed in and threatened to hit him over the head with a poker."

"And that stopped him?" Alice asked as her eyes widened.

"When he turned towards me Maeve threw a glass vase at him and it knocked him sideways and we both ran from the bedroom."

"Good for Maeve! But, Sylvia, are you going to suffer for this?" Alice was now worried about her friend as well as Maeve.

"I told him this morning that I would report him to the law if he ever did anything like that again."

Alice now felt even more concerned for her friend. He could easily kill her, she thought, but kept this to herself.

"What are you going to do?" she asked.

"I've been awake most of the night and I need some advice from you."

Alice nodded. "If there is anything I can do I'd be delighted to help," she assured her, as she patted her friend's hand and then kept hold of it. She could see that Sylvia was very close to breaking point.

"I'm going to leave him!"

Alice was so startled that she moved back. Then she smiled, as it slowly dawned on her that she might be able to help.

"It's strange that you should say that, because just a few days ago I had a letter from Margarita. Sylvia, don't think that I'm a gossip but I mentioned that you were having a hard time with Toby. As I mentioned to you before, my sister Eliza had known him in Midleton and she has always been concerned about you. In Margarita's letter she said that you would be more than welcome to come to New York and stay with her, if you ever felt the need to get far away from him."

Sylvia looked astonished and hesitated before saying, "But I've never been further than England. How could I cope with going so far away?"

"You could take young Maeve with you. She's a very bright girl. You should think about it." Alice was really fearful for her friend, knowing that Toby Ramsay was capable of anything.

"Well, for all I care, he can have the estate," said Sylvia. "It doesn't feel like home to me anymore and it never will while he's living there."

She went on to explain to Alice that she had a big legacy left to her by her grandmother and had no money worries.

"Actually, I don't even have to think about it. I'm going to leave and go to America," she said, smiling for the first time since arriving. "I'm going to leave Ireland and take young Maeve with me, if her mother agrees. But I don't want anyone to know that I'm leaving."

"I'll do anything you want to help you leave. It's about time that you finally had a life of your own," Alice said with relief in her voice, now that her friend was finally fighting back.

"Alice, I believe that you have a coachman in Midleton. I wonder if we could get his help. I know he comes to West Cork fairly frequently and I would pay him handsomely for his services if I could get away safely from here."

Alice was delighted with her friend's request and now she hoped that Mrs. Maguire would be happy to see Maeve get a chance of going off to America. After a while she smiled, her management of travel coming to the fore.

"I'll do more than getting Brendan to bring his carriage. I will also ask my sister Eliza to get someone to organise the tickets for you. I know that Margarita will be delighted to help you when you arrive in America."

On hearing this, Sylvia let the tears flow.

While Sylvia composed herself, Alice was thinking furiously. They had to think of a way that could help Sylvia leave the country without the knowledge of her husband. They agreed to meet again after the upcoming weekend.

When Sylvia returned home, she knew that she needed one person in whom she could trust to help her prepare to leave her family home. When she arrived inside the door, she immediately instructed the butler to ask Mrs. Hayes to join her in the drawing room as quickly as possible. She then made her way to that room to await the arrival of her cook. Úna Hayes had joined the staff as a child over twenty years before and Sylvia had fond memories of her throughout her own childhood. When Sylvia was young, there was always something hot to eat if she passed through the kitchen. When her predecessor had retired, Sylvia had been delighted to keep her in the household. She had always thought that the cook would marry and leave but as she was now in her mid-thirties, Sylvia thought this was by now unlikely. Yet she felt sad that Mrs. Hayes had never had children of her own. She would have made a very good mother, she thought.

Shortly after, there was a knock at the door and the cook entered. Sylvia asked her to sit, as she had something difficult to talk to her about.

"If it's about young Maeve, she told me about it. I'm really proud of what you did to save her. I'm sorry to be so outspoken but your husband has most of the staff in fear of him and I think that he would have found an excuse to get rid of me except he likes his food too much. I just wanted to say that before you tell me what you want me to do."

"Could you turn the key in the door and sit down with me, please."

Although surprised, Mrs. Hayes did as she was asked.

"Thanks to you, plus a few other people, I've finally seen sense with regard to my husband. However, I need this conversation to be private. I will reward you handsomely if you feel that you cannot stay here when I leave."

Mrs. Hayes, with her jaw hanging open, nodded her agreement.

"I'm going to go to America and I hope to take young Maeve with me, if her mother allows it. I'm going to leave the house to him as I have personal wealth and I won't have financial difficulties. Your friend Grace Staunton's daughter-in-law Alice is arranging it but I'll need help in getting clothes and jewellery and other personal items moved from the house without his knowledge. Do you think you could help? If not, I want you at least not to let anyone have any inkling of what I am about to do."

Sylvia waited, watching the changing expressions on her cook's face.

"Lady Sylvia, I've been in this house for over half my life, but the only reason I'm still here since you wed is to look out for you and the other decent staff in the house. I'm not sure how you'll feel about what I am about to suggest. I'm sick of living in this house, with having to watch over the young girls here and not always succeeding. As you know I still have my mother living in the village and she's surviving through the famine only because of the leftover food I take to her. I've thought for the past few years of leaving and taking the boat to America, where I could earn a decent living and send the money home. Would you think I could maybe travel with you to America, Miss Sylvia? I wouldn't impose on you when we arrived, but the fare and a small sum of money to leave to support my mother for a while would be sufficient."

Sylvia looked at her in astonishment. "Oh, my goodness, I would love that! I would love you to travel with us! It would benefit us all if that happened. But could you go without other people knowing, apart from your mother?"

"Don't worry – my mother has been saying for the past few years that I'm wasting my life by staying here. She'll keep her mouth closed because she always wanted me better set up than here, but she knew I loved you too much to leave. I'll give her some money and hopefully we will see an end to this wretched famine soon. Also, if young Maeve is happy to go, I could talk to her mother and if I'm going with you Fiona and her granny might be more comfortable about her leaving."

Sylvia suddenly found herself overwhelmed and close to tears. The kindness of her cook was what she needed if she was to leave the country without her husband finding out. All Sylvia now had to find out is whether young Maeve would join them.

Later that evening Maeve was full of smiles again, delighted with the chance to travel with her boss and was even more delighted to hear that Mrs. Hayes was travelling with them.

"I thought I was going to get sacked by the master," she said, thrilled with the idea of travelling in the company of Lady Sylvia.

Later, when cook came to the bedroom with Sylvia and Maeve's supper, she too had a smile on her face as she told Maeve that she had been to the village and asked her mother if Maeve could go to America.

"Although your mother was sad at the thought of you leaving, she said that she always believed that you would be the one to make something of yourself and she sent her blessing."

With a jump of glee, Maeve catapulted herself into Mrs. Hayes' arms and gave her a big kiss on the cheek.

Mrs. Hayes smiled as she warned the young girl. "She expects you over next Sunday as usual and she's arranged for Micky to be out for the afternoon so it will leave you both time to talk."

Sylvia added her thanks and they chatted about arrangements before eating supper and retiring to bed.

Before they finished, Sylvia made an announcement that delighted them even further.

"When I set foot on the ship going to America, I intend to be known simply as Sylvia. I want you, Úna, to address me just by my name. Maeve, you might prefer to call me Miss Sylvia for a while but, when we arrive in America, we will all just be friends."

Úna and Maeve beamed at each other, now looking forward to getting to the land of the free.

By the end of the following week, the ladies had already begun to use the dressing room as a place to hoard the things that would be taken to America.

One day, as they sorted and mended clothes, there was a sudden loud knock on the bedroom door followed by Toby's voice shouting, "*Let me in!*"

The women looked at each other and Maeve began to cover the large trunk to make the room look normal.

Sylvia called out, "*What do you want?*"

"*I want to speak to you, wife!*" he shouted angrily.

By the time Sylvia opened the door, Maeve was sitting primly in the room, stitching a hem of a garment in her hands.

"I want to talk to you alone – tell your maid to give us privacy," he said, looking with disdain at Maeve.

"I'll finish it in the dressing room, my lady, as I have more work to do there."

"Thank you, Maeve, I'll call you when I need you out here again."

When the girl departed, Sylvia turned to her husband.

"What do you want, barging into my rooms like that? I don't invade your private rooms."

"As your husband, I have every right to enter your room but choose not to as your miserable face doesn't entice me when I can get my pleasures elsewhere. However, I still need you by my side on occasions and next Friday night I want you to accompany me to a charity event at Squire Grimes' home. You are always talking about the poor Irish peasants; well, they will benefit from the night and I will make good contacts with the influential gentry that I know will be attending."

A white-faced Sylvia looked at him with disdain, as she pondered her answer.

"I will join you for the night provided that you will refrain from making sly insulting comments about me to your so-called friends." She waited for his reply.

He started to laugh. "You must realise that many of the women with old husbands are always flattered by my attention to them. They are usually the ones who press their husbands to invite me to their estates, but they don't know that I find most of them almost as ugly and boring as you. So, you have no worries, I will be full of charm on the night as I'll be looking forward to my card game after you are in bed." He smirked as he turned his back on his wife and left the room.

Sylvia couldn't move for a while until the feeling of hatred for her husband subsided, as she told herself that she would be out of his clutches shortly. How I hate him, she thought, and it's strange that I don't have any guilt about my feelings.

As she pulled herself together, Maeve reappeared in the room and walked over to her employer and put a hand on her shoulder.

"It won't be long now before we'll be thousands of miles away from him."

Sylvia nodded and asked Maeve to ring the bell and get a tray of refreshments. I need it, she thought, remembering his hurtful words.

Sylvia sat stiffly at her husband's side as the guests ate venison and drank fine wines, while many of the people in the rural hinterland were either going to bed early without food in their stomachs or scrambling for money to buy a ticket to emigrate. Thankfully, at least, tonight's dinner would raise a considerable amount of money to give to the local Quaker society. The money would help them produce nutritious soup for those who queued. For many of those people it would be the only meal of the day. She shook her head in despair, thinking of these people and she resolved to give a large gift to the local famine charities before she left for America. She felt almost like a traitor to her country by leaving to have a better life and not because of poverty.

As her husband returned to her side, having previously gone to mingle with the titled guests, she woke from her reverie as he excitedly told her of an invitation they had received.

"We've been invited to spend a long weekend next month, as guests of the Earl of Cork and Ossery, at his estate," Toby said, almost overcome with excitement at the chance to move in such exalted circles.

Sylvia nodded and smiled, as was expected of her.

"It's all hush-hush but a select number of his friends are going to shoot deer and feast on our prey over the weekend!" He laughed, seeing the expression on his wife's face.

"Don't worry, they have more tame entertainment for the women."

Sylvia's shocked expression had been only because she never again wanted to go on another trip with her husband, and she wondered how she could get out of it. She could see that he had drunk too much but the excitement for him of being in the company of so many titled people seemed to her to be even more vulgar than usual. She had to remind herself to keep her mouth shut and keep smiling, for now.

"What date is that, dear?" she enquired, still smiling.

"It's four weeks from today," Toby answered excitedly. "Lady Fermoy will be joining the party. She said perhaps you would like to talk to her and discuss what gowns you may need for the weekend?"

"No, dear, I'll leave her alone to talk to her friends, but you can thank her for her kindness when you go by."

Toby walked away; happy he had made an outward impression of being a dutiful husband. Sylvia stared after him, despising him even more for his stupidity in thinking he could still manipulate her whenever he wished. Hearing her table companion speak, she turned to her, and enjoyed a pleasant chat, thankful that her husband had disappeared, hopefully for the rest of the night.

She spent a comfortable night sleeping in the estate dower house, to which her husband failed to return, much to her relief. The following morning, she made her way to the breakfast room where her husband was still holding court with likeminded men. He greeted her warmly and she sat at the table and prayed that this would be the last event she would ever attend with him.

When Sylvia arrived back at the manor, she found that Maeve had made great inroads into packing and concealing possessions that they needed to take to America. Sylvia had already asked Úna to bring tea to the bedroom when it suited and that she was to join them. Thankfully, by now her husband was already asleep in his quarters and Sylvia doubted that he would wake before dawn.

Úna arrived, having earlier prepared dinner for everyone. Sylvia and Maeve had eaten earlier, and the three women now sat around the small oak table covered with a sparkling white cloth, drinking their tea.

The sun was beginning to set and Maeve excitedly pointed towards the window that was facing west.

"That's over where America is!"

The two ladies began to laugh and agreed with her that she was correct.

"I can't wait to see the sun setting in America," Maeve said with the wonder of youth shining in her eyes.

"Well, let's enjoy our tea because we have much to discuss about America when we finish eating," said Sylvia.

When Sylvia had told the others what had transpired at the fund-raising dinner, she went on to say, "Again, let me remind you that I want you both to get used to calling me Sylvia in the confines of this room before our trip abroad. I do not want anyone to know on the journey that I have a title. And I don't want to be known as Mrs. Ramsay ever again when I reach New York. I want to be Sylvia Stewart and, if it is possible, I'll change my name."

The women nodded before Úna asked, "Are you seriously going to go with him next month for a whole weekend?" she asked, feeling worried for Sylvia.

"Of course I'm not!" Sylvia answered emphatically. "That's the weekend that I intend us to set out on our journey to America."

The other two gasped.

"But how are you going to avoid going with him?" Úna asked.

"That's where our three heads come in. I need to come up with a good excuse for being unable to travel, but it will have to be a good one. Has anyone any suggestions?"

The others were quiet as they pondered her request.

Úna broke the silence. "Well, I think you have to be sick and it has to be sudden and plausible."

With this information Maeve piped up. "I know what it can be! It happened to my Granny Maguire before she died and I remember it well because a few years ago I wanted to stay at home one day from school and I pretended the same thing had happened to me and my mam believed me."

"What was it?" both asked at the same time.

"It was my granny's back pain. One morning she couldn't move from the bed, the pain was so severe. She couldn't stand up. The doctor came and said her back had gone into a spasm and other than rubbing it with hot oil and taking medicine to ease the pain, she had to stay in bed until the pain subsided. It eased after a week and she was able to sit by the fire but shortly after that she passed away. It was a doctor from Ballydehob who came over as the local doctor was out on a birth."

The two ladies looked at her before Úna asked, "What happened when you tried it?"

Maeve laughed before telling them. "I told my mam that the pain was terrible and that my leg felt numb. She left me in bed and rubbed liniment on it. However, I got up to go out to the privy in the back yard and my mother caught me walking perfectly! She was fierce cross but agreed it was too late for school so she gave me chores to do. I think she told my dad later but it was never mentioned again."

Sylvia and Úna laughed.

Then Úna asked, "What was what the name of your granny's doctor?"

"Doctor Aherne."

"I know him. He has a good reputation for easing pain," said Úna. "I could easily get the coachman to go over there in the early morning on the day and get him to call. They all come quickly to the houses of squires because they get more money. But, Sylvia, do you think that you could act the part?"

"I can." Sylvia was adamant. "If I read up one of the medical books in the library about the condition, I believe it could work. I think that's a grand idea, Maeve. What would I do without you both?"

They all agreed that they should sleep on it and work out how to best put it all into practice.

The following morning Sylvia went down to see Alice and told her that the date they wanted to begin their journey to Liverpool was the morning after her husband had left for his shooting weekend. Alice agreed to write immediately to Eliza and then Brendan O'Leary could be booked for that whole weekend.

As Sylvia walked back to her home, she looked at the late-autumn leafless trees. Yet seeing the sunlight through the bare branches gave her a nice feeling that maybe if light could peep through those cold and barren trees, perhaps there was some light out there also to see her through to a brighter future.

The following three weeks saw Sylvia meeting with her lawyer and arranging payments to go to both Mrs Hayes and Maeve's mother in the village. She also withdrew funds to pay Brendan and to cover the tickets. She took her jewellery, left to her by her grandmother and being held in the safe of her lawyer's offices, and placed it in her locked trunk. Money was stitched into the dress she would be wearing on the day, for fear of any robberies happening on their trip from Cork to Liverpool.

The ladies left nothing to chance as they carried out their respective tasks, hoping it would eventually lead them to the safety of the liner sailing for America. She hoped with all her heart that the plan would work and she'd rid herself forever of Toby Ramsay.

Chapter Sixteen

On the fateful morning before their departure to a new life, there was a lot of running around inside the manor.

Úna Hayes ran upstairs to the Squire's bedroom and knocked urgently on the door.

"*Who the hell is waking me this early?*" he shouted.

"*It's urgent, sir, your wife seems to have injured herself!*" Mrs Hayes answered.

He opened the door, with his dressing gown still half opened.

"We're going to the Earl of Cork's house later and it is a long and arduous drive. What's wrong with her now?" he asked in an exasperated voice.

"Her back seems to have seized up and she is unable to move from the bed. She's in terrible pain, sir. But don't fret. I've already asked the coachman to send a message to Doctor Aherne in Ballydehob because he's known in the district as an expert on painful backs. I'm sure he'll arrive before you finish breakfast and hopefully he'll have a cure for it."

"He'd better hurry because I'm on the road before noon and whether she's sick or not I'm going for the weekend and you can tell her that!" He slammed the door shut.

Úna grinned in delight as she returned to the bedroom.

"It's working. He'll go without you if you're not cured by noon!"

Sylvia laughed, as Úna warned her to keep a serious face on her.

"Don't make me laugh, it makes my back much more painful!" Sylvia said.

They laughed again, before Úna left to prepare a hearty breakfast for them all before the doctor arrived and hopefully agreed with their own diagnosis.

When Doctor Aherne arrived just before eleven o'clock, Toby was by then in Sylvia's room accusing her of shirking her duty to her husband. She asked him to leave until she had spoken to the doctor.

When Doctor Aherne entered the room, young Maeve went to the dressing room and closed the door, while the doctor insisted that Toby should go outside while he examined his wife. Sylvia explained exactly where the most pain was and after fifteen minutes of thorough testing the doctor recalled her husband and explained to him that his wife had a nerve disease of the lower back that would hopefully improve over time but for the moment it required complete bedrest.

"I have given her some strong medicine to take if the pain gets worse, and I will return next Tuesday and evaluate her progress. In the meantime, she just needs bedrest."

Having seen the doctor off the premises, Toby returned briefly to his wife's bedroom and told her that he was leaving for the weekend and would endeavour to return before the doctor arrived on Tuesday.

"In the meantime, I'll leave your trusted women friends to look after you," he said sarcastically.

With that he marched out the door and, as Sylvia looked at his retreating back, she hoped she would never see him again.

On the previous day the housekeeper, whom her husband had thrust upon her last year, had been given a week's leave by Sylvia, to go and see her family. This was paid for by Sylvia and was pre-arranged some weeks before, as suggested by Úna. Sylvia had explained to the housekeeper that as herself and her husband would be away for at least four days, it would suit the household if she went home as Mrs. Hayes could take over the housekeeping responsibilities.

By nine o'clock that evening, Sylvia's bedroom was a hive of industry with last-minute packing, when there was a knock at the door. Úna entered, followed by two people. It was Eliza and Jack Ryan who had insisted on coming to West Cork with Brendan, to make sure that the ladies would get safely away.

"Alice couldn't show her face here tonight because the staff would recognise her," Eliza explained. "Hopefully we are not known by any of the staff."

Úna pulled up chairs for the two guests and left the room accompanied by Maeve, to fetch some refreshments.

Before any of them sat down, Eliza Ryan walked towards Sylvia and put her arms around her, before stepping back slightly.

"I told my Alice never to tell you what I'm about to divulge but it may help you feel more comfortable about your decision to leave your home."

Sylvia was nonplussed, although she already knew that her husband had not been welcome in Midleton.

"Many years ago, before I married my beloved husband Jack, I knew your husband, having met him through the Beconsford family. One day, when I was walking alone near the bank of the river in the estate, your husband attacked me and endeavoured to push me into the summerhouse. I caught him off guard and managed to kick him and run as fast as I could towards my home. I told nobody at the time because I was ashamed and blamed myself because I had been nice to him when we first met in the Beconsfords' private Regency Lounge in the local Haven Inn. However, later, after I was betrothed to Jack, Toby paid a man to set fire to our new cottage, while Jack was inside. Sylvia, you are right to leave him and I just hope you make a good life in America for yourself. I know my daughter will help you settle in when you arrive."

Sylvia was overcome, as tears flowed gently down her cheeks. Eliza brushed them away with a fresh handkerchief before moving on to the business at hand.

"Brendan will collect you all at nine in the morning. Then we will all leave in the carriage. You are doing the right thing and, when you've done this, I know you'll have the strength to take on the challenge of life in a new country."

Sylvia began to utter her thanks but Eliza just said, "Let us enjoy your last evening as we relax for a while and then we will get you safely away tomorrow."

That evening and the following morning was for Sylvia like walking through a dream or a nightmare, she didn't know which.

Úna had already told the butler that he could stay on late in the village, where he regularly went on a Friday night.

"You can then sleep late in the morning as his lordship is not here," she had informed him. She then set various tasks for the staff away from the front door, telling them that the visitors were collecting some furniture to take to a family in need.

Later Úna opened the front door and beckoned to Brendan O'Leary, who was still sitting in the carriage, to come into the house. Five minutes later, the two men were carrying out the heavy travel chest followed by various bags until all the ladies' belongings were carefully stored in the back of the carriage. Jack and Eliza then quietly left the house and disappeared into the carriage and left the estate, to sleep in the home of Alice and Richard. Úna then told staff members they could enjoy tea in the kitchen where she announced that Lady Sylvia was feeling much better and if she was able, she would visit her friends in the morning.

"Myself and Maeve will go with her and ensure that she is comfortable. We will return much later in the day. She will have eaten with her friends and I will attend to her when we return. So let you all have a quiet and restful day tomorrow."

They all looked at one another, smiling, because they knew that they would have a good day, especially with the housekeeper having gone away also. Úna felt sorry for them because she knew that the wrath of hell would rain upon them when Toby Ramsay returned after his weekend away.

Brendan slept in the carriage that night in a field away from the Staunton's farm.

As agreed, Jack and Eliza walked down to the carriage after breakfast in the morning and at nine o'clock Brendan was knocking on the door of Sylvia's home. When the butler opened it, Mrs. Hayes was standing just behind him.

"Her Ladyship is ready and will be with you in a moment."

Brendan returned to the carriage and opened the door where the other occupants, Jack and Eliza, were not visible. Úna and Maeve came through the door, 'helping' Sylvia towards the carriage. Brendan assisted her inside, followed by her two very happy employees. Five minutes later, the carriage and its intrepid occupants were driving east towards Cork, with the occupants continuing to be fearful of any slip-up. But everything was calm and as they passed the Staunton farm, Grace, Jerome, Alice, Richard and Meg were all standing at the front door, waving and shedding tears for the loss of their good friend Sylvia.

Having left the Ryans in Cork city, where they would spend the night with the Perrott family, the travellers went on to the harbour and boarded a ship that would take them to Liverpool in England and from that port they would leave for America.

At five o'clock that evening, Sylvia lifted her head to smell the sea salt as the ship glided gently out of Cork harbour and she shed a tear for the loss of her home, but her joy at having left her husband was greater. Maybe I am a bad person to hate another human being so much, she wondered. As she stood on the deck, she removed the clips from her hair and laughed as the gentle breeze blew her auburn curls around her smiling face. Then she put her arms around Maeve and Úna, assuring them that she would do everything she could to ensure a good life for them all in America.

It was Wednesday morning before the party finally boarded the Cunard ship going to New York. Later in the evening, Sylvia stood on the deck alone. As the evening light disappeared and the moon appeared in the sky, she finally felt out of the clutches of Toby Ramsay. When she went below deck to her cabin, the freedom she felt in her soul could not be bought for any money and Sylvia knew that she now had two good friends and the hope of a new and better future.

Late on Monday night, an envelope was pushed through the letterbox of the Squire's home. Nobody saw who had delivered it. The butler found it the following morning and placed it on a tray for the master, who had been helped to bed in an inebriated state by his coachman when he had arrived home in the small hours of the morning. Nobody had told him, yet, that his wife and employees had not returned to the house over the weekend and the butler was sure that the letter he was giving to the Squire had been written by Lady Sylvia.

When he woke and read the letter from his wife, the rage that filled Toby Ramsay was so great that many of the staff almost feared for their lives. He could not believe that his slow-witted wife had outsmarted him. She must have got help, he thought. He would be the laughing stock of the county and he wasn't having that. I'll find her, he thought, and give her such a thrashing that she will never do anything like that again.

Chapter Seventeen

Alice knew that since the disappearance of his wife Toby Ramsay had been taking his wrath out on both his staff and his tenant farmers. He was chasing rents from people who hadn't even the money to eat. His out-of-control behaviour worried Alice, as he couldn't pin Sylvia's disappearance on anyone in the locality. Everyone was puzzled, except the few in the know.

As another year dawned, biting cold winds blew in from the Atlantic. Food was scarce, farmers were behind with their rents and fear of another bad year continued to grip the community. Richard and Alice still managed to help some of the locals. Yet life for Alice felt as if she was pushing a cart up a hill before it rolled back down again bringing her back to square one. When everyone else was sleeping, as herself and Richard sat by the fire, he put his arms around her and spoke somewhat sternly to her.

"Alice, what you're trying to do is commendable but we can only help a small number of people because the poverty, death and emigration look like they're not going to end any time soon. Yet I do know one thing. The people in these parts are getting more and more resentful of those with means. Many of the men would kill someone for a loaf of bread if they thought it would keep their children alive. Although there is respect for us in the area, be careful when you're out and about on your good deeds. Nobody is safe anymore. The problems in the country are out of control and we're powerless to do much about it. In addition to that, Toby Ramsay is not a complete fool and he must know that you helped his wife escape and he'd love to destroy us if he got the opportunity."

With tears in her eyes, Alice nodded in agreement. She was worn out from worrying about everyone and everything. She had burned her hand with steam from the kettle last week and tripped up in the garden when she wasn't looking where she was going. Most evenings when she got into her bed in an exhausted state, she couldn't even sleep as she felt that her brain was fried. Thoughts kept swirling round and round in her head and often when she did sleep she had dreams of blackened fields stretching for miles around her and she would be standing in the middle with nowhere to go.

"I agree with you," she said. "I think that I'm just exhausted. It feels a bit like the days after giving birth to Gregory and Emily. I couldn't rest worrying about them for a while, yet I was too exhausted to do things. The same thing is happening now and I find myself forgetting things and making mistakes. I have to take a step back, I agree. I have to remember how lucky I am to have a loving husband and family around me. I need to stop for a while trying to create a good future when nobody, even the parliamentarians and local councils, know what's next in store for us all." She turned to her husband. "Just hold me and let us forget for a little while how the world is and remember how it used to be. Tonight, maybe I'll think of how happy I will be when it's all over."

Richard held her tight but couldn't dispel his own fears and gloom for the immediate future as the famine seemed relentless, especially when bad landlords like Toby Ramsay held people's lives in the palm of their hands.

These thoughts would come back to haunt him even before the week was out.

By the following Friday, the winds had abated and a winter sun shone as Richard joined Alice who was on her way to visit Mary, while Richard went to discuss a fund-raising event with the local town councillors. They were surprised to see horses and riders milling around the junction ahead and they both wondered what was going on.

"It's Jamie O'Doherty's house down there," Richard said, frowning.

"Nelly's baby is due. I hope she didn't have a problem after all the years they've waited for this," Alice said anxiously as they hurried down the road.

Jamie had rented the farm ten years ago from Squire Stewart, after he married Nelly. They had a thriving farm but Nelly never got pregnant until last year and now there was great joy in the village as they were a good hardworking couple. But the blight had struck their harvest badly and everyone knew that money was tight as Jamie tried his best to look after his wife and make enough money to pay the rent.

As they ran towards the junction, Richard let out an expletive as he saw what was happening at the front of the farmhouse.

"It's the bailiffs!" he said as a panting Alice tried to keep up.

"But he's always paid his rent to Squire Ramsay, hasn't he?" Alice said as they slowed down behind the crowd that continued to gather.

"It seems that maybe he hasn't managed now and is being evicted. The stupid man!" Richard said angrily.

"Jamie has too much pride for his own good. He should know that people would try to help, especially to save a good man like him from eviction."

As they moved around the crowd to see what was happening at the front of the house, Alice tried to get close when she saw a very distressed Nellie sitting at the front of the house with a neighbour standing by her side shouting and screaming for help, saying that the baby was coming.

As Alice tried to go through the crowd, Richard held her back. A group of local men from the village were placing themselves in front of the members of the constabulary which forced some of the bailiffs' horses to shy. Some of the local men and women had already moved forward to help Nelly while the local midwife was shouting and trying to get through the crowd to get to her. By now Nelly had collapsed onto the ground. The midwife and even the men stopped as her clothes were suddenly showing a deep red colour that could only be blood. She was shaking and distressed as a friend ran into the house where Jamie had gone to get a covering for his wife. By then chaos reigned. People had put their coats on the ground and the men, including two of the constabulary instructed the bailiffs to move back and let her be moved safely from the ground. As Jamie bent over to put a blanket around his wife, Nelly's whimpering ceased. Her head turned in the direction of Jamie, as she closed her eyes. A cold and frightening silence descended on the crowd as they realised that Nelly O'Doherty had breathed her last along with her unborn child.

Everyone stood transfixed, even Jamie, before he moved back into the house and chaos again ensued as the constabulary ordered the bailiffs to leave. Just seconds after they issued the order Jamie O'Doherty walked out through the front door and raised his shotgun and before he could be stopped, he blasted the bailiff, who was sitting on his horse, straight into the heart. Immediately the horse rose up and the rider slumped to the ground and ended up, lying just two feet from Nelly O'Doherty's body. By now her husband Jamie was again by her side and as he cried out in anguish the uproar of the crowd continued to get louder. Nobody could believe what they were just witnessing. Two people dead plus an unborn baby.

At the back of the crowd Alice almost fainted but felt compelled to join the women as they all prayed, as if they were in a trance. The constable in charge was forced to pull Jamie from his wife's side. He was helped by his colleague as they dragged the wailing Jamie through the baying crowd, towards a cart.

By then Richard took one look at his wife and sat her down, close to the farmhouse wall.

"I am taking you home, love. There are going to be ugly scenes around the townland before this night is out and nobody will stop it. We can do nothing for Nelly or Jamie now but pray that he doesn't hang for this."

Alice felt sick in her stomach and all she could do was nod as Richard gently lifted her up and tucked his arm through hers. They slowly made their way back up towards their own home.

Meg and Grace were surprised to see them return so soon and when they retold the story of what they had just witnessed, they too were in deep shock.

"Two good people plus their little baby. Three lives gone or ruined because of a few months' rent. What a waste of lives! I hope that Toby Ramsay rots in hell because of this!" Meg proclaimed vehemently. "What's this country coming to when things like this can happen and now Jamie will die, too. I feel sorry for the bailiff's family, but I must admit I haven't too much sympathy for him, if truth be told. No good will come of this."

"That's what I said," Richard agreed. "Toby Ramsay has been sending in bailiffs to take possession of more of his tenants' land since his wife left. It's almost as if he's out to punish the locals for supporting his wife's decision to leave him."

Chapter Eighteen

As the sun set in the village, the tavern was full of local men who had been sickened by what they had witnessed earlier in the day. Word had been sent to Bantry earlier to a man whose granduncle had died in the Irish rebellion in 1798. Young PJ Murphy had an abiding hatred of the British occupation and was a writer of covert anti-British pamphlets. He always worked under cover and the men asked for his advice. They wanted to do something but were afraid of being arrested themselves if they were caught breaking the law.

PJ arrived in the inn at seven o'clock that evening. He was brought in through the back entrance and put in a room away from where the local men were drinking. Two of his acquaintances in the village were quietly informed that he was there and they joined him. They told him everything that had happened that morning and informed him of the feelings of the people in the townland. They assured him that the local constabulary and those from Bantry had now left the village, because word had been put about that nobody from Eoinstown wanted trouble. The local constable assured the powers that be that there was unlikely to be trouble before Jamie was put on trial.

"We heard that Jamie is in custody in Cork and will come up before the courts tomorrow morning," Andy O'Connell, an Irish nationalist sympathiser, explained to PJ. "However, I need to explain that this is a law-abiding townland but what happened today has struck the hearts of all the people and they want revenge. Could you suggest anything that would keep us all from ending up in jail?"

PJ digested the information he had been given before responding to Andy.

"I have a couple of men in the region who can help us but it will take until midnight to round them up. In the meantime, I'll give you some instructions for the locals and hopefully we'll all get what we want before the night is out. Take this money and listen to me now."

Andy gratefully took the money and PJ instructed them on what to do. Then PJ disappeared into the dark of the night and the other men rejoined their friends in the bar.

About an hour later Andy asked for hush in the room, knowing that someone would immediately go hotfooted to the authorities and inform them of what he would say.

"You all know how law-abiding the majority of the people here usually are but today has shocked everyone. However, what the majority still want to do is have a peaceful march in the village and a candlelight walk towards Nelly and Jamie's home to say some prayers. We will supply candles before we leave from the gates of the church. Everyone who has enough energy is welcome. The local farmers have contributed food and everyone will get a bit of food tonight and also to take home to your families later. We'll meet just before midnight. As I said, it will be a peaceful walk and troublemakers are not welcome."

The men all nodded and left the inn quietly and made their way home.

When the authorities were informed of the march, they didn't send for any help because even some of them had a sympathy with the outrage felt in the area at the death of a mother and child in front of their eyes that morning.

"We'll go down to the inn and stay around while they assemble, look out for known troublemakers and keep a good eye on them during the march," Constable Archer told his men. "I've sent a message to Bantry to say that it's all peaceful around here and hopefully we'll all be back in our beds before one o'clock."

PJ knew that Toby Ramsay would have protection around his house. On the stroke of midnight, a group of silent men came from all angles towards the manor house and all that could be heard was the occasional tooting of an owl and the sound of silence. They all wore woollen hats pulled over their faces, with slits cut for their eyes, dark clothing and soft soles on their boots. These men were used to moving quietly. The rustling sounds of Toby Ramsay's watchmen in the grounds grew silent as each were caught from behind, had their mouths gagged and their hands and feet bound tightly before they were each dragged to a barn where hopefully they would be discovered later.

PJ quietly moved with a henchman towards the house where the henchman used pliers and a screwdriver to prise open a back window. They both entered the house and were confronted by a terrified young girl and an equally terrified older woman. PJ put a finger to his lips to warn them to stay quiet. He told the older woman to quietly wake all the staff and bring them down to the kitchen. The henchman joined the woman while she heralded the staff into the kitchen, as PJ asked the young girl to show him where the squire was, before he then sent her back to the kitchen. He promised her she would be safe. When they reached his study and she pointed to the door, she fled as if her life depended on it.

PJ quietly knocked at the door and when he heard a grunt asking what he wanted, he just walked in. He pointed his shotgun in the direction of the obese figure of a middle-aged man who roared as he tried to get up from his chair.

"Sit down," PJ told him calmly.

"*Where are all my staff?*" Toby Ramsay roared.

"They are all safe. No one will be hurt, except you. Today, you went a step too far, from what I've been told. I know all about the women you have raped or attempted to rape. Today an innocent woman and her baby died, thanks to your actions. I just hope you rot in hell for your sins and I hope other nasty British landlords take heed."

As Toby sprang from his chair with fury in his eyes, PJ calmly and without any emotion pulled the trigger and shot the squire twice, first to the head, and then straight through his heart. As he dropped to the floor, PJ calmly left the room and, after going into the kitchen and warning the staff to steal nothing from the house, he told them all to leave by the back door.

He went out the front door and signalled his men to do their last piece of work. In a few minutes his helpers had broken the windows in the ground floor of the house. An eerie silence descended for a moment before flaming lamps and oil-soaked cloths were thrown through each window. Not a sound could be heard except the crackling of fire as flames took hold of the curtains and slowly crept through the carpeted rooms, The execution and demolition of the Big House took just fifteen minutes. By twenty past twelve PJ and his followers had melted into the darkness and disappeared into the quiet of the night.

Meanwhile, the vigil for Nelly and her baby was a quiet and respectful event. The constables who walked to the farmhouse were relieved just to hear the sound of prayers coming from the mouths of the men and the few women that attended. As they walked with the glittering glow of candlelight the prayers for Nelly and the baby continued to be intoned. At the cottage, they knelt in prayer again and small posies of flowers were laid on the ground where Nelly and the baby had died. At twelve thirty, as the crowd were returning to the village in quiet contemplation, the pungent smell of smoke hit their nostrils. It was drifting in the wind. Away in the distance, helped with the light of the moon, the sight of black clouds and sparks rising into the sky shocked the majority of the participants in the march.

There was a roar from the chief of constabulary. "*It's coming from the Big House!*"

Everyone stopped, most in shock not knowing what had happened. Richard had joined the parade, having refused to let any of the women come with him. He stood and looked into the distance as the men who were guarding the parade ran in the direction of the house.

As the people from the townland looked at each other one of them spoke up. "Whatever is going on, lads, it's nothing to do with us. Let us all get back to our families and leave it to the authorities."

There was a murmur of agreement from most of those who had walked in the vigil, except for a few of the younger lads who still wanted to be part of the excitement but whose fathers dragged them off home.

Richard had guessed that something wasn't quite right about the night. The meekness of the men had had him puzzled. As he made his own way back to his family, he knew that the authorities in the entire county would be in upheaval and he hoped that their fury wouldn't affect innocent people. Goodness knows, he thought, everyone has enough to worry about at the moment. He entered the house, having decided to keep quiet about his suspicions until they all had a good night's sleep.

Richard was still asleep when a loud knock on the front door woke him. He could hear the voice of Mary talking excitedly to his mother Grace, who was an early riser. He could hear her shushing Mary and warning her that she'd wake the children.

The sound had woken Alice and she sat up in bed abruptly.

"Last night on the way home from the vigil for Nelly, we all saw smoke and sparks in the distance," Richard said quietly to her. "I believe it was Sylvia's home."

"Well, thanks be to goodness Sylvia is in America!" Alice replied as she jumped out of bed and put a dressing gown over her nightgown before making her way swiftly down to the kitchen. Richard followed.

Mary was in full flow but halted when she saw Alice and Richard appear.

"What is it, Mary?" said Richard as he and Alice sat down. "Has the Big House burned down?"

"Burnt to the ground! And Toby Ramsay with it!"

"What exactly happened?" Richard asked.

"I heard it from Bridget who worked in the Big House. She was in serious shock when she got to her mother's house. Two men with guns got all the staff into the kitchen and one of them told everyone to run from the house immediately. He warned them all not to steal anything from the house. They were still in the kitchen when they heard two gunshots. Before they reached the end of the estate, they saw flames coming from the house but they don't know any more except that the constabulary wanted to talk to Bridget later today. If any of them was found with stuff from the house the law would try to blame them."

Alice and Grace looked shocked but Richard was not surprised and knew that it was likely to be the work of Irish rebels. Those at the top of that organisation were very intelligent men and they must have used information from some of the villagers to be able to plan such quick revenge.

Meanwhile chaos reigned at the local Constabulary Headquarters. Top army men from the British military barracks in Cork were already on their way to Bantry and the local constabulary in the region knew that they were in serious trouble. Constable Archer realised that his belief that the village was law-abiding and his assurance to the army officials that no back-up was necessary in Eoinstown was misguided. As he sat at his desk, he knew that he had been outwitted by the locals. It seemed Squire Ramsay had been murdered by someone and he'd find it difficult to pin it on anyone in the village. As well as that, the burning to the ground of the estate house would be blamed on him also. How could he explain the fact that a big number of strangers had entered his territory last night and tied up the security guards. It would all be down to him.

He knew that before the day was out, he'd be dismissed from the force and what he wouldn't know is that the villagers would be sorry for him as he was one of the humane members of the Constabulary and his compassionate views would be lost to the village.

By late afternoon, as British army troops from Cork came into the village, everyone knew what had happened in the estate. Toby Ramsay was dead and it seemed that nobody cared. Thankfully, everyone in the townland could put their hands on their hearts and swear that they had no clue as to who were the perpetrators of the crimes.

The area around Eoinstown was a hive of activity for weeks after the death of the squire. It appeared that he had died from gunshot wounds, although his body was also badly burned by the fire. The local doctor identified his body and nobody, apart from the housekeeper that he had personally employed, turned up at his funeral. It was held in the local church and the rector and the housekeeper made for a sorry sight as they were the only mourners at the graveside. The authorities had to accept that they had been outwitted and they retreated swiftly from the area, frustrated that it was a crime they might never solve, although they had their suspicions.

Meanwhile, the people of West Cork had enough on their plates as another summer arrived with no let-up from the pain felt by everyone and help expected from London was still far too little to make a difference to those in need. The realisation that it could still be a long time before the country returned to some semblance of normality was a sobering thought and brought no solace to the nation.

Chapter Nineteen

New York

Sylvia was surprised at how quickly she fitted into her new life in New York. She had spent Christmas and the new year with Margarita before she decided to purchase a home of her own just down the road from Willow Crescent. Young Maeve had become great friends with Florrie and they all became like one big happy family. Úna regularly took the twins for walks in the park, when Sylvia was otherwise occupied. Sylvia had already joined a couple of charitable groups without using her title and it was still easy for her, with her gracious demeanour, to enter New York society. She began to make real friends for the first time in her life.

Meanwhile, the local school where Rosita attended asked Maeve to help with their younger pupils when they heard of her ambition to become a teacher. The twins were also attending classes for reading and writing, given to them by a retired German immigrant, Frau Richter, who lived close by in Lilac Crescent. Margarita was delighted as it also had the benefit of getting them out of the house each morning for a few hours. She told Maeve that she wished such early-learning classes were the practice in Ireland! Maeve agreed and could hardly believe that she might be on the first step of the ladder to fulfil her dream. Before Christmas, the school surprised her by enrolling her into a training programme that would qualify her to officially train as a schoolteacher. Everyone was proud of her ambition and the contents of her letters to Eoinstown made her mother and Granny Mary very proud indeed.

When the news came through from Ireland that Sylvia's husband had been murdered and her home had been burned to the ground, Margarita hurried around to Sylvia's lovely home in Lilic Crescent to commiserate with her. She was thankfully surprised when Sylvia spoke openly of the tragedy.

"You don't have to feel sorry for me, Margarita. I am not grieving for the loss of my husband. Also, I had grown to hate that house. My memories of it were sullied so much by his presence that it was a blessing to leave it. Maybe it is for the best and, if it's ever rebuilt, perhaps it will be for a family who will be happier there than I was since my father died."

Shortly afterwards, Sylvia openly admitted to the fact that she was a widow and felt no shame at not grieving her loss. On occasions she still wondered how a gentle person like herself could harbour such hatred for one man. That was unfortunately her cross to bear.

As the glorious warmth of summer arrived, Margarita blossomed. She found that she was busier since arriving in New York than when she ran a huge house in Ireland. Looking after the welfare of her three children while also training singers in breathing control made her tired at the end of each day. But it was by now a more contented tiredness. She loved living so close to Sylvia. Maeve now brought all three children to school each day so that Margarita could concentrate on her job, while Mrs. O'Brien kept the household running smoothly. Margarita noticed that Jean seemed of late to have a permanent smile on her face and it appeared she was walking out with a teacher from the local school. Margarita hoped this might lead to something in the future.

The saddest thing for Margarita was when the children talked about their beloved papa. His whereabouts had been a mystery for a long time but a recent letter from Midleton indicated that he may have finally arrived in Vienna looking for help. That fact relieved her mind greatly and thankfully, as she was now so busy, she had little time to dwell on her marriage difficulties. Everything moved at such a fast pace in this city, she thought, as new people from many countries were arriving almost daily. She too had made good friends with some of her neighbours, who frequently invited her and the children to join them in their homes for a meal. Yet she missed her family back in Midleton. Sadly, that town, it seemed, was the only place that would ever truly capture her heart.

Florrie was in her element with time off at night to go dancing and meet other Irish emigrants, and she loved minding the twins when they came home after spending their mornings at Frau Richter's home. It was a contented household and Margarita was ready for a new challenge.

There was a thriving fundraising Irish community in New York and Margarita was persuaded to sing at a fund-raising concert they were holding. These events were held regularly by the various Irish county associations with all the monies raised going straight back to their local parishes in Ireland. The Cork Association had approached her as some of them had heard her previously when they lived in Cork city. She hesitated only for a moment before realising that it was the right thing to do.

"I will do a concert provided that much of the money can go into the townlands in West Cork around Clonakilty and Bantry," she said.

Mr. McCarthy, the chairman immediately agreed and the date was set for Midsummer Night. Margarita dearly hoped that those Irish who had a measure of success since coming to the new world would contribute generously to the event.

On the night of the concert there was a flurry of excitement inside Number 10.

"It's nearly time to leave for the theatre, Margarita," said Jean, fussing. She had made her best effort to ensure that Margarita's favourite concert gown, which had made its way to America in the large trunk, was ready to wear.

"I think you need a properly trained lady's maid to dress for such an occasion," Jean said, shaking her head, as they both laughed. "I love you in red. Your carriage is due in fifteen minutes so you'll need to make haste."

"Could you please bring the children in to me while I finish dressing? I promised them a quick story and it's going to have to be very quick tonight."

The children burst into the bedroom with Florrie running after them, shouting at them not to crumple their mother's dress.

"We only want her to tell us a story about when she was a child," said little Violet.

"Then sit down and I will tell you a quick story about your Great-great-granny Sheila."

They all quickly sat down.

"You all know that she was very wise but she was also great fun. One day she sneaked into her daughter Molly's work in Mrs. Sexton's bakery in Midleton and stole three large cream cakes."

"But stealing is a sin!" Violet said.

"What did she do with the cakes?" was all quick-witted Rosita wanted to know.

Louis was his usual quiet self, just wanting to hear the story.

"Well, that's a good question, because she met her daughter on the way out, so she had to hide the cakes under her cloak. But she had forgotten that all the cakes had thick cream on the top."

"What are you hiding under your cloak?" asked her daughter Molly.

"Nothing," said Sheila, as her face got red.

"So, tell me, Mother, what is the white cream doing falling down your dress and onto your shoes?" Molly asked.

"I have my reasons," she said.

"Then tell me the reasons," Molly insisted.

"Well, I just met three hungry little children outside the shop, but I had no money on me so I told them to wait and I'd get them a treat. I thought you were out the back. I would have paid you tonight, you know!"

Molly couldn't help laughing. "Now you'll have to pay for three cakes that your dress ate!" she said.

Rosita laughed, but little Louis seemed upset.

"Did the poor little children get any cakes then?" he asked.

"They did, of course, my love, because Molly went straight out of the shop door and invited them all in to choose a cake each."

"What kind of cakes did they get?" they all asked together.

"Well, children, if you all go to the kitchen with Florrie now you will find the same type of cakes that the little children got that day. The cakes are sitting on a plate waiting for all three of you!"

As the children hugged their mother and ran for the door, Jean, who had been standing with a smile on her face walked towards Margarita and kissed her on the cheek.

"Obviously you're not just a pretty face and a good singer but you can tell very convincing lies to your children," she said, laughing.

"Lies? Never!" Margarita responded as she winked at Jean.

Margarita and Jean arrived outside the elegant theatre on Broadway, with its tall horseshoe-shaped windows reaching three storeys high and the elegant church steeple beyond stretching even further into the sky. Margarita was pleased to see the sidewalk already packed with theatregoers. The crowd cheered as Margarita climbed the steps and she began to experience a fluttering in her stomach that she hadn't felt for a long time.

"I hope this goes well and that we can make some difference to lives in Ireland. It will also remind the patrons that the famine is still far from over," she said to Jean as they entered through the stage door.

When the concert commenced to a packed audience, Margarita stood listening to the fiddle playing and the more haunting sound from a violin, as she waited with apprehension to go on stage. The cheers of the satisfied audience warmed her heart as she walked on with a smile on her face and a still fluttering tummy. When the applause stopped, she spoke to the attentive audience and thanked them for their support.

"I know that many of you have families back in Ireland and I would be grateful if you could personally send a little extra money home to Ireland to your families, if you enjoy this evening. Every penny helps. For those of you who are better able to contribute we are hoping to set up some extra soup kitchens in the neediest places. The American public have always supported the famine-ravaged people in Ireland. Please continue to do this tonight because you will save many, many lives by your generosity. But enough of the talk, I will now sing!" She smiled as she signalled to the pianist and began to sing a number of popular songs. The audience clapped enthusiastically after each.

Before she commenced singing the Irish and American favourite "*Oh, Don't You Remember Sweet Alice, Ben Bolt?*", she said that many people in Ireland who had suffered great loss resonated to the words of Mr. Thomas Dunn English's haunting song

"It's a memory of long ago. About friendships and love and remembering sweet Alice, who once loved Ben Bolt," As she sang the words, she found tears in her own eyes, as if mirroring the experience of the audience.

"In the old church in the valley, Ben Bolt, in a corner obscure and alone

They have fitted a slab of granite so grey, and sweet Alice lies under the stone."

Margarita had to compose herself as the emotional atmosphere seemed to affect even the hardened men.

She then sang the beautiful "I Dreamt I Dwelt in Marble Halls" from Mr. Balfe's *The Bohemian Girl* which again elicited a huge response from the audience.

She bowed, flushed with emotion, and then continued with other moving songs from popular operas before finishing as always with her theme song, "The Lament of the Irish Maiden", as many of the audience were from County Cork and they appreciated her singing a song written by Denny Lane, a Cork local. As the last strains of the song faded away, everyone stood up to cheer the daughter of Cork.

As the appreciation of the audience continued, she reluctantly walked to her dressing room. She locked the door, before sinking into a chair, feeling both emotionally and physically drained. She finally gave way to the tears that needed to be shed since the beginning of the famine and the trauma of rescuing Rosita and staying strong for everyone. Remembering the reaction to the "Sweet Alice" song brought more tears flowing as it reminded her of the hardship her own young Aunt Alice was going through in West Cork. After a while she began to feel a little calmer and she repaired her face with powder while waiting for Jean to knock at her door when the carriage had arrived to take her home.

Chapter Twenty

Back in 1844, Laurence Flaherty, the son of emigrants from Macroom, had the world at his feet, or more importantly, in his voice. He was tall and handsome with jet-black hair and his tenor voice was breathtaking. Now, five years later, although still a young man, there were flecks of grey in his hair and he had the countenance of an older person. As he walked swiftly from the auditorium of a theatre off Broadway, with his head bowed, hoping to avoid the eyes of the audience, Laurence felt a black cloud descend again. He had hoped that his voice would sound stronger. But thankfully, as he had sung only with the choir, his difficulties were not obvious to the audience. He knew that he wasn't the same singer that had, in the past, graced the stages of New York, as a solo performer. Fed up with the way he was singing he finally realised that he didn't want to share his annoyance anymore with an audience. He would tell his family tomorrow that he had tried to sing, but had failed to hold high notes. All he now wanted was a drink and a meal with his friend Alex before taking a carriage back to his home on the road to Newark, New Jersey.

As he emerged into the street, he heard a voice behind him.

"Laurence, hang on a minute!" It was Alex who seemed to be in a good mood. Alex was always happy singing secondary parts or in a chorus at the theatre, as he had no ambition to make singing his life's work.

As Laurence turned, he saw three females coming towards them. He knew Alex's sister Edna and his wife Lucy. The third was a smiling stranger.

Edna and Lucy were regulars at the theatre. It didn't matter how big or small the production in which Alex sang, the ladies were always there for him. They both loved the excitement that came with attending shows and Alex reasoned that it was worth the money it cost to have them by his side. He knew that his wife needed her friends and leisure pursuits, as he spent his days as a gentleman's tailor while also practising for his singing appearances. Alex always said that singing was for him just a paid hobby that he loved. But he also described himself, tongue in cheek, as a circus performer, bouncing a lot of balls at the one time! Alex didn't take life too seriously. He knew he was lucky to have a small talent and he worked hard at his two jobs to make more money than his parents had ever earned. He'd continue this lifestyle until they were blessed with a family of their own. He confided in Laurence that he wanted to earn enough to put a bit aside for the time when they had children. Laurence envied his friend's home life and exuberance. The two friends were opposites, as Laurence was quieter and more serious-minded. How Laurence envied Alex's happy married life!

Laurence was on his own tonight as he tried to rebuild a previously successful career as a singer. His father and mother were always very supportive, but he never wanted them following him around the country. In the past he had Lisa at his side and that had always been enough for him. But tonight, after his comeback, he was alone but had agreed to join Alex and the girls for a meal and a chat. Yet at this moment he felt like passing up any invitation to eat because of his low mood.

"Laurence, I want you to meet someone," Alex said. "An acquaintance of my sister. She's a singer and is spending time in New York with her children. She was in the audience tonight. I heard her singing recently at a large fund-raising event for the famine victims in Ireland. She loved the music this evening and she wants to meet you because I told her that your parents were also from Ireland."

The smiling women were now by Alex's side.

"I'd like you to meet Margarita Beconsford," he said.

As she stretched out her hand to greet him, Laurence noticed how gracefully she moved. Although her wide smile was warm, he noted that sadness lurked behind her dark beauty. Laurence knew everything about sad eyes and he wondered what had caused her pain.

"Nice to meet you, Margarita," he said, smiling, taking her hand.

They walked to a local restaurant which was frequented by the theatre goers.

Laurence could never recall what his food tasted like that evening. He did, however, catch Alex's eye and warned him to give him a bit of space to talk to Margarita. He wanted to know everything about her singing career.

Margarita was delighted to be in the company of singers. Since she had arrived in America her time was taken up just settling the children into a new routine and then her training of young singers. How wonderful, she thought, to finally spend time with other singers. Usually in America she could not escape from talk about the famine but she felt that tonight, in the company of people who loved singing and the world of singers, she could relax and just chat about her great love.

Yet she soon found herself referring to the famine after all, when Laurence asked her why she had come to New York.

"I've come here because my husband's health was suffering from worry about how his three children would stay safe during the famine – disease is rife in the weakened population," she said soberly. "His daughter, by his late wife Fleur, is now our beloved eldest child and the twins are thankfully still too young to understand fully all the upheaval in their lives."

"You don't look old enough to be mother to three children," Laurence said, smiling. "Parents should look old and serious." He was quite taken with her serene countenance. "How do you get time for your singing?"

"I sing very little now but recently, as you know, I agreed to raise funds for the famine victims. In Ireland, since my marriage, I had been spending time before the famine teaching young singers. In particular, I helped them to control their breathing and to feel relaxed when performing. I'm doing much the same in New York and I'm enjoying it. I remember when I was young and had to perform, my teacher Master Johnson was wonderful in the progressive ways he used to improve my voice. Of course, it was important too that I was very enthusiastic." She laughed. "I remember standing in my bedroom night after night while singing to a mirror and pretending it was an audience of a thousand!"

As Margarita told Laurence about her trip to Paris and Florence to sing, he looked in awe at the young woman who didn't look old enough to have experienced so much in her life. When they finished their meal, Margarita reached into her purse and gave him her calling card.

"Give me a call when you are next in New York. I'm starved of speaking about singing and you could join us for tea."

Having enjoyed her laughter and relaxed manner during the meal, Laurence was impressed by her focus in trying to get on with life for herself and her children in such difficult circumstances. She has brains as well as beauty, he thought.

As he took the card and put it into his inside pocket, he said, "Thank you for your company tonight. I too needed to take my mind off other things."

She thought of how daring she was to give him her calling card. For once she felt that the heady atmosphere of New York had given her a freedom she had never experienced in Ireland.

Laurence then rose and thanked everyone at the table for their company, saying he must leave. "I have to get a carriage back home to New Jersey," he explained.

Having said his goodbyes, he left.

Laurence was going to be thirty-two on his next birthday and lately, more than ever before, he admired his friend Alex for his easy-going charm. He knew that Alex was a very centred and rounded individual. He was not complex. Laurence had to admit he envied Alex's relaxed attitude to life and that in the past he himself was too driven and too impulsive. His mother's words were: "Laurence always wants too much too quickly."

As Laurence stepped inside the comfortable carriage, the driver asked, "Are you sure I don't know you? Your face is very familiar."

"No, no, I don't know you," Laurence murmured as he usually did when people remembered him from his singing days.

The driver droned on as the horses moved forward.

Before long, rain had begun to fall, as the driver called out, "*You know this trip could take us an extra hour as it's getting dark as well as the rain!*"

"*I don't mind!*" Laurence answered impatiently.

The driver seemed to get the message and returned his attention to the road ahead.

As they drove through the country roads, Laurence stared at the road sign pointing to Newark, through the rainsoaked carriage windows. He was left to his thoughts as he stared out at the rain. The water streamed down the carriage window. When it reached the frame, it disappeared but was quickly replaced by the next deluge. Like the constant stream of tears pouring down a face, he thought. Suddenly tears welled up in his eyes. Having enjoyed such a lovely evening, he again felt very low and fed up with life. He tried to stop the tears that wanted to flow. He had to do that a lot since the death of his beloved young wife Lisa over two years ago. Tonight, for some reason he failed to stem the flow of tears as he again, for the umpteenth time, dropped his head into his hands in utter despair.

Life had changed so much since that dreadful time. He still hadn't come to terms with his loss and all efforts to regain some sense of normality in his life had failed.

The rain was still falling heavily as Laurence arrived close to his cottage. Should I ask the coachman to take me on to my parent's home, he wondered. They had invited him to stay over as they would be wondering if the concert had been a success. Or will I sit and spend another lonely night reading and wallowing in self-pity? It's too painful to tell them that for me tonight was not the success that they had all hoped for, he thought. He made a decision to stay in his own home and summoned the driver to stop.

He still lived in the house that he had bought when he married Lisa. It was a warm and welcoming one-storey cottage surrounded by large gardens filled with myriads of flowers and trees. How they had enjoyed their first summer, sitting in the sun and enjoying the peace and tranquillity with just the singing of birds in the trees! Now Laurence felt that a darkness had overshadowed even the brightest sun as he still mourned the loss of his only love. His mother and father constantly begged him to come home to live with them, but he refused. His sister Tess called around most days. She worried constantly about him, as she knew that he was only going through the motions of trying to live a normal life. Sometimes he'd forget about Lisa for a few minutes and then a gnawing pain in the pit of his stomach would remind him of his cruel loss. All his singing friends had rallied around. They told him he should get back to singing. He had tried but today he'd realised that his voice wasn't ready to allow him earn a living at the only job he had craved since he was a child.

He went to bed but couldn't sleep. He tossed and turned but eventually got up again and put more logs on the fire. He sat on the Shaker rocking chair that Lisa had bought for him saying that she'd enjoy watching him rock back and forth when he grew old. But she would never see him in his old age. He sat there for a while, enjoying the rhythm of the rocking chair. He was thinking and wondering what he should do. Do I give up?

The dawn was breaking when he went into his bed and fell into an exhausted sleep.

Chapter Twenty-One

Later in the morning, when Laurence finally left his bed, he knew what he had to do. The previous morning when his sister Tess had called to see how he was, Laurence had told her that he didn't feel like singing in the concert that evening. When she heard that, she had completely lost her temper with him and told him that he should pull himself together and come up out of his melancholia.

"You have to start back sometime. Just go to the concert. Alex is there and it can't be worse than wallowing in your grief!" With that, she stormed out.

Now when a carriage arrived outside the house, he was happy that Tess had returned and was accompanied by his parents, Shane and Eilís. Laurence greeted them with a smile. They were really glad to see that he was out of bed and dressed. He was eating breakfast and asked them to join him.

As Tess sat down, she was delighted to see him looking more cheerful. She wanted to apologise to him because she knew that she shouldn't have shouted at him.

"I'm sorry, Laurence, for being so impatient yesterday," she said.

"You were right, sis. I deserved it," Laurence said apologetically.

They all looked stunned and to break the silence his mother insisted, as always, in making more tea to go with the drop scones she had baked earlier that day.

As they ate, Tess was almost in tears as she explained why she said what she had said to him.

"We have all been very concerned about you."

Laurence looked around the table and was shocked to see that Shane looked upset and Eilís was now crying. It suddenly worried Laurence, as he looked at his mother. How old she looked today and much of that is my fault, he thought, suddenly realising that he hadn't really looked at her properly in ages.

Tess began to talk again but Shane put a hand on her arm and asked her to shush.

Shane turned to Laurence. "We are all concerned for you, son, and we just want to know what you want to do with your life. What do you think Lisa would say if she saw you in such a poor state?" He stopped talking and looked at his son, insisting on an answer.

Tess then reminded Laurence that he hadn't even attended any local concerts with good singers. She touched a raw nerve when she asked if he had thought of perhaps doing a concert in memory of Lisa. They all knew how much Lisa had enjoyed the excitement of concert-going, even when Laurence wasn't taking part.

"Answer your father and give us some glimmer of a future for you, Laurence," Tess pleaded. "We would all do everything to help if you really wanted to return to singing. Your friend Alex is also on board and will help all he can. For goodness' sake, people are queueing up to help you. Everyone loves your voice and they all want to hear you sing again. We all just want you back at the top, Laurence. I'm sure you do also."

Tess had heard him sing recently and thought that his voice would return only when he managed to maybe smile a bit more and put real emotion back into his singing.

Laurence nodded a few times. He was trying to articulate what he had been thinking about since waking that morning.

"I believe I'm ready to do something and I know a voice teacher who might be able to work with me."

"That's great, son! Do we know who he is?" his father enquired.

"It's not a 'he', Dad, it's a 'she'," said Laurence, smiling.

"Do we know her?" asked Tess, frowning because she thought it was unusual to hear about a female voice teacher helping a male singer.

"I met her only yesterday and I've just this morning thought of asking her if she would take me on. You will all love her as she's an Irish lady who is in New York at present."

"Oh, is she young?" Tess looked at him knowingly.

"It's not like that, sis. She is young, but she has three children and she is only in New York to keep them safe during the famine in Ireland. Her husband isn't with her but I believe that he is a lord or nobleman or something like that."

"Well, I hope you don't get any daft ideas about her or her husband would probably fight a duel with you!" she warned him, smiling. "But that sounds right for you, brother. I think it is a very good idea. Anything to get you from under our feet would be fine by me!"

When the family left, all looking more cheerful than when they arrived, Laurence stayed sitting at the table. He took the card that Margarita had given to him and decided to write to her straight away, before he lost his nerve.

Taking paper and a quill from his desk top, he sat down and began to write.

Dear Lady Beconsford,

I wish to thank you for our most interesting conversation when I met you yesterday, in the company of my good friend Alex and his family. I wish also to thank you for your graciousness in offering me your calling card.

I hope you do not think me too forward in writing so soon but I wish to meet you to discuss aspects of my singing that are causing me some difficulties at present. I hope you do not see this letter as an intrusion.

Yours sincerely,
Laurence Flaherty

The following week, Laurence was delighted to get a card from Margarita inviting him to call to her house in the morning of the following Friday. Laurence was, however, still concerned. It's hard to face one's greatest fears, he thought, yet he immediately replied thanking her for agreeing to meet him.

Laurence decided to go to New York on the night before he was to meet Margarita. He would stay in an inn close to her home.

When Laurence arrived in the hotel, he was greeted in the lounge by his friend Alex, who was waiting for him to arrive.

"That's the first smile I've seen on your face for a long time," said a grinning Alex. "What is all the intrigue about?"

"None of your business, friend," said Laurence, joining into the frivolity of their conversation. "I'll let you know when I've spoken to Margarita, but for now I want a relaxed evening in the company of you, my friend, with a glass of brandy in my hand."

Alex was very pleased with this new, more relaxed Laurence and the two friends spent a pleasant evening where, for once, there was no mention of sadder times.

The following morning Laurence asked the coachman to leave him at the entrance to Willow Crescent, as he felt that he needed some air before his appointment. Maybe it would be for the best if I went home, he thought. He knew he was looking for an excuse to run away yet again. He knew also that it was one of those moments in his life when a decision had to be made, and the consequences accepted.

He set off walking in the direction of Number 10. It was a striking redbrick house, three storeys tall. The click of the garden gate as he closed it saw him standing in Margarita's attractive front drive, surrounded by trees and colourful summer flowers in abundance, making the gardens seem cheerful and welcoming. It gave him a feeling that fate had just locked him into something from which there was no return. Yet he was happy.

He resolutely rang the bell. The door was quickly opened by a young woman.

"I have an appointment with Madam Beconsford," said Laurence, feeling like a five-year-old standing in front of a schoolmaster.

Just as he was about to speak again, a door opened and the tall and statuesque figure of Margarita appeared.

"Hello, Laurence, you are welcome to our home," she said with a wide smile. "This is my very good friend Jean who came over from Ireland with me."

Laurence stepped into the house. Margarita walked him towards a door on the left and they smiled at each other before entering the front parlour.

"Would you like some coffee?" Jean asked, slightly concerned that Margarita was stepping over a boundary by having an extremely attractive man alone with her in her home.

"Coffee would be lovely, thank you," Laurence replied gratefully.

Margarita chatted to Laurence about his family, who came from Macroom in West Cork. She wondered to herself if they would be happy about her meeting with their son.

Jean returned with the coffee, excused herself and left.

When the coffee was poured, Margarita turned her gaze on Laurence. She smiled and asked him to relax as she assured him that she didn't bite. Nonetheless, she did wonder if she was competent enough to work with his voice. She had been told how successful he had been in the past.

"Surely you could have had the pick of voice trainers in America, who would have seen it as a privilege to work with you, if what Alex has told me of your talent is correct?"

It would have sounded strange to express it but Laurence felt relaxed sitting with Margarita. Her voice was soft and soothing with her Irish lilt and her smile genuine.

"I am happy to go ahead if you are willing to take me on as a student," Laurence responded, still feeling somewhat apprehensive. "I listened to you last week while we were eating and your interest in breathing and relaxing resonated with me. When I left you, I felt that what you could teach me is what I may need at this stage in my life." As he waited for her to respond, he still felt the pain in his stomach that never seemed to have left him since his wife died. But what was new about that? Indeed, the sense of anxiety and impending doom had pervaded the pit of his stomach from the first morning he found out the seriousness of his young wife's illness.

"Then I would love to work with you," said Margarita. "However, you need to understand that I only have knowledge. You are the one who has to do all the hard work. You also need a belief that it will bring you to a brighter place, when your voice again begins to soar effortlessly."

"You sound confident, Margarita. I hope I will live up to your expectations." Laurence felt himself sagging into the chair as he felt a glimmer of hope that the heavy load, he had been carrying for nearly three years could finally be lifted from his shoulders.

Chapter Twenty-Two

Laurence was the most diligent student Margarita had ever encountered and the most talented. Yet, after several months the progress that she had hoped for was not happening. She knew that there was a conversation they needed to have. After a session, when the training finished late in the afternoon, she decided to address it.

As Laurence stood up to leave, Margarita put a hand out to stop him.

"I'm going to have another cup of tea. Would you stay and join me?" she asked.

Laurence nodded.

When they were sitting again, having been served by Mrs. O'Brien, Margarita tentatively mentioned his late wife, Lisa.

"Surely you have other things to be doing, Margarita?" said Laurence quickly, not wanting the relaxation he felt during the session to be broken by painful memories. "I've already taken up too much of your time today."

"No, no, Laurence. Maybe it's a fault of mine but I never let a singer leave if I think something important needs to be said. I think it's time that you shared something about Lisa with me. I need your help now. I believe that the pain you are carrying around is restricting your voice because of tension in your stomach, your chest and even your jaw. I am not trying to intrude but, sadly, Lisa's death is the reason why you are here now, instead of gracing the opera houses around America and Europe."

Laurence watched as Margarita drank her tea. She exuded an air of someone at peace with themselves. She looked so calm and tranquil.

Perhaps I'm wrong, Laurence thought, as he knew that her husband had some difficulties. We never can tell what is going on in other people's lives, he thought, no matter how relaxed they looked.

He sighed. "Yes, I agree with you. I would like to talk to you about my Lisa," he said, before he had time to change his mind. "Wouldn't you imagine that with all my friends and relatives I could talk freely about Lisa? But I can't. I'm too embarrassed – afraid I'd cry. I'm alone and very lonely most of the time even though my family are always calling around. Yet the paradox is that all they want is to take care of me, but I don't want them around. It's as if their laughter and presence is an insult to Lisa's memory. I don't feel that I have a right to be happy any more. I feel that I lost that right on the day I first got the devastating news of her illness."

Margarita nodded in sympathy, astonished at how freely he now spoke. Perhaps it is because I'm not family, she thought.

"I understand," she said softly, hoping to encourage him to continue with his story.

"We had been to Rome on a very belated honeymoon when she first felt sick. We both believed she was expecting a baby. When the doctor she saw back in Newark asked her to come to the hospital overnight, we hoped there wasn't a problem. I left Lisa in the hospital and my sister Tess insisted that I stay in her house overnight, as she lived close by. I went across from the hospital and she had a lovely meal waiting even though it was near to midnight. It's strange, I couldn't eat and I couldn't sleep on that night. Maybe it was a premonition. I knew, I just knew that the news was going to be bad. I must have slept for a while because I had a dream that I was trying to reach out to Lisa. I seemed to be running after her to tell her something but there were always things in my way. Then she just disappeared from in front of me. I woke up with a terrible feeling of dread and for a few minutes couldn't even remember why I was feeling like that. I can tell you that I've had many similar dreams since then and I nearly always wake up with a dreadful feeling in the pit of my stomach. Yet now, sometimes, for just a few moments, I forget that she is dead and I reach out to take her hand and squeeze it. It's only when I come up against the flattened quilt by my side that reality kicks back in. When I feel really bad, I don't even want to get out of bed in the morning." He paused, bowing his head.

"I believe it's good that you're talking about it now," she said, touching his by now clenched fist briefly.

Laurence tried to get his thoughts together again.

"On that day I sat in a chair by her bed in the hospital while she went for further examination. When she returned, she told me how tired she felt. Asleep she looked so beautiful and healthy, her auburn locks forming a halo around her face. By then I knew that she was not expecting a baby. Nobody who looked so well could be ill, I reassured myself as I stroked her cheek gently. Yet, I was the one who had to appear cheerful then as I saw a terrified look in her eyes when she woke."

Tears welled up in Laurence's eyes and he brushed them away.

"She was dead within a month. Can you believe it? One month earlier we had been hoping that she was expecting a baby but it was a gastric cancer that had grown very quickly. Her tumour was too far gone. They couldn't do anything for her. How the hell could anyone feel that a singing career was important after that?" he said bitterly.

Margarita waited until he got some of his composure back, worrying that she had pushed him too far. I'm not expert enough to be doing this, she thought, but she felt that she was now in too deep to stop.

"Laurence, could I ask you to do something for me? Would you tell me how beautiful Lisa was? Could we talk about her goodness and how she positively affected your life?"

Laurence looked startled but he then began to tell her some lovely stories about the kindness and beauty of his wife.

He had been in Margarita's room for more than two hours when she decided they had talked enough for now. At the front door, she thanked him warmly for opening up his thoughts to her and suggested that on the way home he could try to remember some more of the wonderful memories he and Lisa had shared. As she watched him leave, she believed that she saw a glimmer of a smile around his mouth. She hoped that she'd done the right thing but wasn't sure.

"I would like you to wait for a week before we meet again. By then I hope that you may feel ready to share some more of your good memories of Lisa with me. But if you are not ready, that's fine too," she assured him.

As Laurence made his way home, still somewhat dazed by the afternoon, he found that talking fondly of Lisa seemed to release some of the tightness in his body. Perhaps it is good to talk about your worries after all, he thought.

Exhausted after the day, he went to bed that night, but couldn't get to sleep. He tossed and turned and eventually got up again and put more logs on the fire. Yet again he sat on his Shaker rocking chair that Lisa had bought for him but this time he called out to her.

"How can I go forward?" he pleaded into the night air. "Help me, please!"

As he continued to sit on the chair in the dark night, with the rhythmic movement moving back and forth, he began to feel very sleepy. He could feel her presence in the room. He could hear her laughter in his head. He could see her smile when he closed his eyes. He could almost feel her touch and hear her voice telling him to keep singing.

He must have been sitting by the fire for a long time because the embers were long dead. He felt very cold, yet his mind felt calmer. It was not a nightmare, nor was it a dream, it was an awakening. He now believed that she really was watching over him and would take care of him in the future. The dawn was breaking when he returned to his bed and fell into an exhausted sleep deeper than he had enjoyed for a very long time.

Chapter Twenty-Three

The following months brought a change in Laurence's demeanour that Margarita had not expected. He grew in confidence and stature as his voice again began to soar. He now reached the high notes and held them with ease. Margarita was amazed at how quickly he was moving towards becoming the best singer she had ever heard, either in Europe or America. She was now certain that he would grace the opera houses of the world again.

He was now seen by everyone who lived in Number 10 as a really good family friend. The twins and Rosita looked forward to the regular treats he seemed to pull out of his pockets each time he was in their home and they even called him Uncle Laurence.

Over the following weeks the cold weather of winter arrived in New York. Laurence was now ready to perform and Margarita decided to ask him a favour.

As they sat chatting, which they now did after each training session, because they enjoyed each other's company so much, she began to speak tentatively.

"Laurence, I know that you will be returning shortly to sing professionally again. I was wondering if perhaps you could perform in a Christmas fundraiser for famine relief for the people of Cork? Your relatives in Macroom would get some of the funds, of course."

Without any hesitation he replied, "Margarita, it would be an honour, but there is one stipulation before I agree."

"You will get anything you need, kind sir, as long as you sing," she answered, laughing at the smile that lit up his face.

"That's agreed then, my lady. My only wish is that you sing also and that I can accompany you in a duet or two of your choice."

Margarita looked at him, not that surprised by his request.

"I was always going to sing there," she said, with amusement in her voice. "Of course, I would be proud to accompany you. It looks like we're both happy and I know with you involved, the Irish will be the real winners. I can already see New York society flocking to hear their favourite son on stage once more."

The following weeks were a hive of industry in Number 10. Laurence and Margarita increased the excitement in the house when they practised their duets. On those days, Sylvia and her household usually arrived for tea. The run-up to Christmas became a joyous occasion for all.

On a crisp cold late afternoon in New York three carriages drew up at the entrance to Margarita's house to take everyone from her home and Sylvia's to the fundraiser, except the twins who were taken care of by a neighbour's daughter. Nobody wanted to miss the event of the year in Manhattan. A larger venue had to be found to house the number of people who wanted tickets for the event. Many opera followers were intrigued and wanted to hear how the young widower Laurence Flaherty's voice was after the death of his young wife. Also, a great number of Irish immigrants attended. Word was out that some even borrowed money to be among the great and the good of New York society. In fact, Margarita had discreetly handed out some free tickets which were handled by Mrs. O'Brien. The committee pulled favours from the council and the large hall was decorated to an exceptionally high standard. A new velvet curtain was created especially for the evening performance. Excitement was high even with the workers preparing the venue. The band practised with the singers and as workers and artists alike ate some food before the performance, the paying public were already queuing around the block.

When the concert began, a band of Irish musicians had everyone clapping and stamping their feet in time to the music. The performers backstage looked at each other, smiling. They knew that the audience were going to enjoy the evening's entertainment. An Irish balladeer entertained with the plaintive sounds of "The Croppy Boy" followed by another favourite, "Rody McCorley".

As the expectant crowd saw Laurence and Margarita come on stage together, there was tremendous applause, followed by an expectant hush from the audience. After the two sang Bellini's haunting melodious duet "*Vieni fra queste braccia*" from his opera *I Puritani*, Laurence sang from Mr. Rossini's *Barber of Seville*. He continued with an aria from Donizetti's tragic *Lucia di Lammermoor*. Everyone applauded the exquisite voice of Laurence and as he exited the stage Margarita began to sing the favourite, "Oh, Don't You Remember, Sweet Alice, Ben Bolt", much to the delight of the audience. Margarita got a warm feeling inside her that she had not felt when singing since she had made her public appearance as a young girl in Shelbourne House, back in Dublin. As she reached the last note, Laurence rejoined her on stage. It was then she knew that music had truly returned to bring joy into her life. She squeezed his hand before exiting the stage and watched in the wings.

Laurence then sang the sad and gentle aria, "*Va Pensiero*" from Verdi's *Nabucco*, and finished with an Irish song, "Kathleen Mavourneen".

As he finished, all the participants came onstage and clapped while the audience gave him a standing ovation.

Margarita knew that for Laurence this was much more than a fund-raising event. She knew that the great and the good of the opera world were in attendance tonight, as well as his proud family, and he had proved something to them.

When the final curtain call was over, both Laurence and Margarita were still experiencing the wonderful feeling of satisfaction at the applause he received after each song he sang that evening. Laurence thought he had lost the excitement that he had not experienced in three years, but he now knew he had been wrong. His voice had returned. He knew that Margarita's voice training had given him back his ability to hold a high note. More importantly, being with her had given him back his confidence and his hope for the future that he could again sing in the great concert halls in America and hopefully also in Europe. Yet, he thought, it had come at a price, and he had to address this issue when he next met with Margarita.

Next morning, after a night of great celebration, Margarita had breakfast with the children. Even young Violet and Louis embraced the excitement felt in the house. Everyone had experienced something on the previous night that they would never forget.

"Let me tell you that the biggest success last night was that Laurence was wonderful and got a standing ovation."

"What's a standing ovation?" asked young Violet, wanting as always to be part of family conversations.

Margarita laughed as she stood up and clapped her hands. "That's what people do after a song that they really loved and they did this when Laurence sang 'Kathleen Mavourneen' at the end. And the concert made a lot of money to help your Auntie Alice in Cork, so she can now feed lots of people and help keep them all safe. Now can I enjoy my breakfast in peace? You can go to your lessons and, when you're finished, I'll tell you all about the night and what the ladies were wearing. Alright?"

The children kept up their questions as Florrie tried to usher them from the breakfast table. When they finally left the room Margarita relaxed as she held the teacup in her hands and reflected at the success of the previous night while realising that she needed a few days of rest before she had to think of where her life was going.

As she continued to sit in the cosy warm kitchen Jean came in and passed an envelope to her.

"This was delivered by a hotel bellboy and he asked if you could send a reply if he waits?" That must be from Laurence, Jean thought.

"Yes, of course, take him into the parlour and I'll go to him as soon as I've written a reply." Margarita frowned as she opened the note, wondering why Laurence was writing so early in the morning. She hoped he hadn't had a setback after their wonderful concert last night.

It was a short note and was puzzlingly formal.

Dear Margarita,

I can't thank you enough for everything you have done for me over the past months. It has been a much-needed journey for which I am truly grateful to you.

Would it be possible for me to call on you later this morning, before I return to New Jersey?

I would like an hour of your time if that is possible?

I await your reply,

Laurence

Margarita wrote a quick reply and assured Laurence that he was welcome to come at noon, while the children were still at their lessons, and inviting him to stay for lunch. She went and handed it to the young bell boy and returned to the kitchen.

As she made her way to let Mrs. O'Brien know to prepare for a visitor joining them for lunch, she frowned and wondered what was wrong. At this, she smiled to herself, wondering why she always expected the next bit of bad news!

Laurence received Margarita's reply. He was almost hoping she wasn't available. Yet he needed to do this today before he got on with the rest of his life. He had a new joy in his singing and for that he would never be able to thank her enough.

He arrived at the house at twelve o'clock. He had brought a large bouquet of fresh red roses and small gifts for Rosita, the twins, Jean, Florrie and even Mrs. O'Brien. A beaming Jean opened the door and congratulated him immediately on his success. He thanked her and gave her a gift of a pure silk scarf, which delighted her.

"Margarita is in the front parlour as usual. I'll bring in some coffee for you both."

Laurence smiled. "I'd love that, thank you."

Jean smiled as she opened the door and led him into the comfortable room he had grown to love over the past months.

Margarita rose as he entered. He walked over and took her hand for a little longer than would be deemed appropriate. He then made his way to his usual armchair close to the table situated by the fire. Jean returned carrying a small tray with coffee and two small cookies. When she set it down, she again congratulated them both.

"You two are stars. I feel privileged to have been in the audience last night," she said, smiling before leaving the room and closing the door quietly.

"I'll pour the coffee," said Margarita as Laurence looked at her with a sad expression in his eyes. She felt in her heart that something must be seriously wrong and she didn't want the glow she felt today to diminish.

As the silence continued, Margarita took the lead.

"I'm delighted to see you, Laurence, but this is an unexpected call," she said with a questioning look.

Laurence began to speak with a sadness in his voice. "Margarita, please hear me out because I needed a lot of strength this morning in deciding to come and speak to you. My mother always said that I was impulsive and maybe that is what I'm being this morning. I have had such wonderful times in this welcoming room and I think by now you and I probably know everything about each other. You entered my life like a guardian angel when I was at my lowest point and you saw me through the most important part of my sorrow, which was acceptance. I now understand that while Lisa will always be in my heart, I must now live my life as I know she would have wished, with a song also in my heart. Margarita, I need to tell you that you are so lucky to have three such lovely children. Yet I know from them and you that although you have had problems in your marriage, that you have loved your husband Victor from when you were a young woman. I know also that the love you have for him hasn't diminished, even while you are apart. I can understand why he wanted so much to keep the children safe, having lost Rosita's mother during her birth. You have done that here in New York. I hope that the wretched famine ends soon and brings peace to him and all the other people in Ireland."

Laurence paused for breath, cleared his throat and took his handkerchief from his pocket to mop his watering eyes.

Margarita could hear her heart thumping as she wondered where this conversation was going.

"Margarita, when I first met you, I loved your companionship, your singing, your kindness – the list is too long to continue. The problem is, Margarita, that over the past six months I have fallen in love with you. I know it is not only because we have been thrown together so much. It is because you are one of the kindest and most caring people I have ever met and it's these qualities plus the way you constantly show your affection and love for your children that has made me want such a love in my life."

Margarita went to stand up but as the chair began to slip from behind her, she sat down again suddenly. Her heart was thumping wildly because she too knew that on many occasions during their time together, she had felt a connection with him but she knew that would lead to heartache for too many people if she gave in to it. Perhaps it was only because she had missed her Victor so much that she felt lonely and in need of physical love. Yet she could not reveal any of her thoughts to this lovely man.

As Laurence was about to talk again, she put out a hand to stop him.

"Laurence, it isn't the first time that a grieving person experiences feelings for a confidante. I too have enjoyed our time together and I am deeply grateful for the way in which you have been a positive male influence on my children during the past six months, where they're surrounded by so many women! I hope you didn't feel that I ever gave you any encouragement during our time working on your voice?"

Now it was Laurence who put out a hand towards her. "This isn't about you, Margarita. This is why I have come here today. Recently, I have been in consultation with the man who sourced my singing engagements in the past. He came to see me last night and was very positive about my ability to re-enter the world of music at a high level. He offered me an engagement in Chicago. Earlier he had guaranteed me that if my voice returned, he would give me a chance to tour America. He will honour his promise to me, but he asked me to help him next week and I agreed immediately. I am going to sing in Holy Name Cathedral in Chicago, on Christmas Eve. The singer who was due to take part has been taken ill. I'm leaving in two days. When Mister Comerford confirmed that he was impressed with my voice he got me to sign a deed of contract to tour with him for the next six months. I signed on the spot. Yet when I got back to the hotel, I tossed and turned for hours in my bed and decided to come to you today and tell you the truth. Margarita, my dear friend, you gave me back my voice. You gave me back my hope but I know that you cannot give me your love."

By now it was Margarita who had tears in her eyes. "Laurence, you gave me a real purpose in my life and the money raised last night will make an enormous difference to the people in Ireland. I have grown and learned also from the experience of having you as a pupil."

"I have one last request, Margarita. Could I speak to the children before leaving today, because I have gifts for them and I want to explain to them that I am going away on tour. I want them to understand why I won't see them again."

"Of course, Laurence. They'll be coming home for their lunch shortly and then you can chat to them. The children are all going to miss you, yet perhaps it's for the best. I too have a lot of thinking to do. As I was caught up in so many things during the past month, I just never had time nor inclination to ask myself about the future. So now I too need to start planning."

As they both stood up at the one time, Laurence reached out to her and put his arms around her. He held her close for just a moment. When their eyes met, she gently kissed him on the cheek.

"Thank you for being with me in such a difficult time for us both. I'm going to miss you so very much."

No more words were spoken until they reached the large kitchen where the table was set for lunch.

Laurence joined Margarita and the children for lunch and acted as if nothing had happened, painting a permanent smile on his face.

"I have some presents for you, children, now that you've all finished your food."

There was a cheer from all three as the twins clambered from their chairs and ran around the table to him. The adults laughed as the children all wanted to receive their gifts immediately. Laurence laughed as Jean walked in carrying three wrapped boxes.

There was a scramble as each of the children opened their surprises. Louis, who was obsessed by trains, looked in awe at a big shiny train engine, while Violet squealed with delight as she lifted a large doll from a box. It had a pretty smile, golden locks and clothes that sparkled in the light.

She held it close and spoke in a solemn voice. "Thank you, Uncle Laurence. I will keep her for all of my life."

Margarita shook her head at his extravagance especially as Rosita, who truly thought she was an adult and not still a child, was overjoyed to receive a pair of glamorous fur muffs with a little purse attached to it for her keepsakes and money.

"You're too generous, Laurence. How can we thank you enough?" said Margarita who was now looking anxiously at the children as she knew what was coming next.

"Well, children, you can thank me by being very, very good children for your mama. I am not going to see you for some time. I am going away to sing in a place called Chicago and other big cities in America and that is only because your wonderful mama helped me become a very good singer. So could you all clap your hands and give her a standing ovation, when you manage to put your gifts down!"

This seemed to break the ice as they stood and clapped.

Rosita wanted to know all about the place called Chicago.

By the time Laurence left the house everyone seemed in good spirits. As they all stood at the doorway and bade him farewell, he doffed his cap and bowed. With his eyes on Margarita and sadness clearly evident in their eyes, he promised to meet them all again, sometime, somewhere, in the future.

Chapter Twenty-Four

Margarita spent the next few days fluctuating between sadness and relief as she knew deep down that she had been getting too close emotionally to Laurence.

I'm really missing Victor, she thought. Her anger with his behaviour had abated because she knew he couldn't help himself. In life, Victor had always been the golden, privileged boy who never had a care in the world until his beloved young wife Fleur passed away giving birth to Rosita. Then he just ran away. She had again seen signs of his inability to deal with any type of problem shortly after the birth of the twins, overly concerned if they had even a sniffle or a cough. She now began to understand how much he suffered in his mind when the famine hit. His anxiety obviously weaved a scenario where all his children could die. Although there was still no word from him, she hoped he was still in Vienna. One thing she was now certain about was that she needed to return to Ireland. I will just have to pray and trust that the children will continue to be healthy back in Ireland, she thought. Only then can I find him and care for him as best I can. She would now write to her own and Victor's parents, telling them of her decision to come home.

She thought long and hard before sitting at the desk in the parlour and taking pen to paper.

My dear Mama and Papa,

I want you to know that our fundraising concert raised a substantial amount of money and that it is being sent to your Irish bank for distribution.

Please use your discretion when distributing it, but I would like Alice's famine fund to get a substantial amount as I know the need in their area is still truly great. Of course, make sure that the people in Midleton, but particularly in Macroom, benefit also. Maybe we're being selfish sending it only to Cork as the stories I've been told by the men and women from Mayo and the west of Ireland are truly heart-breaking. Yet I've reasoned that there is only so much one small committee can do and the emigrants from Cork worked tirelessly to make this concert a great success.

The children are thriving in New York, but my heart believes that the famine will shortly end. I'm yearning for my home and family. I hope to give the children a great Christmas in New York and, when the weather improves in the spring, we may return to Ireland, with the wish that the children will all be safe within the walls of the Beconsford Estate.

Send my love to Granny Molly. Tell her I will write in the new year.

Your loving daughter,

Margarita

The following night Margarita sat down with Jean and shared with her the idea that she might return to Ireland in the spring.

Jean hesitated before answering. "I thought that might be happening, Margarita, and I have been waiting for the right time to talk to you. As you know I've struck up a good relationship with Peter Vance, the teacher at the girls' school. In October, he surprised me by asking me to marry him, but I told him I needed time to think about it. I thought you had enough on your mind at the time. I had to make a decision also about the idea of living my life away from Ireland. That was a tough one to make. Yet, I do love him, but before I accept his proposal I would like your blessing. I don't want to disrupt the lives of Rosita and the twins because goodness knows they've all gone through a lot in their short lives."

As she finished, a smiling Margarita jumped up and hugged her friend.

"Why ever would you think I would be anything but delighted? You're too good at minding children to live your life out without having any of your own. You're strong and fit and still not too old to have a family. The famine in Ireland gave people so few opportunities to meet suitable partners. Follow your heart, Jean. I am truly happy for you, but I'd love if you married in the spring so that I could help you, as would Rosita. You have always meant so much to her."

Jean sat down in a daze, knowing that her life was about to change. It was too early to know how she was going to feel when Margarita returned to Ireland.

"Thanks so much for encouraging me. I hope I'm making the right decision. I do know that Florrie will be very happy to be going home. As you know she has been writing regularly to Patrick. That's the lad she met on the boat to England with Victor and Rosita. He seems like a sensible boy and is hoping to purchase his own boat one day. So, I know for a fact that she wants to return home. Although she's not too sure that she will get a good reception in Midleton, having gone away with Rosita."

Margarita assured her that nobody in Middleton would blame Florrie.

"I'll talk to her and reassure her. She was as much a victim in all of that as we were. I will assure her that she will be warmly welcomed at home, as she took such good care of Rosita when they were in England. Now all I want to talk about for the next week is how much fun I want Christmas to be for the children. I'm hoping to give them a Christmas to remember. I have sufficient funds saved from my teaching and Isaac will organise everything that is needed for our return to Ireland. Plus, in the new year we can start thinking about wedding dresses!" She laughed, happy now that good things were happening.

All the residents of Number 10, apart from Mrs. O'Brien, climbed into the carriage.

As they settled down Rosita persisted with the question she had been asking since breakfast time.

"Where are we going today that's such a secret, Mama?"

Margarita smiled. "It wouldn't be a secret if I told you so you will have to wait!" As she looked at her beautiful growing daughter, she thought that she would eventually break many men's hearts, yet she wondered how any man would deal with her strong character. That girl will make history someday, she reckoned.

The weather was crisp and windless as they drove towards Manhattan.

"Are we going to the shops?" asked a now excited Rosita. "Can I get a new pair of shoes?"

"Slow down. Yes, we are going to the shops. Today I want you all to choose some little Christmas gifts to give to all the people you know as presents. I will give each of you some money to spend that your grandparents sent from Ireland."

None of the children had ever experienced anything like the sights of the shops in New York at Christmas time. The windows were all decked out with colourful and cheerful baubles. The prosperous people arriving and stopping their elegant carriages in front of the shops made Margarita feel a pang of sadness that this level of wealth and prosperity was nowhere to be seen in Ireland.

When they alighted from the carriage, the splendour of AT Stewart's department store on Broadway was not lost on the children, as they looked in the windows and exclaimed at all the presents on display. But their greatest pleasure was the array of toys in Tuttle's Emporium where they were each allowed to buy Christmas gifts. Margarita and Jean ensured that the children were able to keep secret the gifts they bought for each other. Two hours later, having spent all their money, much merriment was had by all as the gift-wrapped parcels were carried out to a carriage by an assistant. The day was made more exciting when they went for much needed refreshments to a stylish hotel, where they were served in the opulence of the hotel dining room. It was packed with families, all out enjoying the build-up to the celebration of Christmas. Margarita knew from some of her students that a small orchestra would be playing Christmas music there throughout the afternoon.

At the end of a relaxing day, eating and listening to the tuneful orchestra, the hotel arranged for a carriage to drive them home.

Later Margarita watched the delight of the children's faces as they excitedly hid various gifts in their bedrooms. She said a prayer of thanks that in the midst of the horror of famine in Ireland she had been able to give her young children a normal Christmas in New York that they would hopefully remember throughout their lives. She also promised herself the luxury of putting all her concerns to the back of her mind for a few days of celebration.

Christmas was every bit as wonderful as Margarita had hoped. They dined on roast ham and venison with parsnips and potatoes followed by plum pudding and apple-jelly. Though she could not remove the feelings of guilt completely from her mind that nobody in her family at home would enjoy these luxuries, she was nonetheless grateful that the twins were still too young to dwell on, or even understand, what was occurring in Ireland.

Christmas was over and the dawning of the new year brought snow to New York. Margarita spent some of her time indoors working with the final few students that she would train. It was wonderful, she thought, that because of her success with Laurence she had got a great number of requests from older singers, and her reputation had grown in the world of opera and music. Yet she was now leaving a place that had given her sanctuary and experiences for which she would be grateful for a long time.

Chapter Twenty-Five

It was early summer when Margarita sat at a table in Number 10, Willow Crescent, for the final time, surrounded by all her friends.

Jean had married Peter Vance at Easter, with Rosita and her mother acting as bridesmaids while the twins held the end of her long veil, as the joyful bride-to-be entered the church. After the ceremony, a feast of food was laid out by Mrs. O'Brien and a group of her Irish friends who had come in to help.

Jean now resided in a comfortable flat, situated close to her husband Peter's job. Tonight she was sitting with all her friends to say farewell to Margarita and her family. Sylvia and Maeve also were sad to see their friends depart. Mrs. O'Brien was taking over the housekeeping duties at Sylvia's home as Úna Hayes decided to return to Ireland with Margarita, because her mother needed her in Eoinstown, due to poor health.

Sylvia gave Úna a job in Ireland, which was well due to her after years of devotion. From now on the Stewart land would be rented out at much reduced prices to the farmers and most landholders would get increased acreage. Sylvia decided to let Úna and her good friend Alice get involved in giving the people in the village small plots each, to grow some fruit and vegetables, or even flowers that they could go and sit and admire in good weather. It was her way of giving back to a townland what her husband had taken from them. She also set Úna the task of tracking down the young kitchen maid, Maggie Sinnott, who had ended up with child as a result of her late husband's attack. She wanted a trust to be set up for the child with money to ensure that Maggie had a chance of a good future for herself and her child. Sylvia never wanted to live in West Cork again and she employed her lawyer and an estate manager to look after the rents and to help Úna and Alice deal with the needs of the local people.

Maeve Maguire loved her teaching job in America. In fact, she was so good at it that the board of managers had given her a bursary to attend Colombia College where they hoped she would gain a qualification and that she would return with increased knowledge to teach at their school again. Sylvia was especially proud of her as she always saw Maeve as the daughter she never had. Sylvia had promised Maeve's mother that she would always take care of her and she believed she was well on the way to doing this.

As Margarita looked around the room, she felt a fondness for America in the way it opened its arms to strangers and gave them a chance to reach for their dreams. As she raised her glass, she spoke to the whole group.

"I'd like you all to drink a toast to a wonderful country – America!"

As they all raised their glasses with tears in some eyes, it turned to laughter as young Violet wisely asked, "How can you drink toast, Mama?"

The rest of the night was spent singing and dancing with the children given permission to stay up late. Margarita knew that for the majority of the Irish, such as Mrs. O'Brien and her friends, few of those emigrants would have the luxury of returning to their native home.

Later, as she lay in her bed and watched the moon cast shadows on her lovely garden, Margarita was grateful for the luxury afforded to her to go back home. Tomorrow she would be returning to her native land.

Chapter Twenty-Six

The sun rose in the eastern sky promising a beautiful sunny morning as Margarita sat in the Secret Garden, beside the Big House, alone with her conflicting thoughts. The signs of a good crop of potatoes heralded a new dawn for the island of Ireland and the relief in believing that the murderous potato famine was now passing brought joy to her heart. Thankfully most of the community around the estate had survived, through diligent efforts to keep them in food. However, many of the townspeople had passed away, mainly from the fever that had spread when the workhouse was flooded with sick and hungry women and children from the city of Cork.

Mrs Sexton, who had been in the bakery all her life and during the famine had worked as a helper in the soup kitchens, had died a year earlier. Thankfully in her own bed in the home she owned. Margarita, Eliza and the Beconsford family all had fond memories of their younger days when Mrs. Sexton chaperoned the girls in the Regency Room attached to the Haven Inn. She died as she had lived, helping people in the community.

Margarita and her family had returned safely in the early summer of 1850. When bright weather arrived in the early spring of 1851, shoots of hope grew within the people that the famine that had decimated the population of Ireland through both death and emigration, was at an end. Yet her husband had still not returned home to Midleton.

Victor Beconsford, who had been in communication with his family for over a year, continued to live in Vienna, until his exasperated father Isaac decided that it was time to have a showdown with him. Margarita was grateful for his intervention because she did not want to leave the children and go to Europe. Isaac travelled to Vienna in the spring of 1851 to tell him that the dawn of a good future was forecast for Ireland. He wanted to emphasise to him that the family were all now safe and healthy.

Before seeing his son, Isaac first met with Doctor Mateo Bauer, who had treated Victor so well after the death of his wife Fleur.

The doctor shook his head many times as he spoke about Victor. "I have done everything I can for him. It is a disease, I believe, over which he has no control. There are no medicines I can give him. His system may be damaged beyond repair. Although he is still a very young man, I am not sure that he has the resilience he displayed when he first came to me many years ago. I can just wish him and you luck when you take him home. He needs to be with his family."

It took several weeks for Isaac to persuade Victor that the famine was gone, that the children had thrived while in America, that everyone was in perfect health and that his wife was bereft at his continued absence.

Victor looked like an old man as he sat in the bedroom of his home, with his hands over his face, anguished.

"Are you sure everyone is safe?" he asked.

"Yes, Victor, as I said, everyone is in full health and the farm has begun to return to normal. It's all over, son. Please come home."

"Did the Irish get an apology from the English parliament?"

Isaac wondered where this was going. "No, they didn't."

"Well, they should have. I've been reading the newspapers in Europe and I know that over a million people died in Ireland in the last five years and way more than two million emigrated. They say that the English decimated the population of Ireland. The newspapers that tell the truth say that the English Parliament never did enough for Ireland."

As Victor continued to rant, Isaac put his head in his hands, feeling exhausted and exasperated by his son.

"You know, Father, how people were so pleased with Queen Victoria giving two thousand pounds to famine relief. I bet few people realised that the young Sultan of Turkey, Khaleefah Abdul-Majid, whose friends I know in Vienna, offered ten thousand pounds to the relief fund. He was stopped giving so much money by the British embassy and told to donate only one thousand pounds as it would offend the Queen if he sent more than her! Father, that money would have fed the whole of Ireland back then. I know that he did send three shiploads of food to Ireland and the English courts tried to block that but the Ottoman sailors secretly got it in to Drogheda. I hear that it saved the lives of many people."

As Isaac looked at the ashen pallor of his son's face, he put his arm gently around his shoulders. "I knew about some of what you have just said and I too feel shamed at what happened and I agree that we were let down by the government. But, Victor, like I often said in the past, throughout those years I just did the best I could do, given the circumstances I was in. I couldn't save a whole nation, son. I just got on with things and helped as many people as I could. Your children are all safe, so just come home, son, and help us all to make people's lives better in the future."

"But, Father, are you going to at least ask the British government for an apology?"

Isaac shook his head. "Victor, there's too much work and restoration to be done in the country for recriminations. We have to move on and look to a brighter future. You can be part of that when you return home." He was trying to keep patience with his distraught son. "Well, Victor, what is it to be? Do you see your future in a downtrodden set of rooms in Vienna or at home where you are loved by many people who have been waiting patiently for your return?"

It took three days of persuasion by Isaac and Doctor Bauer for Victor to eventually get on a train that would take father and son across western Europe. Throughout the journey, Isaac became as perturbed regarding Victor's physical health as he was with his mental state. Doctor Bauen had expressed serious concerns, telling Isaac that his son would need a lot of care and attention and he had to stay away from alcohol as there would be serious consequences if he didn't. Isaac assured him that everyone would do their best to return him to health.

Chapter Twenty-Seven

When Victor returned from Vienna, the joy in the Beconsford estate was immense. Margarita showered him with love and everyone made an effort to understand what the doctor in Vienna had said. They secured the services of a young Cork doctor to take care of him. Doctor Lewis said that he had a disease over which he had little control. The family hoped to build him up with nourishing foods and broths and they were all patient and solicitous when dealing with him.

During the first few months, when Victor stopped drinking, everyone in the house lived through many halcyon days and a euphoria was felt that this crisis had now passed. Margarita, Victor and the children were inseparable. The twins sat at his feet, with small arms around his legs, giving him and them comfort. They all loved being so close to each other, while Rosita read endless books out loud. Margarita always finished the family time together by singing his favourite songs. On a few occasions husband and wife sat close together in the Secret Garden, both lost in memories of days long gone. At night she held him close to her heart where they each spoke of their great love for each other.

But as another autumn passed, so did Victor's willpower. It faltered because his body regularly shook uncontrollably. In the past when that happened, it stopped only with the help of a soothing drink of alcohol. As the cold weather arrived, Margarita realised that the fairy tale she had hoped for now seemed out of reach. Her heart felt that a lead weight was pressing down on it when she thought about her husband. He had now turned into a shadow of the young man that she had married ten years earlier. His shrunken face and yellow pallor showed the evidence of the drinking he could not seem to live without.

His growing twins now asked why their papa didn't play with them much anymore and Rosita, who seemed to be wise beyond her years, was the one who seemed to bring him the most joy. She read the books he loved each morning, as he now spent his day sitting close to his bed, watching the world of the estate, as if blind, through his bedroom window.

He took no interest or joy in the increasing prosperity of the estate and surrounding farms as life in Ireland returned to a semblance of normality. Before his afternoon sleep, Margarita told him the good stories from the estate, but each night he lost himself in the end of a bottle of brandy. It seemed to help him sleep. The family knew that his heart was in turmoil and his body was in pain. The saddest thing that Margarita felt for him was the shame she knew he carried at not knowing what to do to stop his excessive drinking. She often thought that maybe at the start of the famine she could have been tougher with him but sadly the love she had felt for him since she was young did not include the mental strength to call him out with harsh words. His father Isaac and mother had tried to pull him out of his despair with tougher love, but all they both got were worry lines etched in their concerned brows. Isaac now had a head of snow-white hair, which seemed to have happened almost overnight.

As she continued to sit in the garden, she reflected on her determination to make her marriage work when she had returned from America. Sadly, the hard work in getting a family through the end of the famine had left her with too little energy to save the most precious man who had held her heart for so many years.

She was pulled out of her reverie by the voice of her beloved mother Eliza, walking towards her.

"You look pensive, lass, on such a lovely morning," said Eliza with a concerned look on her face.

"I'm grand, Mama. I just got caught up thinking of too many things."

"It's about Victor, of course, isn't it, love? You know the doctor is doing all he can but there's little that you can do now. Victor has to take responsibility for his own drinking. Mind you, I agree with Doctor Bauer in Vienna when he says it's a disease. If that's true then Victor can't be blamed and there's little you can do but be there for him."

⚜

As December approached with no improvement in her husband's health, Margarita reflected that it had been nearly eight years since there was joy in the estate over the Christmas holiday time. This year was no different. Her husband now seemed to get more warmth from the earthenware hot jars that Jenny kept replacing than from the warmth of her body close to him. On many nights, it did not even seem to register with him that she was lying close to him. The quiet tears she shed on those occasions brought her near to despair.

For the sake of the twins, the family put a big fir tree in the hallway, as they had done every year since Deborah had married Isaac.

The lighting of the candles on Christmas Eve was a family tradition, and the children screeched with joy as they opened their presents that were laid out under the tree. As the family sat down to dinner on Christmas Day, plates full of meats and vegetables, topped off with rich gravy, were enjoyed and appreciated by everyone at the table. It had been many years since such an extravagance had been seen in the Big House.

Yet it was far from a joyous day as Victor's declining health kept him in his bedroom. The children visited him for a short while on Christmas morning, but even the twins seem to have sensed the pall of sadness surrounding their father and they seemed subdued as they climbed onto his bed to kiss him.

As the sun set on a difficult Christmas Day for the Beconsford family, it was a solemn group that sat in the drawing room late into the night. The atmosphere was muted, there was no singing but thankfully the happy, exhausted twins' exuberance, as they played with their new toys, had kept everyone's spirits up during the festive day.

On the following day, the feast of St. Stephen, Victor seemed to take a turn for the worse so they called Doctor Lewis.

They sat in the drawing room while the doctor examined him. Margarita was sitting with her parents, their arms around her protectively. Isaac and Deborah sat opposite, comforting each other. There was the silence of unshed tears surrounding the room, broken only by the knock on the door before Doctor Lewis entered.

They all looked towards him. They were tense and fearful as they waited for him to speak. Having sat down close to Margarita, the doctor broke the silence.

"My, lady, I wonder if you would like to join me?" he asked. "I would like to speak to you alone and then I will return and explain to the rest of your family. Victor is resting but he wants you by his side."

Margarita smiled hopefully as she addressed Doctor Lewis.

"That's a good sign, isn't it?" she asked with hope rising within her.

"I'll let you know about his health when we get to his dressing room."

Margarita walked slowly beside the doctor. They climbed the staircase. Thoughts were swirling around in her head. She prayed to God and promised that she would never again be harsh with her husband, or do anything wrong in her life, if He saved him. She continued to pray in her head. *Please, please save him! His children all need him. I need him. Please keep him alive!*

Doctor Lewis gently helped her into a chair in the small dressing room and sat opposite her. He began to speak.

"Victor was always a very strong man, but the famine seems to have sapped all his energy. As you know he began seriously drinking again even before he went abroad. Doctor Bauer in Vienna wrote and said that his nervous system is compromised so he hasn't the mind or energy to fight his demons with the alcohol. I promised him, before he went into a deep sleep that you would sit with him while he slept. Just keep talking to him. He told me that he loves to hear the sound of your voice and the touch of your hand when you hold his."

Margarita kept her eyes closed all the while the doctor spoke. Please help me not to cry, she begged as she endeavoured to stop the tears flowing. I must stay strong for him. She nodded her head and stood up to follow the doctor into the darkened room, lit only by gentle candlelight.

Our bedroom always had a warm feel to it but it feels cold in here tonight, she thought, or is it just me? She wrapped her warm shawl around her shoulders and sat by her husband's bed. He was sleeping, his breathing soft and low. She took his cool hand in both of hers as she bent over and gently kissed his warm, damp forehead.

Doctor Lewis discreetly left the room.

"I know you can't hear me but I need to tell you how much I've always loved you," Margarita said. "Lately, I've had too much time to think. Yet, since you got sick, my world has shrunk inside my head. I don't think about wars around the world, of local news or gossip. I'm full of thoughts of you suffering so long alone and how cruel fate can be. There is no laughter in my head and I find it difficult to be a good mother to our beautiful children because I'm afraid they will see the worry in my eyes. I cannot feel joy in music which was a comfort to me in the past. I feel a weight in my heart all the time. It is sorrow. Sorrow that I gave up on you when you took Rosita to England. I did not see beyond that moment. During that time all I felt was anger with you for everything that you had done wrong. I forgot the beautiful boy that I adored since my childhood and I forgot the lovely man who fought his demons to come back to me and make me the happiest girl in Ireland when he married me. The wonder of having the twins and Rosita in my life sealed my happiness forever. I forgot all that too when I

AFTER THE DARKNESS   215

left you to fend for yourself when we went to America. All I now want is for you to get better and try to forgive me."

Margarita could not now stop her tears flowing. She squeezed his hand and got no response. She sat looking at him, hunger for his voice making her heart feel like it was breaking in her chest. As the quietness mingled with Victor's slow breathing, Margarita's head fell beside his and, when her eyes closed, she fell into a deep sleep that only exhaustion brings.

Margarita jerked her head upwards as a knock on the door sounded. The door opened just a little as if someone was peeping in. Then it opened to reveal Hilda Bowe, who had proved in all ways to be a great replacement for Jean. Hilda then retreated and came in bearing a tray with tea and hot buttered toast. She placed the tray on the table by the window and poured some tea.

"You need to take a cup of tea, love, and something to eat. You must try and keep your strength up," she said quietly.

A shaft of morning light sent a ray of early sunshine across Victor's face, as Margarita wearily sat upright in the chair. As she took Victor's cool hand, she said a prayer of thanks that he was still with her and hoped that the light in the room was a sign of hope.

Hilda brought her a cup of tea. She drank some tea and, with Hilda's encouragement, began to eat the toast, though it felt like cardboard in her dry mouth. I have to keep my strength up, she thought, for the children and for Victor. Yet I feel that all I want to do is to curl up in a ball and shut the whole world out until the pain in my heart goes away. A picture suddenly jumped into her head and she saw herself and Victor, smiling and laughing as they walked out of the Secret Garden and watched their three happy children playing and having fun. Why did that wretched famine come to Ireland? She knew that it tore so many families to shreds with deaths, disease, emigration and the dreaded workhouse. Is it also going to take my heart and soul?

She was interrupted in her thoughts as Doctor Lewis asked if she would go and rest as he wanted to examine Victor. She kissed Victor's forehead and reluctantly acquiesced as Hilda took her by the hand and led her through the doorway.

"Margarita, it's still very early but your parents are already in the drawing room having breakfast. Would you like to join them or would you prefer to go for a rest?"

Margarita thought for a moment before answering.

"Tell them that I will join them. Perhaps you could be on hand if Rosita wakes and bring her down to join us for breakfast? Tell Florrie to keep the twins in the nursery and I'll go to them later. I know I've been neglecting them but I must stay strong for Victor for now and when he's stronger I'll be a better mother again."

Hilda looked sadly at her, thinking that Margarita was fooling herself about his ability to turn his life around. She left her with Eliza and Jack, who both looked as drained and tired as their daughter, sad for all those good people who hadn't done anything to deserve having to go through such pain.

"You look tired, Mama," Margarita said, as she kissed them both before sitting down beside them.

"We're not who matter at the moment, love, just you and Victor," Jack said, feeling despair at the way their only child's life was so cruelly in the balance. He couldn't get his head around the possibility that his beautiful, talented daughter could be widowed in her thirties. He also had to deal with the fact that his wife Eliza was trying to stay stoic for everyone's sake, especially the exuberant twins who now spent most afternoons in their home, with Eliza trying to keep a semblance of normality in their lives. The Big House was such a silent place at present, with Isaac and Deborah too traumatised with worry to either work or care what went on around them.

Jack could only imagine the pain they felt at the thought of losing their only child.

Another night began, followed by a weary day where Victor had moved from restless sleep to agitated wakefulness, when he made no sense to anyone. Only Margarita's hand holding his seemed to ease the aggravation he felt in his body.

It was late on a bitterly cold evening, just three days after celebrating Christmas, that Doctor Lewis summoned all the family together.

"I would like you all to come to the bedroom together. I have administered a high dose of laudanum to ease Victor's torment. He is now resting peacefully but you all need to be with him."

A stunned silence descended on the room, broken only when Margarita jerked to her feet.

"I want Rosita with us. She was his firstborn and he lived for her safety always. She knows how ill he has been. Could someone get her and bring her here to me before I go in? You go on ahead and I will follow."

Hilda, as always in these trying times, was hovering close by. When Jack left the room, he asked her to fetch Rosita.

Margarita needed the time alone to try to make sense of her thoughts. There were intense feelings of sadness at the possibility of never again talking, laughing or just holding her first love, as she recalled her childish feelings when she first heard that Victor was to marry his wife, Fleur. Her Great-granny Sheila had said to her that what didn't kill you made you stronger, but she hoped on this night that nobody spoke comforting platitudes, because tonight was different to then. She knew that after this hour she might never again see the shining light in the eyes of her beloved husband. How could she face it?

The door opened and Hilda walked in, her comforting arm around the tall, beautiful Rosita who seemed throughout her short life to have had wisdom beyond her years. The young girl walked quickly to embrace her beloved mama. They clung to each other before Margarita guided her stepdaughter to sit close to her on the chaise longue. As she placed a protective arm around the girl, they remained silent until Margarita squeezed her arm, before speaking quietly.

"You know how much we all love your father and how he has been suffering for a long time. Soon he's going to leave us and he'll never feel pain again. You know he always wanted only to keep his family safe. Sometimes his judgment was wrong but never forget how much he loved us all. Before we go in to be at his side, I'd like us both to remember some of the good things we did together. If he's awake when we get in to see him, you could remind him of these times?" Margarita held Rosita even closer as she began to speak.

"Do you remember the first day that we all went down to Letty's father's farm and I was allowed to climb the tree with Papa? I recall your smile as I waved to you from a sturdy tree branch and then how nimbly I came back down. Papa was so happy that he swung me around and around with the two of us laughing until we both fell down onto the grass, as you and the twins continued to laugh. The twins wanted the same and Papa swung them around too. You had brought a picnic, Mama, and we all sat under the tree eating it. I don't remember what we ate but I recall the twins running all around with Papa chasing them." Rosita nodded her head and smiled as the memory of that day came back to her.

"Keep those thoughts about your papa in your head and let them be your memories of your life with him. Let us go and be with him and always remember that everyone in this house loves you and loves your papa. That love will always be there."

Margarita entered the quiet bedroom clutching Rosita's hand. She could smell a whiff of laudanum as she watched the agony on the faces of Victor's parents. She moved quietly to where Jean had placed a chair at each side of Victor's bed, close to where his thin parchment-like hands lay on the bed cover. Margarita and Rosita sat on either side. They each took a hand, but Margarita felt no response as she gently squeezed his hand in both of hers. She looked as Rosita stroked his hair as quiet tears ran down her cheeks.

Isaac sat motionless beside the bed with his arm protectively around Deborah, their heads down to hide their grief. No one spoke as a clock in the distance chimed midnight.

As the slow, uneven breathing of Victor pierced the cold night air, it was followed by a truly deathly silence. Victor Beconsford had breathed his last. It was four o'clock in the morning of the 29th of December, 1851, just four days after the twins had enjoyed showing their Christmas toys to their papa. Now he was gone. Yet the silence continued, nobody prepared to admit the inevitable loss of a man, so young, until his first-born child bent over his now still body and kissed his cheek.

"Good bye, Papa." Her words, spoken so gently, were so wise for her years. "You were all so lucky to know him so much longer than me, but I promise you all that I will keep his memory alive for as long as I live."

Margarita kissed his cheek, terrified that at any minute she would start wailing and never stop. "Rosita, you and I will leave for a while so that your grandma and grandpapa can say their own goodbyes to their boy. But first I will say a prayer that your papa will find peace." She knew exactly the right prayer to say.

"Oh, heavenly one, our eyes are sad, we plead for your forgiveness
You see the beauty that lived in his heart, his frailty as human weakness,
Please wrap your cloak of love and warmth and keep him in your arms
And help us accept that he has gone, to freedom from pain and harm."

Margarita tried to hold her composure as she left the room with Rosita but, as she ascended the stairs with her daughter, she heard the agonising sound of Deborah's plaintive crying, coming from the room they had just left. It would be a long time before that sound would leave Margarita's memory.

For everyone in the Big House, the week that followed was so traumatic that they hoped this kind of pain would never envelop them again. The loss of an only child left everyone in the county who knew the family in complete shock. The future Lord Beconsford would now be young Louis, who sadly wasn't even old enough to mourn his father nor attend his funeral service.

The funeral of Victor Beconsford brought hundreds of mourners to the estate church. Isaac had opened the grounds to everyone from the village to allow them pay their respects also. During the church service Richard sang, as Master Johnson played the organ. When the funeral cortege finally left the church, the schoolchildren and their parents lined the gravel path, while the coffin was carried to the graveyard beyond.

As Victor Beconsford was finally laid to rest by the side of his first wife Fleur, his wife Margarita and his eldest daughter Rosita were the first to place red roses on the coffin. As the rest of the family followed suit, the sound of Rosita crying in her grief brought tears to the eyes of the watching congregation.

Later the guests joined the family in the house. Unfortunately, this day lacked the usual celebration of a long life fully lived. Victor Beconsford had died too soon and had left a bereft family in mourning that would last for a long time.

The loss of Victor as a husband, a father and a son, took its toll on all the grieving family. It hit people in so many different ways. The twins bounced back in no time what with the love and attention they received from everyone. Rosita was different. She held on to her suffering in silence. Margarita just felt guilty. Guilt, especially for not being there for her husband throughout their marriage. No matter who told her that she was not to blame, the feeling that she could have done more for him stayed with her for a long time.

In Eoinstown, they too mourned his loss and Alice racked her brain to know how she could help Margarita, but Richard and Meg kept telling her that only time would heal Margarita's suffering.

"You can't take everyone's burden on your shoulders, like you tried to do during the famine," said Richard, knowing that Alice had come close to cracking under the strain of everything when the famine had continued into its fifth year.

"You have enough to do now with the children and Sylvia's grass-plot committee to keep you occupied. Let Margarita's two families help her, love. You can be there again for her when she's ready to heal."

Alice nodded in agreement. "You're right, as always saving me from myself!" she said wryly. "We have a committee meeting in the morning and I'll forget about sorrow and think about how Sylvia's gift to the townland is making people smile again."

The following morning, Alice, Úna, Mary and her daughter Fiona, joined the land agent and the lawyer, Mr. Robson, in the agent's house on the Stewart estate.

Alice, as chairperson, spoke on behalf of the group. "The famine now seems like a bad dream to most of us in these parts because I know that many small farmers around Eoinstown now have more resources and are all supporting each other. They share men, horses and equipment when harvesting, sheep-shearing and when someone is ill. The Stewart land is rich and harvests are good. All of us on the grass-plot committee are really excited at the enjoyment the locals are getting out of their small piece of land with only a peppercorn rent. As I thought would happen, some have even built sheds to house tools and chairs to sit on when the sun shines. Others are growing vegetables and most of the children who spent time up there with their mothers or fathers are planting small flower beds. Some are even selling their produce at the Saturday market in Ballydehob. We send news about all the people regularly to Sylvia and I know that it warms her heart. Also, and this is private to this group, we located the young girl who was cruelly raped by Toby Ramsay. She has a beautiful young son and neither will experience poverty again, thanks to Sylvia. It's funny that out of the evil perpetrated by Toby Ramsay, such good has come. Maybe the death of Nelly and her baby was not after all in vain. Plus, there's good news about Jamie. Her husband was not hanged but was transported to Australia. Word has come back that he has a good farm boss and in ten years, with good behaviour, he might be a free man. Some of the farm bosses in Australia were not impressed that the bailiffs were sent in during a famine, especially with Nelly's baby due. Maybe someday he'll return to Eoinstown, although I doubt it."

When the meeting ended, Mr. Robson thanked them for their diligence. After the two men left, the women went into the local inn where tasty meat pies were available and they enjoyed one of their regular outings, without a worry or care about children or work.

The famine was over and, for now, Alice was determined to have some fun and enjoy herself and not worry anymore about the future. Her children were growing up and her husband was getting paid again for singing.

Chapter Twenty-Eight

It was now over two years since the death of Victor and Margarita was slowly beginning to come out of the lethargy she had felt since his death. Hilda was always by her side as, sadly, her husband who always had poor health succumbed to a fever. The doctor said that neither his heart nor lungs were strong enough to fight it. Hilda had now moved full-time into Beconsford House and both Esme and Lizzy lived in also. Florrie had finally married Patrick and she now lived with his mother in Rosslare where Patrick was still saving to buy his own boat.

━━━ 〜 ━━━

As Margarita sat having a leisurely breakfast, the post arrived, just in time for her to enjoy it with her hot cup of tea. She was delighted to see Alice's writing on the envelope. When she opened it, she glanced quickly through it before reading it properly and her eyes came upon the name Laurence Flaherty. It was a shock and she had to put the letter down for a moment to calm her shaking hands. When she had composed herself, she read it very carefully.

My dearest Margarita,

I hope you are feeling good and that you are getting out and about, with the arrival of summer. I envy you the Secret Garden at this time of year. Sometimes I close my eyes and picture the roses blooming in the sunshine. I can almost smell the perfume and hear the gentle sound of water from the fountains. I'm hoping to experience it for a few days next month and now I'll explain why that might happen.

    Mam and Grace have been at me for quite a while to take a long holiday, now that there is little to stop me. They want me to go with Richard when he goes to sing in London. However, that is only the half of it because Richard also wants us to go to Verona in Italy! There is a reason for that and I think it might interest you and get you out of Midleton, now that your children are also more self-sufficient. I'm sure Isaac and Deborah or Eliza and Jack would love to have the twins staying with them.

    You will remember the man in New York that you helped with his singing, Laurence Flaherty? Well, Richard met him in Paris last year and they now communicate regularly. Recently, he wrote to Richard to tell him of his excitement at being given the opportunity to sing inside the walls of the famous Arena in Verona. He mentioned in his letter that you once joked with him that he would play in the opera houses in Europe. I don't know if you remember saying that to him. Then he went on to invite myself and Richard to join him at his expense when he is in Verona. But didn't he also go on to extend an invitation to yourself and Rosita, if you wanted to join the party! Margarita, I don't want to accept until I get an answer from you. However, I strongly warn you that I will be deeply unhappy if you do not agree to go to Verona. Surely you would love to see and hear some wonderful opera performances again? This is a chance in a lifetime for me and after the famine and everything that's gone on in both our lives, I think you and I deserve a holiday without children crawling all over us and looking for attention.

    I felt almost like jumping into a carriage and going up to you because I feel you'll need some persuading, but I don't have the time at the moment as I'm getting ready to go to Europe!

    With love to everyone in Midleton,

    Your loving young aunt,

    Alice

Although she had a knot in her stomach reading the letter, she had
to smile at Alice's exuberance. She realised that nobody but herself and
Laurence knew of the closeness that they had experienced in New York.
She heard how much he was achieving only when Sylvia wrote. Also, when
Victor died, Laurence sent a formal card with his deepest condolences.

A week later, Margarita sat alone in the front parlour. She still had
conflicting feelings about whether or not she should accept the invitation
to Verona. She did not mention it to anyone for a few days but when she
mentioned it to Deborah, she was kissed and hugged by her.

"Go, go, go, Margarita! Rosita would love it and you both need and
deserve it. The twins will be fine with all their grannies and granddads. It's
a chance for you to listen to music that you love. Maybe it will give you the
motivation to start singing once again. You know that we don't want you
mourning Victor forever. You deserve a second chance at life. Take it."

Yet here she was now with no clear thoughts in her head as to where her
life was going. Years ago, she would have walked over to her Great-granny
Sheila's cottage and sat with her and sang to her and in return would have
received enough wisdom to keep her going until her next visit. She made
a decision to walk to the village and visit the now semi-retired Master
Johnson, her teacher and friend.

Arriving at the cottage, she was met with a wide smile as Mrs. Johnson
opened the door.

"Well, this is a sight for sore eyes," she said. "My husband, as always, is
sitting in the music room. He still loves to be surrounded by his piano and
his memories. Go and join him and I'll bring in some refreshments for you
both."

"Could you please join us, Mrs. Johnson?" Margarita asked. "I'm
looking for advice and a female listener may help."

"Of course, I will, I'd love that," she answered, intrigued as to why the young lady of the manor would be asking for her advice.

When they had finished eating a delicious plate of cream pastries and drunk coffee, Mrs. Johnson asked Margarita how they could help.

Margarita hesitated before answering. "I'm not really sure myself but I know that if I spoke to my mother or father they would, as usual, start worrying about me and wanting to fix the problem. I'd just like to share my thoughts with you. I've known you for most of my life and I always loved coming here even if it wasn't for singing lessons." She paused before continuing, "I feel that I've come to a crossroads in my life. Anyone looking at my life would probably think I'm being selfish but, since my beloved husband died, I've been living in a world in which everyone has tried to keep me safe and free from any more distress. I don't seem to know anymore how to manage my own life in a way that gives me a future. The problem I have is that I've got an invitation from Alice to join her and Richard to see some opera abroad, including watching the man I helped when I was in New York, Laurence Flaherty. He is singing in the Verona arena. You remember I told you about him. They have also invited Rosita. I just can't seem to make up my mind as to whether or not I should go."

As Margarita paused again, Mrs. Johnson said, "Margarita, myself and my husband have always felt that you were the daughter we never had. Every time things went well for you it made us very happy. Now with everything you have been through during and after the famine and the death of your beloved Victor, we have, like your family, felt deeply for you and I am grateful that you thought of coming to us now."

Margarita smiled gratefully at Mrs. Johnson.

"I know what my husband would say and I agree with him," Mrs. Johnson continued. "That you should begin to sing again. However, only you can decide how you approach that. For now, you need to experience the world of music at its best and you can do that by going on this trip. You know that you still have the talent to become an international opera star, but would you want all the effort or commitment that achieving that requires? Go on this trip and see if your love of music is still in your heart. Maybe then you could consider how much joy your singing would give to people, with recitals, or just for charitable events. Everyone knows what wonderful concerts you gave in New York during the famine."

Margarita nodded as Master Johnson smiled at his wife.

"My dearest, I couldn't have put it any better myself and I agree with all your sentiments," he said. "Margarita, you are too good a singer to spend your life teaching others, like I have done. You are still a young woman and the training you have given has kept your own voice in shape. Think about what my wife said and, when you go home, do a little exercise that I give to students who are at a crossroads in deciding if singing or a different career is what they want in life. Sit, alone, in that beautiful Secret Garden of yours and try this exercise. I still do it when I can't make up my mind about something. So, ask yourself three questions on all the options open to you in relation to Verona. Firstly, ask what is the worst outcome, then ask yourself what would be wonderful if you decided to go and finally ask what it needs from you if you decide to go, or stay at home. Just listen to your heart and follow what it tells you. I first did that exercise when I was young and I discovered that my life was more fulfilled in handing on my musical knowledge to others and I have never regretted my choice. Finding a singer such as yourself was one of the highlights of my career, Margarita, but it included years of satisfaction also from just passing on a skill to the next generation. So, whatever choice you make will not guarantee that you won't meet obstacles, but you've lived through many of these in your life and have come out the other side."

Margarita had tears in her eyes as she told them, "I had been thinking of the loss of Great-granny Sheila, because she always gave me such good advice and a listening ear. Now I know I have a replacement for her. Thank you both."

As she took her leave of her friends, they hugged each other in turn. It felt emotional for all three and no more words were needed.

Margarita took the Johnsons' advice and took time before coming to some tentative decisions about her future. Having received the emphatic seal of approval both from her parents and the Beconsfords, she sat down, put pen to paper and wrote to her young Aunt Alice in West Cork.

Alice was already making preparations for her trip around Europe. Each night she said a silent prayer that Margarita would have the courage to get back out into the world. Almost two weeks passed before the letter arrived.

My dearest Alice,

Of course I remember Laurence Flaherty. He had a wonderful voice. I have spent the last while wondering how to reply to your invitation to join you on your holiday in Verona. I have made a decision. Myself and Rosita will travel with you, on one condition. I want you to stay with us for a few days in Midleton before we travel, because I've decided that I need a manager to tell me what to take in my luggage!

I cannot contain Rosita's excitement at the moment, so with the twins surrounded by family and staff here in Midleton I think I can safely leave them while I am away.

I feel sure you will also make all the necessary travel arrangements for us and you will be reimbursed on arrival in Midleton. I'm quite looking forward to having a manager looking after me again!

Our love to all in Eoinstown,

Your loving niece,

Margarita

Alice had tears of laughter on her face as she reread the letter to the family at the breakfast table before lifting it in the air and dancing around the table singing tunelessly, "*I'm off on my holidays with my niece Margarita!*"

Her growing son Gregory got red with embarrassment, while Emily joined her mother and they both continued to dance around the table.

The excitement in the house didn't die down until the day arrived when Alice and Richard left on their trip to Europe. As they climbed into the carriage, having hugged the children and promising presents from Italy if they behaved for their grandmothers, Alice had a moment of worry.

"Have we done the right thing leaving them for over a month, Richard?"

He laughed as he put his arm around his wife. "Well, it's a bit late to think of that, now that we're in the carriage. I leave them almost every week and like me you have to trust that they will be fine until we return. You, more than anyone I know, deserve this holiday. Enjoy it because I certainly will."

Alice was often amazed that Richard could so quickly switch his thoughts to what lay ahead and didn't worry needlessly about things that might happen to everyone while he was away. Maybe it's a man thing and their brains work differently, she thought. After all, she reasoned, since the world began men have risked their lives out hunting while their wives took care of the children. She had always found it harder to switch off her brain and get to sleep if the children had even a cough or a sniffle, while Richard slept peacefully beside her each night.

The carriage ride was very comfortable but Richard took her out of her reverie as they went through Macroom. He reminded her that Laurence Flaherty's parents came from there. As she looked out the window at the busy street with shoppers carrying their loaded bags and shops with windows full of enticing goods, she remembered how grateful these locals had been when they had brought the proceeds of the famine fund-raiser in New York to the town. As they passed through the main street, she made a decision: I'm just going to relax and enjoy this trip and maybe I'll learn not to worry so much about everything and everyone.

Rosita loved to call Alice "grandaunt", just for fun and as she pleaded for extra luggage space Alice said, "I'll give you another square foot of space in my bag if you promise to address me as Alice from now on."

Everyone was in good humour as they waited for Rosita to reply.

"Alright, Grandaunt Alice, I will never call you grandaunt again," said Rosita, grinning as she heaped more clothes into the already overcrowded trunk.

At the end of July, during a summer spell of glorious sunshine, the intrepid group left Midleton for England. Having enjoyed the hospitality of Margarita's relatives in Hertfordshire, two carriages of relatives joined them to listen to Richard sing in concert in the splendid surroundings of the Royal Opera house in Covent Garden. They all enjoyed the experience hugely, especially listening to Richard's warm and graceful tenor voice soar. Margarita thought that his voice had matured beautifully and that he had a long career ahead of him.

The prolonged warm and sunny weather continued into August as the happy travellers finally left England and sailed to Calais and the start of their journey to Verona.

Chapter Twenty-Nine

The large imposing palazzo in Verona, arranged and paid for by Laurence was, when inside, a cool refuge from the heat of the sun. It was situated opposite the Arena. The imposing rooms on the ground floor led to a secluded garden filled with palm trees, with cool wrought-iron chairs placed in the shade. The vista from the bedrooms upstairs had views as far as the city skyline. The River Adige could be seen in the distance meandering under the iconic Ponte Pietra bridge.

The travellers from Ireland delighted in the luxury they would enjoy for the next few days. Laurence was staying with the other performers and he left a message to say that he would meet them in their hotel once he had finished his performance. The tourists spent the afternoon walking through the labyrinth of narrow streets. The following day, they went sightseeing where they admired the opulent interior of the Basilica di San Zeno and the wonderful Piazza   delle Erbe with its magnificent fountain and ancient town hall the Torre dei Lamberti, before returning for early dinner to ensure they would be well on time for the performance.

Margarita entered the arena with Alice and Richard and a star-struck Rosita. The setting evening sun cast welcoming shadows on the immense stage. Elegant ladies walked beside their handsome Italian men. Margarita had never seen so much glamour in one place. As she looked around in awe at the circular walls, she dropped her head, giving thanks to whoever created this place that was now opening up its doors to opera music for all to enjoy.

"We're sitting very close to the stage. I can't wait to hear Uncle Laurence," Rosita whispered to her mother, with wonder in her voice. That's the first time she's called him "uncle" since America, Margarita thought. It could need a bit of explaining if she said it in front of Alice and Richard. Margarita had conflicted thoughts about the evening. It was a strange feeling inside, almost like not feeling, or was she suppressing fear because she had to confront some of her past? Numbness, she thought. That's what I feel.

Alice's delight showed as she looked around her.

"This is all happening thanks to my wonderful husband who knows so many great singers. Even Napoleon Bonaparte didn't have such good seats when he came to the Arena!" Alice, smiling, moved to kiss her husband's cheek. "I thank you, kind sir!" She smiled as she endeavoured to bob him a deep curtsey.

Nothing was going to diminish Alice's exuberance tonight, thought Margarita. I wish I could be a little like her and just enjoy the moment.

"I cannot wait for the performers, especially Laurence," Alice went on, "but I'm so excited to be here just to see the Arena."

Margarita needed no reminding that Laurence was going to sing, because she could think of little else.

As they sat on their cushioned seats, Richard handed them sheets with the participants for the evening. The orchestra pit was already beginning to fill up, with around one hundred musicians warming up their respective instruments. For Margarita, the names of most of the Italian singers were unknown to her but in their midst her eyes were glued to the name of Laurence Flaherty. Her stomach slowly began to tingle with anticipation at the opportunity to once again enjoy the melodic sounds of his voice.

As the conductor took the baton and signalled to the musicians to begin, Margarita was transfixed by their overture. It had hardly begun before her skin began to tingle with expectation. After the applause ended for the orchestra, the audience was in awe as a choir of over one hundred walked onto the stage. Their soaring harmonious voices singing Nabucco's *"Va Pensiero"* entranced the Arena and afterwards the audience called for an encore. As they again sang the chorus, the Arena filled with the flicker of candlelight, offered up to the sky by the grateful listeners. As the moon rose in the darkening sky, tears of joy glistened in the eyes of the audience. As the aria ended, with shouts of '*Bravo! Bravo!*' the feast of music continued. Tenors, sopranos and baritones walked on and off the stage, all to tumultuous applause. Margarita shed tears when she heard Bellini's *"Casta Diva"* from the opera *Norma*. She recalled the awful night of the big wind when her Granny Molly nearly died and old John the herb man passed away. She had sung that song to them, as estate workers strove to save them both from death. She was still reminiscing when she heard his name being called and the smiling handsome man that had captured her confused heart in New York came onstage.

Margarita's body returned to a state of numbness as she watched the handsome singer raise his voice effortlessly and smile often. This was something she had witnessed rarely when in New York. He looked like a new man whose fame had raised his stature as well as his profile around the world. As he finished, the applause was deafening from the mainly Italian audience, who rarely appreciated American singers. Yet they seem to have taken Laurence to their hearts.

When the performance ended and the people exited the Arena, the Irish party all had smiles on their faces with the memory of the music still making their hearts beat faster.

As they walked slowly across the large square outside the Arena, Rosita was jumping up and down with excitement.

"That was brilliant, Mama, but I think that you are a better singer than most of the sopranos!"

They all laughed at her exuberance as Richard asked, "Am I better than Laurence Flaherty?"

"Well, Uncle Richard, I think maybe you're equally good," she answered diplomatically.

They were all in good humour as they entered the hotel, where they were escorted to a parlour with a round table set for the party of five. The large glass door at the back of the cosy room was an exit to the garden. Margarita loved her seat, facing the garden. She knew that she would be sitting with Laurence and did not know what to think or do when he arrived.

As Richard poured drinks for everyone, Laurence entered the room. Everyone clapped and Rosita ran up to him and gave him a big hug.

"Uncle Laurence, you were wonderful tonight and I still have the muffs you gave me in New York, but it was too hot to bring them here!" She grinned as he stood back and looked at her.

"Is this beautiful young woman the girl that used to steal the twins' sweets from my pocket even before I took them out?"

Rosita grinned. "Sorry, Uncle Laurence, I remember that, but I thought you hadn't seen me!" As they continued to joke with each other, Alice gave Richard a knowing look and they both raised their eyebrows.

Margarita looked a little flustered. To hide her embarrassment, she walked over to Laurence, smiling.

"I'm so proud of you. Your voice was magical tonight and you obviously now have a world reputation. Do I now have to bow to you?"

Laurence laughed as he replied. "Definitely not, my lady, but can I give you an Italian welcome by kissing you on both cheeks?"

She smiled as he held her shoulders and planted an elaborate kiss on each cheek.

"Do I get one?" said Alice, walking over with hands outstretched. "I'm her Auntie Alice."

"I am so delighted to meet you. I have heard so much about you, firstly from Margarita and later in Richard's letters. I believe you are a very special lady. Of course I'll give you an Italian welcome!"

"Not too much of a welcome – she is my wife!" Richard jested.

By the time they all sat down to eat their meal, it felt like they had all known Laurence for ever. Alice was glad to see that Laurence had no pretensions. Of course, he wouldn't, she thought – his Irish parents would keep him grounded. She also wondered about the familiarity between Laurence and Margarita. I must ask Sylvia about it when I next write, she decided.

It was very late when the meal ended and coffee had been served.

Rosita was the first to express her desire to retire. As she did Alice pushed gently against her husband's leg and said, "I think we will retire also. You two have a lot of catching up to do. Why don't you have a last drink together as our time in Italy is nearly at an end?" She rose and almost dragged her husband out of the room, as earlier he had looked as if he'd stay talking all night.

"There's definitely something going on between these two," she whispered, after they saw Rosita to her room and went towards their own bedroom.

Richard nodded sagely.

"Wouldn't it be grand if there was?"

As they closed the bedroom door, they both let their imaginations run riot as they collapsed laughing onto the bed.

"I knew you could do everything, Mrs. Staunton, but I never put you down as a matchmaker!"

As Margarita and Laurence sat in the dining room, the concierge made sure a fire was glowing brightly. Italian stone houses, with their shutters keeping out the summer heat, had a chill in the late evening. They sat close to each other in the warmth and cosiness of the room. Feeling replete after the delicious food, Laurence poured a brandy for himself and a sherry for Margarita. As he sipped slowly, he could feel the warm glow reaching his throat and his body relaxed. He leaned over and gently kissed her cheek. She wanted to respond but instead put up her hand to stop the intimacy. He watched as she moved away from him, but still decided to take the plunge.

"Would you come and sit for a while in the garden?" he asked. "It is only at night that you can enjoy the magnificent perfume of the flowers in Italy, especially the gardenia."

As Margarita nodded, glad of the diversion, Laurence removed his jacket and draped it over her shoulders.

"It's sometimes cool at this time," he said, just trying to make conversation.

As they entered the garden, Margarita breathed in the mix of perfumes rising into the soft night air.

"I agree with you – the scent is more beautiful than can ever be created in a factory. I will remember it because my father Jack loves to hear about anything to do with gardens."

"Shall we sit for a while and drink in the atmosphere?"

"Yes, let's do that."

They sat down on a seat for two people.

Margarita didn't know what to think, as his closeness made her cheeks burn as she tried to deal with the feeling being with him brought. She found herself blustering a little.

"When I decided to go to Verona, I was so excited that I wrote a little poem about this special place of which I knew so much but had never seen. Would you like to hear it, Laurence?"

"Of course I would. Anything that keeps me here talking to you is fine by me," he jested.

Margarita took a slightly crumpled piece of paper out of her pocket and said, "It's called 'The Arena':

Its circular walls hold sounds from the past
Voices that lift everyone towards the heavens,
Flickering candles glow to toast the sweet sounds of music,
Each person touched by the stillness of beating hearts,
The silence broken only by tumultuous applause
And the chanting of 'Bravo! Bravo!'
Sing on, Verona, you are still young!"

Laurence gently touched her hand as she finished. "Now I know you can do more than just sing. It is a lovely tribute to a beautiful place. I, too, never thought I would be here. Being with you makes it so much more special."

Margarita was beginning to feel embarrassed by his words, not knowing how to answer.

"I won't stay out too long as Rosita might worry if she doesn't hear me going into my bedroom," she said, knowing that she was shying away from any possible intimacy.

"Margarita, do you mind if a ask you a question?"

"Of course I don't," she said.

"I'm going to ask you a question and I want you to answer, but I need you to answer only with your heart."

"Don't keep me in suspense, Laurence," she said nervously.

"This question I'm going to ask you, I will ask only once and if you say no, I will fully understand."

"What is it, Laurence?" Her voice betrayed her tension.

"Will you marry me, Margarita?"

Margarita's heart leapt in shock. She hesitated for a long time before answering. She knew the answer she had to give him. In her heart she realised that she was far too fragile to marry this talented man. She would hold him back because her heart still felt like a heavy stone that only she could handle at this moment. As the sound of silence sat heavily in the night air, she answered.

"I'm sorry, Laurence. I'm still recovering from the manner of Victor's death. I believe that I let him down in his hour of need and I can't trust myself to love anyone at the moment. I don't know if I ever will."

Laurence reached out and took her hand as he saw the sadness in her eyes, just as he had felt in the past when Lisa passed away.

"I understand fully, Margarita. You know, when I was very young my parents always said that I was too driven and always wanted the best and always focused on getting it. I felt that I had to try again tonight, but this time I understand. From the moment I got the chance to perform here in Verona, I knew that the only person I wanted there was you. I'm deeply grateful that at least that part of the dream has come true. Do you remember telling me that you'd come and watch me in the opera houses of Europe? I didn't believe you at the time but being able to meet you here will have to be enough. Could I ask for one thing, just so that I have a real memory of tonight?"

"Yes," she whispered.

"Could I hold you for just a few moments?"

Margarita looked at the sadness in his eyes, moved closer to him and laid her head on his shoulder. He put his arm around her. She didn't stop him as he gently stroked her hair. They sat in silence, each savouring the moment of intimacy, which had been missing from both their lives for a long time. If only it could last just a little bit longer . . .

Chapter Thirty

The return trip from Verona to Midleton was surprisingly enjoyable for Margarita. Richard was excited because he had made contacts in Italy, thanks to Laurence. He was likely to receive invitations to sing, both in Milan and Florence. Alice enjoyed the holiday so much that she told Richard that they would bring the children with them to Europe in the future and Rosita said that she had definitely fallen in love with travel and would do it for all her life. Without any singing commitments, they stayed in Paris for a few days with Alice insisting on hiring a small private boat to tour the canals, as a memory of her trip in 1839, when she was the tour manager for Richard and Margarita.

When they returned to England, they again enjoyed the company of Lily and her family in Hertfordshire, before taking a train to Liverpool where they boarded the steamship back to Ireland.

Margarita found the fun and camaraderie of the group infectious, and it allowed her little time to think of what might have been with Laurence. When they finally arrived back in County Cork, the delight of Louis and Violet in Midleton and Gregory and Emily in Eoinstown made them all appreciate how lucky they were to have such wonderful children, who had all thankfully survived and even thrived while they were abroad.

When Margarita returned home from Italy, something had shifted inside her. She wanted to start looking forward, instead of backwards. Within weeks she had returned to teaching, but only for one day each week.

The death of Victor Beconsford had left such a deep void in the lives of three generations that it was hard for everyone to pick up the pieces, rebuild lives and feel hope for the future. They say that time heals and this is true for many but the sadness felt by Deborah and Isaac, having buried their only son, struck deeply into their very souls. Margarita had exhibited a stoicism that she did not feel inside, as her way of coping. With the help of Hilda Bowe, who now acted as Margarita's companion and friend, plus her own parents, she spent most of her time with Rosita and the twins. Now, having returned from Verona with her body relaxed and her soul replenished from the music she had experienced, she was again looking outward.

Louis, who would be the future of the estate, was being groomed for this job by Isaac, and his governess was preparing him for an academic life. He was a good child who accepted his future, but his mother hoped he wouldn't miss his family too much. Margarita knew that he would soon go to England to Eton College and she didn't have any fight left in her to try and keep him in Ireland. She was just grateful that Violet would still be tutored in the house and, like Rosita, could spent her childhood in a more normal environment.

Nonetheless, Rosita had her own views about her future. She made this clear when she made an announcement at breakfast one morning.

"I know that I can never be a doctor because men make that impossible, although I think it is outrageous," she said with scorn in her voice for the restrictions under which she, as a woman, had to spend her life. "However, I know from my Grand-aunt Lily in Hertfordshire that a lady called Florence Nightingale has been serving the troops who were injured in the Crimean war. I want to do what Miss Nightingale does even if I'm not allowed to be a doctor like any man can!"

There was a shocked silence in the room and Deborah was the first to break it.

"Young lady, I don't want any more of that ridiculous talk in this house. Do you hear me?" she said with fury in her voice. "I lost your father and I am not going to mourn your death on a battlefield during my lifetime!"

Isaac put a steadying hand on her arm as he asked Rosita, "Why not get more involved in the charities helping those who have been poor since the famine. You could do a lot of good here arranging fund-raising for these people. You could even take over the foundation that I created many years ago."

It was now time for Rosita to get angry. "Thank you, Grandfather, but no thanks. I don't want to spend a life beholding unto the county gents and ladies in the hope that they'll donate something that they don't even want, but do it only because you are my grandfather. I want to leave Ireland and see places that I've only heard about and I want to help people properly. I know how progressive the people in America are, having met them. I want to be beside people when they are sick or dying. I'm not afraid of hard work and being able to help injured soldiers who have offered their lives in wars would be an honour. I want a different life from the suffocating sadness of this house since Papa died. I want to make a difference to people who are not privileged. I really am fascinated by the work of Florence Nightingale and if I can go to England when I'm a little older, that is what I would love to do. Grandaunt Lily has already promised that she'll help me at least meet some of the nurses that follow Miss Nightingale."

Margarita was stunned by the ferocity of her daughter's outburst, but she admired her for having a vision of her future.

"Maybe you could take things a little slower for the moment, love," she said, placing a hand on her daughter's arm. "Perhaps we can find some people in Ireland who have an insight into this kind of work. If so, I'd be happy to support you in trying to learn a little about caring for the sick, before you make a leap into the dark in England. It will give us all a chance to get used to the idea that you may leave us to work abroad."

"Alright, Mama, I'll do that, but the only thing I don't want to do is to attend parties where there might be an eligible man who wants to marry me. I do not wish to get involved with any man and become his possession, even if he is a good person. As a woman I want to be my own person and if I ever marry it will be my own choice and in my own time."

Margarita had to hide a smile as she listened to her strong, independent stepdaughter. She recalled the girl who was abducted by her father and lived in fear in the depths of Devon, when she not only coped but almost took over the role of adult in a place where the only adult was incapable of making good decisions.

"Well, Rosita, I would like to be a fly on the wall when the first man asks for your hand in marriage!" Margarita said and it released the tension in the room, as Isaac and even Deborah both chuckled. "Let us now enjoy the rest of our breakfast and later maybe your grandmother and yourself can join me and we'll go down to my mother Eliza. She knows everyone and she always has a solution to problems."

As Margarita had promised, Eliza helped and supported her granddaughter.

"By the time she is eighteen, she will either have lost her enthusiasm for tending the sick or she will follow her dream," Eliza said to Margarita.

Eliza asked Doctor McNally in Cork city, who knew the Beconsford and Ryan families well, if Rosita could shadow him as he visited his patients. He agreed.

"But try to keep her away from any serious infectious diseases because you could have a murder to contend with if her other grandmother comes chasing after me, if Rosita picks up an illness!" Eliza said laughingly.

"She can shadow me for three days each week, to start. She will have to learn how to roll bandages and dress small wounds at the start. As she watches me doing my work, I will soon know if the sight of blood turns her away from helping the sick. If she's alright with that, I'll get her to help my midwife, when she's supporting me with the delivery of babies. I'll do my best to keep her safe, as cleanliness is one of my top priorities when tending patients, but if she ends up tending injured soldiers in the future, it's then you can all start to worry about her. She seems independent-minded enough to do whatever she wants with her life and being that headstrong can be a hard life for a woman in a male-dominated world. However, for now you can assure the family that I'll safely equip her with enough knowledge to start her on her journey."

True to his word, Doctor McNally taught Rosita well, as if he was training a young man who wished to be a doctor. Having three daughters of his own, he knew how restricted the lives of women could be if they had an ambition to be something other than a homemaker. Her level of inquisitiveness fascinated him and over the following year Rosita spent more time at his family home, enjoying the company of his daughters, particularly Jennifer who was of a similar age, than she did in Midleton. Doctor McNally often smiled at the dinner table which regularly turned into either a quiz on medical matters or an argument about women having more rights over money and life choices.

Chapter Thirty-One

In September 1856, the Beconsford family sat down for breakfast as a family for the last time before Louis went to school at Eton. He looked so grown up and handsome with his blond curls and his serious countenance. Rosita would be travelling with him. Their grandfather Isaac was accompanying them on their journey. Rosita would stay in Hertfordshire with her Grandaunt Lily where, hopefully, she would make the acquaintance of Miss Nightingale and take advice from her and her followers on how to best involve herself in helping the sick. Rosita had loved every minute working with Doctor McNally.

When the morning came that they were due to leave, Margarita felt bereft. Her world was changing dramatically and she knew that she needed to find some purpose in her own life as she would now have only Violet living with her. But today was all about the children and only when they had safely arrived in England could she take time to breathe and think. Yet she knew that she just had to let them go. She would imagine them happily living their futures, as she closed her mind to all of the bad things that could happen. Young Louis still felt like her baby. He was a placid and contented boy and she knew that he would be liked by friends he would make in the future. She could just pray that going into a new world wasn't too painful for either Rosita or Louis.

"Rosita, make sure that you keep hold of your brother's hand at all times as your grandfather will have enough to do with the amount of luggage that you are both taking with you."

"Don't fuss, Mama," both children said together, laughing.

"We'll be perfectly safe," said Rosita. "We're used to travelling to London and I guarantee that Louis will be perfectly safe and I will visit him every month at least, if he isn't too embarrassed by his older sister arriving." Rosita smiled as she leant over and tickled her adorable young brother, much to his annoyance.

"I don't need minding," he said, frowning.

"We all know that," Isaac said, "but I'll have a lot to do with all the luggage we're taking and if I know that you're safe then you'll make me very happy, as I'm getting old."

"Sorry, Grandpa. I'll help with the luggage because that's a job for the men, isn't it?" said Louis, brightening up at the thought of pleasing his beloved grandpa.

As the women all smiled Deborah went over to Louis and put her arms around him.

"You will make me very happy if you help take care of Grandpa on the journey. I need him to come back safely to me, and I know you and your sister will help each other in keeping him safe."

Rosita and Margarita both wanted to chuckle but kept serious faces as Isaac nodded his agreement.

"Well, that sorts everything. My grandson and heir to the Beconsford Estate has finally begun to look after me."

Louis lifted his head and almost grew in stature as he accepted the complement from his grandfather.

"Didn't I tell you all I was grown up?" he said proudly.

Margarita playfully ruffled his thick head of hair and agreed that he really was growing up.

As the hallway clock chimed twelve noon, the carriage was at the door and the luggage had been loaded. There were tears and hugs and smiles as his four grandparents, plus his mother and sister, were joined by the household staff who all came to say goodbye to the children that many had taken care of since they were small babies. Louis decided that it would look babyish to cry and refused to give in to the sadness he felt at leaving his mother. But he knew that he had to go away to school. His cousins in England had told him great stories of the pillow fights, the games in the fields and the midnight feasts that they often had when they had got money sent to them by their parents. He was looking forward to those things. He was even secretly glad to get some time away from his two very bossy sisters and he knew that his family would visit him often and he'd return for the long school holidays each year.

Nobody left the steps of the house until the carriage went through the estate gate and disappeared from sight.

Later, as she sat by the window of her bedroom admiring the abundance of colour in the Secret Garden, Margarita gave way to the tears that she couldn't shed in front of her children. Her head was filled with memories as she tried to recall the good times, in particular those that included her beloved Victor. Losing her children was a completely different pain to that felt when Victor died yet her heart still felt broken as she now felt she was losing control of two of her children who would now have so many other people in their lives who would make decisions for them. She could just pray that the majority of people who came into their lives were good but she also realised that she wouldn't be around for them when they are in pain either emotionally or physically. She wondered what her old Great-granny Sheila would have said and smiled when she thought that even she wouldn't have the words to bring comfort today. It's funny, thought Margarita. When someone dies all your family and community surround you with love, yet for this type of loss most would say I am lucky to have children who are so privileged they can afford a private education.

Yet today she didn't feel lucky but knew that she had to deal with it and get on with the rest of her life.

Two weeks after the children left for England word had come back that Louis had settled into his school and Rosita was enjoying the freedom of spending time with her cousins in Hertfordshire. She had not yet met her heroine Miss Nightingale but it would happen soon, wrote the optimistic Rosita.

Louis had made a "best friend" already called Darian who slept next to him in the dormitory and he had already enjoyed a midnight feast with the money he had been given by his grandfather.

During breakfast that morning Margarita asked Isaac and Deborah if she could have a quiet word with them after lunch and immediately Deborah asked if there was a problem. Margarita assured her that there wasn't and Isaac said that he would clear any work by two o'clock in the afternoon. They agreed to meet in the library and Margarita made sure that a warm fire was set early, and coffee and chocolate slices would be left in the room by the cook.

Margarita took a light lunch with Violet, who was between lessons that seemed to be going well with her trusted tutor Miss Nesbitt. Margarita had promised herself that she would spend more time in the company of her daughter but was surprised that the youngster had learned well from Rosita and seemed to be growing up fast. It's funny, she thought. Louis seems far less mature than Violet and he's certainly behind what Rosita was when she was his age. Her youngest daughter had now made friends with children of her own age and announced that she was going to a friend's home for the afternoon.

"But you can collect me after four, Mama. Miss Nesbitt will take me down. As we go through the estate, she teaches me all about the different plants and trees and she makes me remember their names. So, it is like having a lesson, Mama! Also, Grandpa Jack thinks that I might have a good eye for growing things and thinks the lessons I learn going through the estate are very important!"

Margarita could only feel amused. In some ways having Violet with interests of her own could make it easier for her mother to move on with her own life. It's funny, she thought, that her own young child had begun to get on with her life while she still felt stuck in the past. She knew this would have to change.

Margarita was already in the library and was sitting close to the fireplace when she was joined by her apprehensive-looking in-laws who sat close together on the large couch opposite her. As she poured coffee, she smiled at them both.

"I was hoping you wouldn't look so worried, but I'm not sure how you'll feel about the suggestion I'm about to make."

"We will be worried until you let us know," Isaac said with a warm smile, seeing two of the most important women in his life looking anxious, as he encouraged himself to stay calm and just listen.

"Thanks, Isaac. You both know how much I love this estate, having been born here and grown up surrounded by its beauty. Well, I hope to live a long life and to continue to watch the changing of each season within the estate."

Isaac and Deborah were relieved to hear her say that as she continued.

"However, I am still only in my thirties and since the death of our beloved Victor I haven't seen any future for myself. I seem to be stuck in a fog of memories, regrets and what-ifs. Since Rosita and Louis left, I've been doing a lot of thinking and want to have some purpose in my life which has not been happening for some years now. One of the problems is that by living in this house, everywhere I turn around I am reminded of Victor. While up to recently these memories felt like a warm blanket surrounding me, I've begun to realise that I cannot live forever in that past and I must begin the task of moving on with my life."

Isaac asked what way she wanted to move on, as he saw that Deborah was beginning to look increasingly anxious.

"This estate and house are eventually going to be owned by Louis and hopefully his wife. Although I love living in this house with you and Deborah, I would like, if you are both willing, to be allowed to move to the Dower House in the estate. I would live there with Violet and Hilda and just a small number of staff."

"Have I caused you to feel an outsider in this house?" Deborah asked, looking worried.

Isaac put an arm around his wife as he said, "No, love, she just wants her own space and somewhere to put her own stamp on. Here everything has stayed the same for years. Am I right, Margarita?"

Margarita nodded, grateful that Isaac seemed to understand. "Maybe that's part of it. I'm hoping to again start helping students with their voice training. Master Johnson wants me to ease his workload although I see it also as somewhere I can continue to practise my own singing. Therefore, I would love to create a comfortable music room in which to work."

Isaac kept his arm protectively around his wife, squeezing her gently as he spoke again.

"We would be delighted if you do that, wouldn't we, Deborah?"

His wife nodded. She would be sad to lose her daughter- in-law from the Big House but understood that she needed to begin to live her own life again. Maybe I should take a leaf out of her book, Deborah thought.

"Thank you both," said Margarita. "Would you like me to let Violet continue to go up to the Big House for her education with Miss Nesbitt?"

Isaac breathed a sigh of relief.

"I'd like that very much, Margarita," Deborah said smiling. "Perhaps she could stay for lunch with us each day, if that was alright with you?"

"Of course, she can, Deborah. I know how much she loves being with you both. I think she would enjoy that very much. It would also give me more time for my music."

"Well, if that's settled, even though it's afternoon, I think we all deserve a glass of sherry to celebrate your return to music," Isaac said, thankful that the women in his life seemed happy with their decisions.

Chapter Thirty-Two

Margarita's life slowly changed as she kept herself busy. She now taught in her newly furbished music room in the Dower House but more importantly she began to practise singing in her spare time. When she told Master Johnson, he insisted that she return to his home to allow him help fine-tune her voice. At Christmas time she sang in the church and began to give a few charity recitals in the county. The children were all growing up and she began to believe that sometime in the future she might again return to sing on a bigger stage.

As a new year came and spring arrived, it brought a renewed desire within Margarita to follow her musical dreams. On a bright day in early May she sat watching the sun go down, and finally made a decision about her future. She put pen to paper and began to write a letter to her good friend, whom she hadn't seen for what seemed like a very long time.

My dear Sylvia,

I hope you are continuing to enjoy your life in New York and that Maeve is well also. I write regularly to Jean, who is very busy looking after her husband and her two young children. I hear regularly from her about how helpful you are, taking presents to the children and taking them for walks. She is very grateful to you.

I have something to ask you and hope you might be able to help. I am considering making a trip to New York, with the idea of possibly resurrecting my music career by singing in a couple of charitable events. I know you are forever involved in charitable pursuits with your friends and I could perhaps

help by singing for one of them. I also want a chance to attend some shows in
the concert halls. It would be best in September as I would have enjoyed the
holidays with Louis and Violet, before they return to their studies.

I think that I need a break for a while from Ireland to see if I still have
the voice, plus the hunger, to return to my singing. It would be lovely to spend
time with you, if you have can find room for me in that large mansion of
yours!

Otherwise, I am keeping well, but feel that I need to start to plan the next
phase of my life.

Keep sending me all your news.

I await your reply.

Regards to everyone from your Irish friend,

Margarita

Having sealed the letter, she then turned her attention to writing a note
to her young aunt Alice in West Cork.

At her home in Eoinstown, Alice woke on a bright early-summer morning
to the singing of the birds and the sound of the letter man lifting the latch
of the garden gate. She was awake before the children and decided to enjoy
the quiet time and have a cup of tea before her real day began. She waited
until the tea was in her hand before opening the letter, which she knew to
be from her beloved niece Margarita.

My dearest Alice,

I'm delighted to hear that young Emily is now enjoying her schooling.
Pretty soon Gregory will be making career choices and I know that he's out
helping on the farm. Maybe he's going to be a farmer? I know that Barry
seems too settled in America to ever return. I don't know how the years have
flown so fast!

Everyone in Midleton is well and I'm looking forward to young Louis spending summer with us in Ireland. He's enjoying his schooling as Grandaunt Lily and her family take him to their home very often and of course Deborah's family in Hertfordshire love to spoil him, given any chance they get. Violet is really happy with her tutor, Miss Nesbitt. They have formed a great relationship and she encourages Violet to explore many diverse subjects.

I have some news that I believe will make you happy. I've just written to Sylvia to ask if I could stay with her in New York in early September. I want to see many concerts and maybe I might even sing! I hope to see you in Midleton soon and make sure to bring Gregory and Emily with you as everyone wants to see them. It is wonderful that Richard's singing career is going so well.

Well, that's all my news for now. Keep writing, I look forward always to your letters.

Love, Margarita

As Alice finished reading the letter, Richard entered the room asking, "What's making you smile so early in the morning?"

"It's Margarita. She finally seems to be returning to some kind of normality because she is proposing to go to New York in September and maybe sing again. For charity, of course." Richard looked at her in astonishment.

"That's the best news I've had in ages. Her voice has been lost to the world for too long. Has she asked you to go with her?"

Alice looked at him for a moment before she smiled broadly at her husband.

"You have just given me a great idea. The two children will be attending school in September and you don't have any bookings yet for that month. Could we both take a holiday and join her there? Margarita could be travelling alone."

Without a moment's hesitation her husband answered. "That's a great idea. I might even do some singing there myself and earn enough to pay for the holiday!"

"Hmm … there are other ideas about this holiday that I'm now thinking about, but I won't tell you until I've checked a few things out!" Alice said, looking fondly at her husband.

"What are you planning now, I wonder? Are your organisational skills going into overdrive?"

"You don't have to worry, beloved husband, I will reveal all when I'm ready. But now I have to reply to Margarita and then I want to write to Sylvia in New York. That's enough information for the time being!" she said, pushing her husband playfully. "Have your breakfast and get started with your work, as I need time to think!"

Margarita was delighted when she received the news from Alice that she and Richard would join her on her trip to America. It put a smile on her face for the rest of the day and, for the first time in a long while, she felt that she had some focus on a viable future for herself.

It was the following month before she heard from Sylvia.

My dearest Margarita,

I was thrilled to receive your news about a trip to New York. Of course, you are welcome to spend as long as you wish in my home. Maeve and Mrs. O'Brien were overjoyed to hear that you are coming over and your room is already being prepared! I had a letter from Alice and Richard and I've written to them today to tell them that they too are welcome to share my home. However, I have a favour to ask you in return. I think that I would like to return to Ireland in mid-summer for some weeks. My lawyer wants to tie up loose ends as I'm now happily settled in New York. If it was possible to stay in your home, I would love to visit Midleton. Although I will make at least one trip to West Cork, I need to spend some time closer to Cork city. Also, though Alice wants me to stay with her, I do not wish to spend too much time in West Cork as all memories of the area are still very painful. I still pray for my soul at night because I'm so happy that my husband came to a sorry end. He had affected too many lives negatively and I even now wonder how I was so naive to allow myself be forced into marriage with him. Thankfully, I now meet some wonderful people who have no knowledge of him and that pleases me greatly.

I have already spoken to the Cork Association in New York and they are delighted that you are coming over. Apparently, they all have a great fondness for you due to the amount of help your fundraising and Lord Beconsford's trust gave to so many communities in the county during the famine.

I hope that your children are all well. Please write soon and let me know if you can accommodate me.

I am looking forward so much to seeing you soon,

Sylvia

Margarita could not wait to put pen to paper to say yes, yes, yes to Sylvia. It pleased her greatly that Sylvia would stay with her in the Dower House.

Margarita spent a joyous month with Sylvia, as did the children. Sylvia had proved a great help in entertaining the twins. She even showed Louis how to play the game of rounders where she ran as fast as any of the children. Margarita thought that she would have made a wonderful mother and wondered if she might find a kind man in America who would give her the life that she deserved.

Before they knew it, the time had come to make their journey to New York. Although Margarita had many anxious moments about the trip, Master Johnson gave her confidence by reminding her that her voice had matured with a new depth of feeling that came from her many varied life experiences. He had an uncompromising belief in her ability and she kept reminding herself that she could do it.

"Talent does not disappear, Margarita. It just sometimes hides away until it blossoms again. Just like the flowers that awake in the spring," Master Johnson said, on the eve of her departure to America.

***

"Sylvia, have you any space in your trunk for the rest of my clothes? My performance gown has taken up so much room that I've little room left for my day and evening wear!" Margarita pleaded.

"Of course, I have. I brought a lot of things from New York to give to the people in Eoinstown so I have plenty of space in my trunk for you. Just make sure that you have a good gown for the first dinner on board the liner as I've managed to ensure that we will be seated with the captain on our first night at sea. I think two Ladyships in our party did the trick!" Sylvia said, laughing. She hoped that the excitement ahead would finally take Margarita out of her lethargy.

"I must make sure that Violet has everything she needs before I leave her," said Margarita. "She's looking forward to having Gregory and Emily here for a few days until Meg takes them back to West Cork. Once Violet is happy, I shall be ready to begin my adventure."

"It was so wonderful visiting the beauty of Cork and Kerry during the past month. The children will remember the seaside towns for a long time. I don't know how you had the energy to build so many sandcastles with them, Sylvia. I was just happy to sit watching the sea and reading my book, so I have much to thank you for this summer."

"I loved being with them and you must consider bringing them both to New York when you next visit."

"I feel tired even thinking of taking the twins on a ship. I think I'll wait until Rosita is back in Ireland to attempt anything so adventurous."

By noon the carriage was packed and the travellers began to take their seats. Margarita suddenly felt concerned that she was doing the right thing. Louis had happily returned with his Grandad Isaac to England and as she hugged Violet as tightly as she could, she knew that Deborah and Eliza would take good care of her while she was in America.

"Let you be good while I'm gone and I will bring you back some presents."

Deborah and Eliza told her not to fuss and finally, the carriage was on the road to Dublin to connect with the Ferry to Liverpool before joining the ship that would take them all to America.

It was a weary group of travellers from Cork that arrived three days later to Liverpool dock, having endured a rough crossing of the Irish Sea in the British and Irish steam packet company ship. They spent a much-needed night in the Adelphi hotel to refresh themselves before their American adventure began.

The sight of the ocean-going liner close to the dock wall had Alice and Richard incredibly excited. They were the only two who had not previously sailed in such a ship. Sylvia explained that it was the same ship on which she had travelled to America during the famine.

Well rested after their stay in the Adelphi, they boarded the liner in the late afternoon where they were shown to cabins situated close to each other. Staff helped everyone to settle in and after a light supper the group stood on deck as the ship left the harbour. With no hint of the bad weather that they had experienced on the trip from Ireland, they stood on the deck and watched as the setting sun cast colours and shadows across the rippling waves. Sylvia reflected on her mood when she had previously taken this ship to America. On this occasion, she felt a lightness in her mind and body at the prospect of returning to her home and life in America. They all agreed that an early night's sleep was essential, with the comfort of experiencing still waters, as nobody could predict the weather for the remainder of the crossing.

Early in the morning Alice knocked on Margarita's cabin door and, as always in the past she entered with an exuberance that Margarita envied.

"It's beautiful on deck and Sylvia has just received an invitation for us to have afternoon tea with the captain!"

Margarita looked at her, frowning. "Aren't we supposed to be joining him for dinner?"

"That's why I'm so excited. This is in addition to the dinner invite. He wants to get to know us all before we meet later in the company of the other travellers," Alice answered.

"Very well. So, what does my event manager suggest I wear this afternoon then?" Margarita asked, knowing Alice would suggest something suitable.

"I want you to wear that delicate red silk dress with the silver cashmere shawl around your shoulders. You look elegant and alluring in it."

"Do I need to look alluring for the captain?"

"As an opera star travelling to America, of course you do!" Alice said, pushing her playfully in the arm. "You're not wandering around the town in Midleton now. I need to see the new you walking out of this cabin for afternoon tea!"

Alice continued to chuckle as Margarita shooed her out of the room," saying, "Well, let me at least enjoy breakfast before I dress like an opera goddess!"

They hugged before Alice left. I wish I had her ability to enjoy the moment, Margarita thought. She's back to her old self since the famine ended, thank goodness. It must be a skill that I haven't got, as I'm always either remembering the past or worrying about the future, while always questioning if my decisions will turn out right. Shaking her head, Margarita decided to try for once not to overthink everything.

Having eaten breakfast, they walked together on deck where, of course, Alice stopped to enjoy some games on deck with other passengers. They agreed that a light lunch would suffice before they took tea with the captain in the mid-afternoon.

Alice insisted on Margarita allowing her to sweep her hair up in a way that made her alluring. As she placed diamante clips into her hair, which shone in the light, she was satisfied that Margarita looked her best.

Alice, Richard, Sylvia and Margarita chatted happily as they made their way to the captain's quarters. Margarita was surprised at the opulence of the room. It was a large space with mahogany panels and pictures adorning the walls. In the centre of the room a good-sized table sat, covered by an embroidered white tablecloth. The table was laid for six people and as they entered the room a splendidly dressed gentleman walked, with outstretched hand, towards the group.

"I'm Desmond, captain of your ship, and it is my pleasure to welcome you to my quarters. It's lovely to see you again, Sylvia." He bent over and took Sylvia's hand in his, before kissing it and holding it for a while, much to the embarrassment of the blushing lady.

Alice and Margarita looked at each other with eyebrows raised and smiles on their faces.

The rest of the formal introductions were made. Desmond led them to the table, placing Sylvia at one side of him and Margarita at the other. Drinks were passed around and when everyone raised their glasses, the captain toasted the guests, especially those whom he said had not been on his ship in the past. Everyone was in a good mood when the tea arrived. Delicious sandwiches and slices of salmon on delicate biscuits were brought to the table plus the obligatory pastries and dainty chocolate slices.

Margarita found the chat warm and welcoming and she relaxed, realising how much she was enjoying herself.

As they sipped tea, replete after the lovely spread, Desmond said that he had a request to make to Margarita, but first he wanted to tell her a story.

Margarita smiled at him and said she'd be delighted to grant his request, thinking it was probably to sing before they reached New York.

"Thank you very much, my dear, but first for my story. My name is Desmond Bates and I don't know if that name rings a bell for you?"

Margarita shook her head.

"I have a connection with you, my lady."

Margarita looked at him in astonishment, wondering what was coming next.

"The connection goes back to 1816. My uncle was a ship's captain sailing out of Liverpool, from where he sailed all around the world. Whenever he returned to shore, he regaled me and the rest of my family with his stories. However, it was only after he retired that he told me this story. It was around the time when I decided to make a life at sea for myself. I'm glad he told it to me because, soon after, his memory began to fade. He died some years ago and his ashes were scattered by me at sea, with his family by my side. It was his lifelong wish. The story he told me was about a young man who joined his crew at eighteen and stayed for three years. He was a somewhat troubled lad and my uncle advised him to go home to his native land and make a life for himself. He even organised a free passage home for him to his native city of Cork in Ireland. To the horror of my uncle, that ship, along with two others sank in the Atlantic Ocean near the south coast of Ireland and that lad's name was never given as a survivor."

As Margarita listened, goose bumps were running over her body.

"Yet this story did have a happy ending because Jack Ryan was his name. Your father, Margarita. I know from my uncle that they communicated some years later, but Jack didn't want to disclose his past to anyone and my uncle respected that."

Margarita's eyes were shining. "My father told me his story when I was about sixteen. The only reason he kept his name quiet from the authorities is that he feared he might get your uncle into trouble for getting him an illegal free passage on a troop ship. That's how caring my father is. He never wants to hurt a soul. He's full of kindness and care towards everyone who crosses his path."

Alice and Richard looked astonished as they didn't know this story.

"Margarita, when my uncle died, I saw a letter from your father among his possessions," Desmond continued. "In it he said that he needed to thank my uncle, because if fate had sent him safely home to Cork, he would never have met his beloved wife Eliza and also being blessed with a beautiful daughter called Margarita, whom he said in the letter had the voice of an angel."

There was silence in the room, broken only when Sylvia spoke.

"I learned of this story only on my crossing from America on Desmond's ship and I felt that Margarita would love to hear it. I hope my judgement was correct, dear friend?"

Margarita looked at her friends before turning back to Desmond.

"Thank you for that. I'm very happy to hear that during that period of his life, about which he never spoke openly, was a happy time for him with a man like your uncle caring about him. He had previously had a difficulty at home, due to his father's excessive drinking. Thank you, Desmond, I am deeply honoured to hear that story. I can't wait to tell my father and I'm sure he would love to meet you one day."

He looked at her with a grateful smile. "Now it is time to ask you a favour. I have a man on this ship who has asked to meet you. We have a mutual friend in New York. The man is very interested in promoting singers in America and during the famine he actually heard you singing in the Cork famine fundraising concert in New York. Your voice made an impression on him and when he discovered that you were travelling, he asked for a meeting with you. I know him just as The Maestro and I think it might be beneficial for you to meet him. He will be joining us for dinner tonight, but wished to speak to you before then."

Margarita smiled indulgently at Desmond. "I'd be delighted to meet him, Desmond. Where would you like us to meet?"

"He will come to my suite next door and I will bring you through as soon as he arrives. In the meantime, your friends will stay drinking the good wine in this room while you meet him, as I must return to make sure that this ship stays on course!"

Within a few minutes the captain's attendant opened the adjoining door and announced that the captain's guest was waiting.

As Margarita walked to the door, she turned to her friends and announced, "If I come back as an international opera singer, please all stand up and bow. I will expect no less!" She laughed as she stepped through the door.

Margarita was surprised that no introductions were carried out. As the door closed, she saw a gentleman, dressed in a stylish jacket, standing with his back to her. He was looking at the ocean through a porthole.

Margarita hesitated before speaking. "Maestro?" was all she said as the man slowly turned to face her. As he stepped towards her, Margarita almost collapsed in shock.

"Laurence? Laurence? Is it really you? I thought I was meeting someone else," she said lamely, not thinking straight.

He took her hand, led her to a chair and sat down beside her.

"Margarita, if I have offended you by meeting in this clandestine way, I sincerely apologise and I assure you that I won't bother you again. Please let me explain. I have been friends with Sylvia since you left New York and when you wrote to say you were coming over, it seems that Alice wrote to her also wondering if it would be possible to arrange a meeting between you and me, when you arrived in New York." He gave a faint smile as he continued. "It was Alice and Sylvia who suggested I meet you in this way, quietly and while you were not under any pressure," he said ruefully. "I met Desmond through Sylvia and it was only recently that I heard the story of

Desmond's connection with your father. I took that as an omen that we should meet in this way."

Margarita had her usual mutinous thoughts about Alice and now Sylvia, as she tried to recover her composure. "Laurence, where were you, before you got on this ship?"

He laughed before answering. "I've been visiting all my many Irish relatives from Cork right up to Mayo, and during this week I had two recitals in Manchester before boarding the liner."

Margarita shook her head in astonishment that all this was happening behind her back.

"Margarita, when I arranged to meet you in Italy, I foolishly had a hope in my heart that meeting you in Verona would give me a fairy tale reunion with you. That illusion was shattered when I looked into your large sparkling eyes which I had remembered from New York and saw not even sadness, but a deadness there. I understood that you were still in love with your late husband and didn't yet have room in your heart for me. I have loved you for many years and this daft attempt to let you know is my final attempt to woo you. If you are unable to be at my side in the future, I will understand and leave you to become the brilliant singer that you were and always will be."

Margarita listened in bewildered silence to this most unexpected turn of events. The only thought that was going through her head was a meeting she had with Victor in London around fifteen years ago when he declared his love for her. Was this another man whom she would love, for it yet again to end in heartache? She knew she still needed time to think, knowing that she had feelings for Laurence when she was in New York, but had buried them when she returned to Ireland. Now she knew she had to deal with these feelings again. Laurence deserved at least that much.

She lifted his warm hand, held it between both of hers and looked into his eyes which had more sparkle in them than when they had last met.

"This has all come as a shock to me, Laurence, but in a good way because I am delighted to see you again. I am honoured that you have opened your heart to me because I know the courage that needed. I'm flattered at the amount of trouble you have gone to in orchestrating this meeting. I would love to spend the time before arriving in America and when I am in New York in your company – and I am going to spend that time considering your proposal. But first I must have a severe talk with my young Aunt Alice for trying to sort out my life for me! In order to do that, let us both go next door and start having a little fun!"

As Laurence stood up, Margarita put her arms around him and they hugged in silence before smiling at each other and walking through the door.

That night those seated at the captain's table were envied by the other passengers. Fun and laughter was the order of the evening. The group were all entertained with stories of famous people who previously sat at this table. It emerged that the English author Mr. Dickens loved to cross the Atlantic with his wife and they usually danced the night away to the sounds of the ship's orchestra.

After dining, Margarita was delighted to take to the dancefloor with Laurence, as the rest of the group smiled with delight at the happiness of the pair. Margarita was overjoyed to see the captain ask Sylvia for the first dance and, as she watched carefully, she noticed how close Desmond was holding her and it warmed her heart. Maybe Sylvia would finally find happiness with a loving man.

During an idyllic period of weather on the Atlantic, the guests enjoyed shuffleboard and tug of war competitions on the deck where Alice turned out to be the champion of most events, much to her delight.

As the ship finally entered the Hudson, Desmond Bates was a happy man, having finally got permission from Sylvia to escort her while he was on shore leave.

Margarita gazed in delight at Sylvia's large, three-storey residence situated just a short distance from her own abode when she lived in New York with the children. Mrs. O'Brien was bustling about ordering the coachman to be careful with the luggage, while Maeve was hugging Alice and asking for all the news from Ireland. Jean would join them later, a meeting that Margarita had been looking forward to since agreeing to make the trip.

Mrs. O'Brien was radiant as she greeted her previous employer. "It's lovely to see you back, my lady, and if I may say so you're looking wonderful. The rooms are ready and I will ensure that you are all well taken care of while you are guests in this house."

The visitors smiled, enjoying being greeted by her warm lilting Cork accent. They all felt at home as soon as they entered Sylvia's house.

"I am preparing a meal for you all later, but tea and refreshments will be available all afternoon in the parlour. We have other Irish staff in the house, all looking forward to having visitors over from Ireland."

Later Margarita sat alone, in the parlour, sipping tea. She had a feeling of restful contentment, as she sat by the window and watched the world go by. She had spent many nights during the voyage considering her future, as she continued to do now. She was looking forward to her first singing event in America, already organised by Sylvia. It would be among people she knew. It was hoped the event would raise large sums of money to help rebuild homes and lives of people still living in poverty back in Ireland. Since they met on the ship again, her thoughts kept returning to Laurence. She had been puzzled by her worries that history was repeating itself when

Laurence declared his love on the boat. Sitting here, she was now sure that this was different to the night Victor had declared his love for her in London. She realised that Victor Beconsford had become a broken man after the death of his beloved Fleur. He had found solace only in living while staring at his future through the prism of alcohol. This in turn changed his thinking and for a long time before he remarried, his mind and thoughts had been wrapped in a carousel of warped judgments. A good man damaged by grief in such a bad way found that life gave him no chance to repair either his body or his mind. Whereas, Laurence dealt with his grief with rightful tears of sadness and long moments of despair. His talent for singing disappeared along with his beloved Lisa. Yet he fought his despair with determination to learn to sing again. He had moved to celebrating her memory and he didn't succumb to dark and devious ways of coping.

Yes, she concluded, Laurence is a strong man and I know I can trust him with my future.

Four separate carriages drew up at the entrance to Sylvia's home on the afternoon of the concert to be held in the newly built Academy of Music, the Manhattan opera and concert hall where the four thousand seats were fully booked out. The presence of Laurence Flaherty brought opera lovers whereas the Irish would turn up in their thousands to listen to Margarita and Richard. Sylvia had been responsible for organising the prestigious venue, but the Irish committee, as they always did, made the occasion seamless for the performers. Excitement was high as the enormous crowd took their seats. The orchestra had a long rehearsal with the performers on the previous day.

Two hours before the concert was to begin, Margarita, Laurence and Richard walked through the performers' entrance to the theatre, each feeling nervous. They ate lightly, before retiring to their respective dressing rooms to prepare their voices. Margarita was helped by Alice to don a new dress in her favourite colour, red. It was made of Italian lace with a wide underskirt of white silk. As Alice placed a simple silver tiara to her head and fixed her favourite locket, given to her by her parents for her ninth birthday, around her neck, she sighed with happiness. Margarita looked beautiful and was ready for her performance.

When the performance began, the orchestra commenced with the overture from *The Barber of Seville* and the first cheers from the audience came as Laurence made an entrance and sang favourite arias from Mr. Rossini's opera. The orchestra then continued with the haunting prelude to Giuseppe Verdi's new opera *La Traviata*. But the Irish audience members were not forgotten as it was followed by musicians playing well known tunes with fiddles, violins and bodhráns, all making a true Irish sound.

Richard followed with many of the Irish favourites that were always requested, including "The Croppy Boy".

Before the interval Margarita came onstage to the sound of audible murmurs at her beauty and her attire. She too wanted the Irish to hear their favourites. She told the audience about young Denny Lane and his beautiful lyrics for "Lament of the Irish Maiden", before she began to sing her favourite song.

"*On Carrigdhoun the heath is brown,*
The clouds are dark o'er Ard-na-Lee
And many a stream comes rushing down
To swell the angry Owen na Buidhe..."

As the audience clapped, she finished with her favourite aria from Traviata, "*Sempre libera*", as Laurence hauntingly sang off stage. As she reached the last note, Laurence rejoined her on stage, to celebrate with her and to hold her hand as she exited to thundering applause.

As they left the stage together for the interval break, Margarita found that a red carpet had been laid on the ground off-stage and a grinning Alice and a beaming Sylvia stood at either side of it. Margarita laughed and shook her head at them both but as they reached the end of the carpet, Laurence swung around in front of Margarita and took her hand in his as he knelt on the ground. As he looked up into the eyes that had haunted his dreams for many years, he put the question to her.

"Margarita Beconsford, will you do me the honour of becoming my wife?"

By now a grinning Richard was standing by, with his hands behind his back.

Without a single moment of hesitation, Margarita answered, "Yes."

Laurence jumped up and kissed Margarita properly for the very first time. He then held her close to him, afraid that she might change her mind.

Richard pulled a bottle and two glasses from behind his back. Filling them, he handed them each a glass. Everyone backstage cheered and clapped. Chairs were pulled up and as the opera singers would not be returning to the stage again until later in the second half, drinks were passed around.

Yet again, Margarita tried to scold Alice, telling her that she knew all this madness was her doing. Alice just laughed and said that Sylvia was a big part of it and Margarita had to wonder at the difference there was in the now smiling, excitable Sylvia compared to the lost woman who had arrived from Ireland during the famine. She gives me hope for the future, Margarita thought. Maybe it is time to stop allowing the pain of my past mar the possibility of a happy future, with a good man by my side.

As the singing, dancing, clapping and music came to an end, Laurence joined Margarita on the stage and announced to the audience that he wanted to sing a song for the Irish emigrants but in particular to the lady by his side.

"I sang it for her once before and know that she loves it. It's called *'Kathleen Mavourneen'*."

The audience clapped enthusiastically and Laurence began to sing.

"It may be for years and it may be forever,

Then why are you silent, Kathleen Mavourneen?"

After the last words were sung by Laurence, there was more cheering and clapping for the American-born son of an Irish emigrant, before silence descended, as Laurence put a hand up to quieten the excited audience.

"I have waited many years to be reunited with *my Kathleen Mavourneen* and, although she is not named Kathleen, I have finally been able to sing again with Margarita. But, for me, tonight is even more special. Although I am American born, my soul is Irish, passed down to me by my parents and my ancestors. I will soon be returning to Ireland with my betrothed, Margarita Beconsford, because tonight she agreed to become my bride! At this moment, I believe that I am truly the luckiest man on the planet."

The audience again erupted into applause and all stood up to cheer, as the rest of the cast came back on stage. Immediately the band burst into an Irish jig and everyone clapped. Nobody seemed to want to go home. Finally, the curtain came down, but those in the audience and on stage knew that tonight they had experienced a very special, unique evening. Two people whose hearts had been broken in the past could now heal as one.

Epilogue

Margarita sat in the parlour in Beconsford House on the day before she was to marry Laurence. Good weather was expected to continue as everyone in the estate prepared for her big day. Laurence was staying in the Dower House and Margarita had moved back into the Big House until the day of her wedding. As she looked through the window, she saw a rainbow with its myriad of colours ending inside her beloved Secret Garden. That's a good omen, she thought, smiling to herself. As she reflected on the way her life had woven its way towards this day, she wondered how full would be the pot of gold, if she were to go into the garden and pick it up. She wondered today also about her life experiences and how they had shaped her. Would it be possible for her to leave the parts of her past that pained her, behind? She yet again wished she had the exuberance of Alice and thought back to her mother's sister Lily, who was described as frivolous. Perhaps, like her mother Eliza, she was too conscious of being reliable and sensible. She wondered if other people were able to allow the future blossom without worrying about it. As she looked again at the rainbow, she imagined herself picking up the crock of gold and feeling its weight. It would have her beloved children and parents in there, and now the love of a good man who was willing to see her blossom again with her singing because she now knew that a life for her would forever be enhanced by the sound of music.

The following day the sun continued to shine on the small number of wedding guests, as they made their way to the estate chapel. Carriages had arrived on the previous day bringing everyone from Eoinstown to Midleton, while Laurence's parents and his sister Tess arrived with some of their relatives from Macroom. Sylvia and Desmond Bates, whom she would shortly marry, had arrived from America, much to the delight of Margarita's father Jack.

Before the wedding ceremony commenced, Margarita's twins scattered flowers in the path of the bride, while her beloved Rosita stood by her side as chief bridesmaid. Although Margarita knew that Rosita would shortly go overseas again, still hoping to join the nursing corps attached to the military, it made her very happy to have the independent young woman at her side on this important occasion. Margarita wore a long gown of ivory, designed for her by Alice and there was joy in her heart as her father Jack proudly handed his daughter to Laurence, while her mother Eliza shed tears of joy. For Isaac and Deborah, it was a bittersweet day but they were pleased to see Margarita finding joy in her life again. Richard enhanced the ceremony with his soaring tenor voice. He was accompanied by a proud Master Johnson on the organ, before the minister finally pronounced Laurence Flaherty and Margarita Beconsford man and wife.

It was a relaxing day for all the guests, with little fuss, as they enjoyed the wedding banquet in the Big House, while the estate workers made merry in the gardens. It was nearly midnight before Margarita and Laurence walked away from the Big House towards their future home in the Dower house, having refused a carriage. Margarita stopped Laurence in the middle of the estate lawn and asked him to look up at the stars in the sky.

"My father told me that on the night my twins were born, he held my mother and said his only life's ambition was to stand on the rich soil of Ireland and watch the sky and give thanks for his life and his family. Tonight, I too want to say thanks – for getting another chance to again find love. Thank you, Laurence, for waiting for me. You truly are my sun, my moon and my stars."

As Laurence held her close to his heart, in the quiet stillness of the night, he wondered how Fate had allowed him on this night to hold the woman he loved, who had given him a second chance at living his dream. He silently said his own prayer into the starry night. It was that he would live a very long life with his new bride by his side, always. They had both got a second chance at love. As they walked on into the night, they knew that soon they would seal that love, forever.

Printed in Poland
by Amazon Fulfillment
Poland Sp. z o.o., Wrocław